An Unf

Incident

Julie McLaren

With thanks to all the members of my family who have read this novel in various stages of its development and have offered support, ideas and encouragement. Thanks also to my sister, Ginny Constable, for the cover design. I'm grateful to Kath Middleton for beta reading and other members of the KUF authors' forum for many different forms of advice.

DECEMBER 2016

The moment she sits down she is assailed by doubts. Whatever possessed her? It's one thing exchanging a few cheery messages online, but this? This is madness. What can they possibly say to each other after all this time? And, more to the point, what about the things they can't say? Yes, there will be some old memories to revisit and some gaps to fill. A lot of gaps as it happens; nearly fifty years of gaps. But how much of that does she want to talk about anyway? She tries to remember the thought processes that led her to reply in the first place. It must have been boredom, she thinks, or loneliness. But really, she knows. From the minute she read those few lines of text there was never any doubt about how she would respond.

Her coffee is still too hot to drink comfortably. If it were a little cooler she could gulp it down and make a run for it. It wouldn't be the first time she'd entered a cafe and completely failed to join the ranks of chilled-out people who sit there for hours reading, apparently oblivious to anyone around them. Maybe she could just leave anyway. Who would notice or care if she slipped her coat back on and walked out, leaving the full cup of coffee steaming on the table.

But then it's too late. She hears the dull ting of the bell, a relic of the time when this cafe was a thriving baker's shop, and there she is. She looks completely different - completely different to anything Alice has imagined she might look like now - but yet it is unmistakably her. There is something about the way she stands there, careless of the blast of cold air she is causing to swirl around the two couples at the table nearest the door. There is nothing in her physical appearance, absolutely nothing, that is remotely the same as the last time Alice saw her. Yet something beyond the physical is there, immutable by time and circumstance.

But goodness! Time and circumstance have certainly played havoc here, she thinks. The woman in the doorway has her head swathed in a dull-coloured scarf and her coat looks too thin to keep anyone warm in this weather. And how long is she going to stand there, freezing everyone to death? Alice decides to take matters into her own hands and rises. Her table is at the back of the cafe, where the lighting is muted and there are no other customers. Maybe she is hard to see, with the cold light of the low winter sun streaming through the windows.

By the time she gets to the door, the two couples most affected by the draft are visibly annoyed. Luckily, they are too polite to do anything other than mime exaggerated signs of imminent hypothermia and mutter under their breath. She approaches the woman.

"It's Georgie, isn't it?" she says, touching her briefly on the arm. "Shall we go and sit down?"

SEPTEMBER 1963

We weren't allowed to go to the funeral. I couldn't understand why, as plenty of people I knew had attended at least the wake when their grandparents died. David Baker had been to the whole ceremony and had even been encouraged to look into his grandfather's coffin. He regaled us with the gory details at school the next day, with the cheerful unconcern children often display at the death of elderly relatives. I'd been looking forward to seeing for myself, to judging the extent of his elaboration, but no. We had to stay at home, even though I was eleven and perfectly capable of conducting myself sensibly. We had to be looked after by Auntie Val, a family friend who became visibly irritated the later it became and sent us all to bed at the same time, despite the fact that Janey was only six.

Not that we stayed in bed. We played spying games, sneaking downstairs to peek into the lounge where Auntie Val was sitting with one eye on the tv and the other on her sewing. I'm sure she knew we were there, as my sisters made very inadequate spies with their tendency to giggle or snort at critical moments. But she pretended not to see us anyway, even when the dog got to his feet and started to wag his tail in expectation of some fun.

We scrambled upstairs and dived into bed when we heard the slamming of van doors that signalled our parents' return. We waited quietly, listening for the fading of the conversation and the click of the back door that would indicate Auntie Val had gone and the coast was clear. However, by the time that happened, I was the only one awake. So I crept down alone and was allowed to stay up while my parents made a start on unloading the van.

That's how I know it was September 1963 when Georgie came, even without my diary. It was two days after the funeral. Two days after my parents carried in a load of my grandmother's possessions, including her dressing table. This was installed in my bedroom where it stood and sneered at the rest of the furniture. It was a wonderful piece – or so I thought at the time – highly polished wood with a beautiful grain. Its three mirrors provided endless views of yourself from a multitude of angles, which may or may not have been a good thing.

We had only been in school a couple of weeks when she arrived, but we had already begun to form our little cliques. It was a matter of necessity really. We'd been ejected from our village schools of perhaps a couple of hundred pupils and thrown into an environment so much bigger and more challenging. You had to acquire at least one friend, and fast, or you would be the one with no-one to sit with at dinner or no-one to pair off with in PE. I had attached myself to a girl called Caroline. I didn't particularly like her and I doubt she particularly liked me, but it was a friendship of convenience and I suppose we were both grateful for it at the time.

Caroline was the tallest girl in our class. She was also very thin and thus quickly earned the unoriginal epithet 'beanpole.' Unfortunately, she was otherwise unremarkable. I have had no success in recalling much about her other than her height, but not so Georgie. I can see her as she came into our form room that morning, as clearly as if it were yesterday. It was as if someone had introduced an exotic bird into a flock of pigeons. It wasn't just that she was wearing a school uniform that bore little resemblance to ours. It wasn't just the shock of dark, frizzy hair that cascaded around her olive face and over her shoulders or the fact that her fingernails were painted red. Those things changed over the following days. It was her expression, the tilt of her chin. The way she looked around the room as if she already possessed it and all that it contained. That didn't change. The flash of her grey eyes didn't change either, even when she wore green like the rest of us and her hair had been tied back and partially tamed.

Miss Houseman had taken the register and was about to conduct an inspection of our ties. I was never quite sure whether it was a greater sin to have your tie too long or too short, so I intended to measure the comparative intensity of Miss Houseman's displeasure as she moved amongst my classmates, her ruler at the ready. However, she had not left her desk when the door opened and Miss Garfield, the Headmistress, walked in with Georgie in tow. But no, that's not right. That's not how it was. Georgie was not in tow. She may have entered the room second, but she held herself as if she had the right to walk into any room she chose and she just happened to have chosen this one.

"Ah, Miss Houseman. Sorry to interrupt you, but I have a new girl for you," said Miss Garfield, gesturing at us to sit down. We were expected to rise every time a member of staff entered a classroom, and this was even more critical when it was the Head.

Miss Houseman bore an unfortunate resemblance

to a small rodent and thus her nickname had been predetermined before she ever stood in front of a class. She smiled an uncertain smile and her invisible whiskers twitched. I don't know whether it was normal for parents to turn up with a child and for that child to be admitted to school there and then, but that is what seems to have happened. The surprise showed on Miss Houseman's face. She obviously had no idea Georgie was coming. Thirty pairs of eyes turned to look at the new girl and the new girl didn't flinch, nor did she blush. She scanned the classroom as if she did this kind of thing all the time, then looked back at Miss Garfield.

"Girls, this is Georgia May. She has recently moved into the area and she'll be your new classmate. I'm sure you'll give her the kind of welcome we expect here at Victoria Lane and help her to settle in."

We nodded dutifully and said 'yes, Miss Garfield' more or less in unison. This seemed to satisfy her and she left. As she did, she placed a foolscap envelope on the desk and said something about Miss Houseman's capable hands that caused her to flutter and glance down at them as if she had never considered them in this way before.

So that was the start of the Georgie era. I watched as Miss Houseman chose a couple of girls to sit with her in lessons and help her to find her way around school. I had no particular desire to be chosen so there was no disappointment as Miss Houseman indicated Mary and Barbara. However, they glowed with pleasure at the prospect. They were big girls, with breasts already visible under their jumpers. They begged to be chosen for even the most mundane tasks. They were like irritating little dogs in great big girls' bodies. I don't think they had ever spoken to me and I had no expectation that they would. Girls like Mary and Barbara thrived on public acclaim and that was something I would be unlikely to offer them.

There was a quiet buzz of excitement as the bell rang. Tie inspection had been abandoned and Miss Houseman spent the remaining five minutes of form time perusing the contents of the envelope. As we filed out, she handed it to Mary with the instruction to pass it to Mrs Hunt, who was taking our first lesson. Some of the girls tried to get as close as possible to Georgie as we left, but others held back so they could talk about her without being heard.

"Did you see her nails? She'll be in big trouble when Mrs Hunt sees them!"

"I know, and that hair! I can't believe Miss Garfield didn't say anything!"

The first lesson was English. Mrs Hunt was so old that she was well on the way to being mummified, but she had a reputation for ferocity and was highly respected in the school. We were the top set, or we would never have been taught by her. She had made it clear from the start that there would be no nonsense in her lessons.

We sat down and awaited the explosion with a heady mixture of pleasure and fear. Amanda Purdy had been sent out on the first day for having her hair loose in Mrs Hunt's lesson even though it wasn't her fault that her elastic band had broken. There was no way Georgie was going to escape. Mary and Barbara were visibly tense, as if some of the fall-out from the inevitable retribution would settle on them, but minutes passed and nothing happened. Mrs Hunt set us some quiet reading while she leafed through the contents of the envelope, glanced at Georgie with an expression that gave nothing away, then continued the lesson as if nothing was any different. She talked, she questioned, she wrote examples on the board with squeaky chalk and spidery letters and still nothing happened. She even chose Georgie to answer a question and praised her when the answer was correct. Mary and Barbara relaxed, but the rest of the class were incredulous and more than a little disappointed, especially Amanda Purdy. What was going on here?

It was the same in the next lesson and the one after break. The teachers appeared to have been afflicted with a communal and very specific visual impairment, leaving Georgie to sit between her two minders seemingly immune to any kind of criticism. She was obviously bright and answered every question put to her, but she didn't seem anxious to please. If her hand went up it was with a laconic motion that implied she was unconcerned whether the teacher chose her or not. There was no squeaking or waving from Georgie, no desperation to gain the approbation of the teacher or the other girls. The consequence of this was that the teachers seemed to choose her to answer far more often than would have been normal, but their response to her answers was strange. It was as if they were testing out some kind of theory and were surprised to find out it was true.

By lunchtime, Mary and Barbara were glowing, basking in the reflected glory of being Georgie's friends. Barbara had loosened her tie and undone the top button of her shirt and Mary had taken off her jumper and draped it round her shoulders in what she presumably hoped was an artful and casual way. They stuck to Georgie's sides like a couple of bodyguards, glaring at other girls who tried to talk to her or reminding them that they had been especially chosen for this task. I didn't see what happened later. I had a packed lunch and they all had school dinners, but Caroline told me while we were lining up outside our form room for afternoon register.

"Apparently she turned to Barbara and said something like, 'Look, I'm sorry, but I'm finding all this a little oppressive. Thanks for looking after me, but I'll be fine now. If I get lost, I'll ask someone. It can't be that difficult.' And then she gave them a smile and a little wave and she was gone. They're both mortified."

Caroline smiled. I wondered whether this was due to her pleasure at witnessing Mary and Barbara's fall from their elevated position, or the fact that she had used such a good word to describe their discomfort. Mortified. That was a very good word indeed. I resolved to use it myself as soon as possible.

So Georgie sat where she chose for the rest of the day. She bestowed her presence on different girls as the afternoon progressed and then she took it away again. She didn't sit with me and Caroline, but that was no surprise. Instead, we played a little game in which we guessed who she would sit with next and awarded ourselves points if we were right. I can't remember who won, especially as the system became rather complicated in PE, the last lesson. It was difficult to know whether she had chosen her partner or acquired her by accident. In any case, it helped to pass the time and I felt a genuine pleasure in Caroline's company for the first time as we said goodbye at the end of the day and I went off to get my bus.

I had no idea that Georgie would be getting the same bus. It simply hadn't occurred to me, but there she was, sauntering down the drive a little in front of me. She was on her own but I didn't approach her. She had shown no interest in me and I certainly had no desire to provide her with an opportunity for a rebuff. I was skinny and under-developed and looked young for my age. I was resigned to being ignored by girls who were more physically mature. This was their loss, I told myself, and mostly I believed it.

The bus was an ancient double-decker provided by the council. It coughed and spluttered its weary way through the outskirts of town and then through two villages before ending its journey at the crossroads half a mile from my house. There was an unspoken rule that the top deck was reserved for the older girls and Georgie seemed to have understood this. She was seated half way down the lower deck as I got on. Obviously I had no intention of sitting beside her, but our eyes met as I passed and she stopped me with a smile.

"You're in my class, aren't you? Come and sit with me, I could do with a friendly face."

I'm not sure that my expression had been particularly friendly. I hadn't intended it to be, but I sat with Georgie and we talked. To begin with it was all her, but soon I found myself telling her where I lived and answering her questions about my family. She told me they had only moved to the village a week ago and were still settling in, and then she told me the name of her road: Templars Way. It was the main road into the village from the east and it was lined with expensive, detached properties with large gardens. My house was on an estate much closer to the village centre and I had never met anyone who lived on Templars Way.

"Is it big?" I asked, instantly regretting my words.

"I suppose so," she said, "but not as big as our old house. That was huge, but when Daddy …" She stopped, and I couldn't help thinking she was going to cry. However, when I glanced across she was still smiling. She leaned closer. "Look, this is kind of secret but you seem like someone I can trust. My father isn't living with us at the moment as he works for the government and he's on a special mission. That's all I can say and I shouldn't really have said that. It's why we had to move right away where nobody would know us. You won't tell anyone, will you?"

Later, I tried to think of a word to describe how I felt when Georgie told me her secret. Shocked, surprised and even astonished were quite inadequate. I needed a word that was as good as mortified and eventually I settled on flabbergasted. I also liked dumbstruck and stunned and decided to keep them in reserve, although I had no idea when I would be able to use any of them in conversation, as I had been sworn to secrecy.

Of course there was no reason why I shouldn't tell my parents about Georgie. As long as I kept her father's secret career to myself, I could tell them about the way she looked, the way she seemed to be so much older than the rest of us and how she had shrugged Mary and Barbara off as if they were irritating puppies snapping at her ankles.

"You should've seen their faces," I told my mum, bending the truth a little for dramatic effect. "They were mortified."

DECEMBER 2016

She leads Georgie to her table at the back. She is aware of how the light catches the silky, red lining of her own expensive coat, thrown casually over a chair. She wishes she had dressed less smartly, now that it is obvious that all her expectations about the elegant woman she was due to meet were spectacularly wrong.

"What can I get you?" she asks, rummaging in her handbag for her purse before there can be any awkwardness about who should pay. "Coffee? Tea? Something ..."

"Tea, please," says Georgie. It is the first time she has spoken, and her voice has the husky timbre of a smoker.

"How about a nice cake?" says Alice. She hears the patronising false jollity of her voice and wonders where that came from. "I know we shouldn't, but if you can't indulge yourself sometimes ..."

"No, thank you."

There is a finality in Georgie's answer that does not invite the kind of persuasion to which Alice herself is only too susceptible when it comes to cake. She has been looking forward to the excuse for enjoying the very good lemon drizzle cake they serve here, but it is not to be. There would be little pleasure in sitting there munching away when Georgie won't join her, for whatever reason. Certainly, she doesn't look as if resisting cake is a problem for her. She is as thin as she was when she was eleven. But it is not the healthy physique of an active child – for that is what they were in those days, not mini adults – it is a scrawny thinness that hints at meals missed or poor appetite.

Alice returns with Georgie's tea and places the little tray on the table in front of her. It has taken an age to get it, but she welcomed the queue building up behind an elderly man confused by too much choice. She used the time to think of what she could possibly say to this person who bears no resemblance to the Georgie she has imagined. Sadly, she has come up with nothing interesting.

"So," she says, picking up her own cup but putting it down again. "How long has it been then?

Do you think we should dare to work it out?"

"Since we last saw each other? That would be 1967. Fifty years, give or take."

Alice picks up her cup and swallows a mouthful of coffee. It is luke-warm now. How did that happen so quickly? She hopes the remaining time will pass at the same speed. This is clearly going to be hard work and she has no intention of raking up what happened in 1967.

"No, I was thinking of that first day. When you started at Victoria Lane. D'you remember? We all thought you were so grown-up, so … sophisticated, I suppose. And then we started chatting on the bus ..."

She stops. What is the point of dredging all this up? In her mind those days are still drenched in a golden wash of sunlight and expectation. Despite everything that happened later, she can still conjure up her eleven year old self, reaching out to grasp the promise of everything the friendship with Georgie seemed to offer. Such days. She does not want her memories blighted by whatever Georgie's life has done to hers.

There is silence. The moment is not quite long enough to be awkward, as Georgie is occupied with pouring tea from the stainless steel teapot and Alice still has a mouthful of coffee to drink, but it can't go on for ever.

"Are you still local?" asks Alice. This would appear to be less potentially difficult territory and might just trigger a conversation sufficiently anodyne and long enough to fill whatever time it will take Georgie to finish her tea.

She pushes aside the vision of this encounter she enjoyed as she drove into town. The Georgie of her imagination was an older version of the girl she once knew, well-dressed, confident and grinning from ear to ear as they met. Just like she used to. They would chat about the good times, somehow completely avoiding any mention of how it all ended. It would all be pleasant and civilised and they would, at last, meet on equal terms. It might end with a goodbye and an insincere promise to keep in touch, but it might not. But that was impossible. How stupid she has been! She should never have agreed to meet.

"Not exactly," says Georgie.

"Oh, I hope … You should have said. How selfish of me!" Alice is uncomfortable. Here she is, in her favourite little cafe, having driven only fifteen minutes or so. In contrast, Georgie looks as if she may have trekked for an hour or two to get here. "I should've asked before we arranged anything. Well, at least you can let me drive you home. It's the least I can do. Whereabouts do ..."

"Actually I'm in transit today," says Georgie. Her headscarf has slipped down and Alice can see that her hair is brittle, with a grey stripe down the centre where her roots have grown through.

"You mean you're moving house? Today? Oh, my god, I feel even worse now! You should have said! I could've made it another day – any day!"

"It's ok, it's not your fault. You couldn't have known. It's complicated. Like I say, I'm in transit. I was going to look for somewhere round here for a couple of days, but ..." Georgie takes a quick swig of her tea and Alice can see how her hand is shaking. "Actually, I was wondering, I don't suppose you know anywhere … ? No, listen it's ok. Of course you wouldn't."

Alice doesn't. She tries to think, but there's only the small hotel in the High Street and she doubts Georgie would be able to afford that. Not if her appearance is anything to go by. Alice rarely has guests, and, if she does, they stay in the house. It's big enough, after all.

"Really, forget I said it," says Georgie. "I'll get a local paper. There's bound to be a B & B somewhere."

Somehow, the words come out of Alice's mouth before they have even registered in her brain.

"You will not look for a B & B!" she says. "I've

got a perfectly good spare room and I'd welcome the company. No, I won't listen, I insist."

OCTOBER 1963

It was the day before half term and Georgie and I were on the bus. A whole week of freedom stretched ahead of me but I had mixed feelings about it. Who would I play with? My best friend out of school had been Christopher, who lived next-door-but-one, but now we were at secondary school a huge chasm had opened up between the boys and girls in the village. He had started to look away when he saw me. No more running around the fields and woods with him. No more damming the stream or making camps in the long grass. No more climbing trees and sitting there quietly, waiting for other kids to come along so we could drop twigs and cob nuts on them and make scary noises.

That part of my life seemed to be over. It had been illustrated perfectly the weekend before, when Christopher's cousin Stephen came to stay with him.

Normally they would have included me in their games, which were always more exciting. Stephen was a year older and liked to range further afield than our usual haunts. I had been hanging around outside with nothing much to do when Christopher's mum saw me.

He's gone up to the woods with Stephen," she said. "Go on, you'll catch them up if you run."

So I ran, up the street, through the alley and there they were, just a little way into the field.

"Christopher! Stephen! Wait for me!" I shouted, my breath coming in sharp, painful bursts. I had a stitch in my side and needed them to stop for a minute. They looked round.

"Sorry, no girls," called Christopher. They turned their backs and carried on walking, leaving the words with me in case I wanted to hear them again.

I felt as if I had been stabbed. It wasn't the stitch, although that still hurt. It was the pain of rejection that almost took what was left of my breath away. No girls! It had never occurred to me that being a girl was a problem, certainly not for Christopher. Ok, some of the boys in primary school had teased us and they tended to play separately, but that didn't feel like exclusion. Certainly it had never happened out of school. I walked back slowly, trying to stem the flood of burning tears. Christopher's mum was still in her garden, doing something to the roses.

"Didn't you find them?" she called as I slouched past, head down.

"Yes, but they wouldn't let me play," I mumbled, and ran inside. I hated Steven for turning Christopher against me and I hated Christopher for allowing it, but I was powerless to do anything about it.

So I wasn't looking forward to half term with quite the same pleasure as usual. My sisters would be delighted to play with me but there was no excitement in that. I didn't really know anyone else well. There were no girls from my school year living nearby, and I had never made any attempt to play with the others. It had always been Christopher and me, for as long back as I could remember. Now I had to start from scratch.

"What are you doing next week?" asked Georgie.

"Oh, just the usual," I said. I couldn't admit that I was probably going to be monumentally bored, even though that was an impressive phrase I had stumbled across only the night before and this would have been a good opportunity to use it. Doubtless her family would be doing something interesting. I had no idea what this might be, but it would be the kind of thing families with fathers who went on special missions did. Families who could afford to live on Templars Way didn't hang around being bored for a week.

"Well, I am going to be bored out of my tiny little mind," declared Georgie. "My mother seems to think unpacking crates is a good way to pass half term, but I think I'd rather be at school. Don't suppose you'd like to come up to mine sometime? You'd be doing me a huge favour."

I was so surprised that I forgot to answer. Then Georgie started to say I shouldn't worry, it was only a thought and of course I would have better things to do. So then I had to say that I'd love to and make her believe it, before the whole thing fell apart. It was ok in the end, but it was awkward for a minute and I couldn't believe how close I'd been to messing it up. Me, doing Georgie a favour by coming to her house! Now I would need an even better word than flabbergasted when I wrote my diary that night.

When Monday came, I got out my bike and prepared to cycle up to Templars Way. Georgie's house was too grand to have a number, but was called Penhaligon for reasons that were unclear.

"It's a ridiculous name for a house," she'd said. "But anyway, it's the fifth one along on the right if you turn left at the top."

I looked at my bike and wondered if it would be better to walk. It was a long way, well over a mile, but my bike was an embarrassment. It was second-hand – all my parents could afford for my eleventh birthday – and although my dad had spent hours renovating it and replacing many of the parts, I could not get over that fact. The brakes were sharp, the gears were smooth and it sailed up the hills, but my dad had painted it red and it was the wrong kind of paint. Other kids had bikes with shiny, metallic paint and lettering on the cross-bar. Mine was covered with what was left over from the last time the front door was painted. I felt sure Georgie would notice.

In the end I swallowed my pride and cycled. It would be a long slog up there, and I would have to come home earlier if I walked. I wanted to spend every minute I could at Georgie's, so I dumped my bike in the bushes just inside her gate when I got there. I doubt Georgie even saw it.

I stood there, looking down the drive. This was a real drive, indeed. It wasn't like ours, which was effectively just a narrow strip of concrete about the width of a car. It separated our house from next door and led to a pair of asbestos garages. In contrast, Georgie's drive was a wide, gravel arc, lined with trees and shrubs. The house wasn't even visible from the gate. I felt as if I'd been transported into a film, or the setting of one of my favourite adventure books. I imagined myself the heroine, poised on the threshold of a place that would hold unimaginable secrets and hidden dangers.

Eventually, I dragged myself back to reality and walked up to the house. It was certainly not what I had been expecting. The paint on the front door and window frames was cracked and peeling and the front porch was littered with discarded shoes. I was about to raise the heavy, brass knocker when the door opened and there stood Georgie. A big smile lit up her face and her hair, now loose, was curlier than ever.

"Am I glad to see you!" she said. "Come in and rescue me from this eternal unpacking."

She led me inside and I began to understand what she had been talking about. We were in a huge, wood-panelled hall, with several doors leading off and a wide, impressive staircase. An enormous grandfather clock looked magnificent despite the fact that it believed apparently that the time was six o'clock.

I had never been in a house like this and my astonishment knew no bounds when I looked up and saw an ornate chandelier hanging above us. There was not an inch of floral wallpaper to be seen. Despite all this, the overall impression was one of chaos. Wooden packing crates were stacked up against one wall and almost every stair was home to a teetering pile of books, clothes or other assorted possessions.

"See what I mean?" she said.

I didn't know what to say. I felt bad about agreeing that her house was a mess but equally bad about contradicting her. In the end I said something about it being sorted out soon, but she only snorted at that.

"George, is that your visitor?" came a voice from one of the rooms off the hall.

Georgie rolled her eyes. "Come on, you'd better come and meet my mother. You mustn't mind her. She's an artist and she's completely mad. Now you can see what I have to deal with."

I laughed. Obviously she was joking. We were all disparaging about our parents, emphasising their faults and foibles and playing down their strengths. That was normal, so I followed her into the kitchen where a tall woman with a patterned scarf only partially controlling a shorter version of Georgie's hair stood at the table. This was a large, farmhouse-style centre-piece to the room. It was completely covered with what I could only describe as junk, although I vowed to research a better word later.

"Don't just stand there, George," said the woman. "Introduce us! Have you forgotten everything they taught you at Hawfield?"

Georgie glared at her mother but proceeded to make introductions in an overly formal manner. Then she offered me a glass of orange juice which I accepted, although I regretted this immediately when I saw Georgie's expression. Clearly this had been included as part of the ceremonial formalities and I was expected to refuse politely. Unfortunately, it was too late now. I squirmed as Georgie took some time finding a glass. She washed it out and poured the remaining dregs of some squash into the bottom before filling the glass to the top with slightly luke-warm water.

The resulting drink was revolting, with only the slightest hint of orange, but I drank as much as I could. Meanwhile, Georgie's mother returned her attention to a large slab of clay which sat on a metal turntable at one end of the table She was using a wire tool with a wooden handle to carve off slivers that curled and fell as she worked. The table was smeared with watery clay and other tools were scattered around. I was fascinated and moved closer to watch. Was she going to make a pot? I had watched a potter create a vase on Blue Peter and had always wanted to have a try.

"We're going up to my room," announced Georgie, walking purposefully towards the door. I was obliged to follow. Georgie's mother didn't reply or even look up from her work.

We picked our way up the stairs, trying to avoid the piles of possessions that would surely have created some kind of domestic avalanche if one of them had been disturbed. There was a landing at the top but it was more like a gallery, as it formed three sides of a square and you could look down on the hall below from each point. Rectangles of lighter coloured paint on the walls marked the previous homes of large paintings, now absent. I was overawed by all this, but here was Georgie, seemingly immune to its faded splendour. Whatever must her previous home have been like, for her to be so casual about living here?

Georgie's bedroom led off the part of the landing farthest from the stairs. At least, that's what I assumed when she opened the door, but then I saw a staircase winding its way up to another floor.

"Come on," said Georgie. "My room's up here. Servants' quarters. You wouldn't believe the trouble I had getting my mother to agree to it, but I just went on and on until she gave up. She usually does eventually. It's my sanctuary."

We climbed the stairs and there was Georgie's sanctuary. I knew what that word meant, although I looked it up later to be certain. The official definition seemed a little dramatic, however chaotic the rest of Georgie's house appeared. 'Refuge or safety from pursuit, persecution or other danger,' it said in my concise Oxford Dictionary. I couldn't see that she was being either pursued or persecuted, but were there dangers I didn't know about? Was she telling me something in a coded way?

For the moment though, I was charmed. More than that, I was entranced by Georgie's bedroom. It was indeed an oasis of calm and order away from the chaos of the rest of the house. It was also quaint and quirky. The ceilings sloped almost to the floor and a leaded casement window opened out onto the back garden, which appeared to be a wilderness. There was a little window seat with a lid that opened up to reveal a storage space, and there was a half-sized door leading into the eaves. This was like an illustration from Alice in Wonderland and I was grateful that Georgie made no attempt at a joke referencing my name. The roof space was not boarded, but Georgie had put some bits and pieces of wood across the joists to provide further space for her things.

"It's, it's ..."

It wasn't often that words failed me. They were my armoury. But no adjective I could think of was adequate. I was delighted, jealous and amazed all at once. Nothing Enid Blyton – the source of much of my fantasy life - had described could match Georgie's room. The only things that could have improved it were a talking parrot or maybe a tame but mischievous monkey sitting on the bed. It was absolutely perfect, with none of the childishness of my own room.

The walls were simply white-washed. Georgie had put up some pictures and photos, but there were no pink flowers here. A one-eyed teddy-bear squinted at us from its position propped up on a chair in a corner, but this was the single visible sign of her childhood. Maybe the rest of it was in the eaves, put away in the many cardboard boxes, an indication that she had left all that behind her. In contrast, my childhood still hung on tenaciously, refusing to give up gracefully. Anyone who had entered my room would have seen that straight away.

It would take too long to describe all the fascinating things I found in Georgie's room. How many eleven year olds have a fully-functioning microscope sitting on a desk? Not a child's version, but one that could have come from a lab? How many eleven year olds have a large collection of fossils and can tell you all about them, including their names and how old they are? How many eleven year olds own so many books that they have to be stacked, two-deep, against one wall, with their own reference system devised by the child to enable them to be found when needed? This was Georgie's room, her haven. It also included her own record player in a box with a lid and a crystal radio set that worked with an out-sized pair of headphones.

"You can get Radio Luxembourg up here," she said. I nodded enthusiastically, although I had no idea what she was talking about.

I probably could have stayed in Georgie's room all day without tiring of it. The sun moved round until it shone right through the grimy leaded glass and bathed everything in a soft, dusty glow. I sat on the bed like a disciple while Georgie played her records. Mostly they were old – crackly, croony songs by people I had never heard of – but she also had "She Loves You' by the Beatles and a couple of other recent hits. How could this be? It had never occurred to me that I could actually own a pop record. This was something that older kids did. Yet here was Georgie stacking them on the spindle of the record player then leaning back against the bed, legs stretched out in front of her, as if this was something she'd been doing for years.

Eventually, I had to ask. I had to find out if this was something I could aspire to.

"Are they expensive?" I said.

"I'm not sure, they're mostly my brother's," she said, "but I think they're about four or five bob."

This was disappointing. I received pocket money

most weeks, but when I did it was less than half that amount. I would need to spend little or nothing for at least a month to buy just one record. No sweets, no comics, nothing for all that time. My vision of a pile of singles sitting next to my parents' extensive collection of classical records faded and died. But then I was struck by something else Georgie had said.

"Did you say they were your brother's? I didn't even know you had one!"

Georgie paused before replying and I saw her lips tighten.

"Oh, yes, I've got a brother alright. Hilary. He's at university, thank God. Cambridge. He's an insufferable idiot and I detest him."

This was said with such vehemence that I could think of nothing to say in reply. Instead, I filed away the word 'insufferable' and pondered over the fact that not only did Georgie's hitherto unknown brother have a girl's name, but he was also at university. This family just got better and better. I wished so badly it was mine that sometimes it actually hurt. At that moment, I knew that I would do just about anything to remain a part of it.

Eventually, Georgie replaced the records carefully in their paper sleeves and put them back on the shelf.

"Come on, I'm hungry. Let's go and see what we can find to eat."

So we went back downstairs and into the kitchen. I don't remember whether I was expecting Georgie's mother to have behaved as mine would have in that circumstance and prepared some sandwiches and cake for us. If that was my expectation it was soon to be dashed. The kitchen was in exactly the same state of disarray it had been when we left it more than two hours earlier. The only change was that the slab of clay was now no longer a slab, but the head and shoulders bust of a young girl with a mane of wild hair. It was rough and unfinished but it was unmistakably Georgie.

"Look, Georgie, it's you," I said, perhaps unnecessarily, although it did provoke a smile from Georgie's mother.

"I'm not entirely happy with it, but I'm glad you can see the likeness," she said.

"You're never entirely happy with them, mother," said Georgie. "That's why they all end up back in the clay bin, every time."

Georgie's mother looked up. For a minute I thought there would be an argument. Her eyes flashed in a very similar way to her daughter's, but clearly she thought better of it. Maybe she didn't want to admonish Georgie in front of me. I would never have got away with speaking to my mother like that, even if half my class had come to play at my house. There was a frosty silence for a moment, then Georgie took a loaf from a battered tin and some butter and cheese from the fridge. She carried them on a tray into the garden, summoning me to follow with a jerk of her head.

It was a bright October day, but chilly. Georgie saw me shivering and went back inside for our coats. Then we ate lumpy cheese sandwiches at a rickety wrought iron table on the paved terrace that ran the width of the back of the house. Weeds had thrust their way between the paving stones and rusty garden implements were lined up against the wall. There was a statue of a young girl holding some sort of pot on the overgrown lawn and a weeping willow beyond that. The garden seemed to stretch further than my eyes could see.

"What an amazing garden," I said, thinking of the neat square of grass at the back of my house, with its well-tended borders and crazy-paving path. True, there was a world beyond that, with fields, woods and streams all at my disposal, but Georgie's garden seemed to be a world in its own right. A magical place just waiting to be explored.

I don't know if anyone had tried to tame that garden since Georgie and her mother moved in. If they had, it was to little effect. The grass was long and brambles had overrun the shrubs and bushes that formed the borders on either side. We found a few late blackberries in a sheltered spot and devoured them, examining them carefully for maggots before popping them into our mouths and biting down to release the explosion of sweet juice. Our fingers were purple and I had several tiny thorns embedded in mine, but I didn't care.

Georgie found a scythe propped up against an overgrown greenhouse and slashed a ragged path down to the fence right at the bottom. We could hardly even see the house from where we were. Here, there were more trees and rotting apples hiding in the grass, waiting to spurt sour-smelling juice over our shoes. A few drunken wasps made half-hearted attempts to dive-bomb us but they were on their last legs and they seemed to know it. This was where Georgie dropped her next bombshell. She was leaning against an apple tree, her feet soaked by the long grass and her head tipped back as if she were searching for something in the twisted branches above her.

"I suppose I ought to tell you," she said.

I stopped trying to pinch the end of a thorn between my thumb and fingernail. Her voice had changed.

"My father's been captured."

"What? Captured by who?"

"The Russians, of course," she said, looking at me as if I were utterly stupid for not working that out for myself. "We only found out last week. We were expecting him back, but then someone from the government came and said his cover had been blown and it might take months or even years to release him. Just thought I should tell you, in case you wondered why he still wasn't here. But you mustn't tell anyone else. You must promise, or we could all be in danger, even you!"

My heart lurched and began to race. Of course I wouldn't tell anyone! This had become more than just a little vicarious excitement. This was serious. I didn't know much about the Cuban crisis just a year before, but I did know it had been critical and that the Russians were involved. There was talk of nuclear war and the destruction of everything. My parents had even discussed emigrating to Australia, as if somewhere that far away would somehow be excluded from the end of the world. Then it had all blown over and they had stopped talking about it. However, the Russians remained the universal bad guys in films and TV programmes. I knew better than to get on their wrong side.

"I swear on my life," I said and I meant it, I really did.

DECEMBER 2016

Now it has been said, there's no unsaying it. For a moment she thinks Georgie will refuse and all will be well, but she doesn't. She protests only to the degree that makes it obvious she is yearning to accept, so Alice keeps her smile pasted on all the time arrangements are being made.

Georgie's possessions are somewhere else. It is not at all clear where they are or how many of them are involved, but she is adamant she will deal with them herself.

"Where are you parked?" she says. "Wait there for me and I'll come to you." For a few seconds, Alice thinks the old Georgie has returned. She was always telling Alice to 'wait there' but it is only momentary. "If you're sure that's ok? If you're sure you don't mind?" she adds, destroying that illusion.

So Alice waits. She sits in her car for - how long? It must be half an hour or more. She begins to wonder whether the whole thing is some kind of elaborate hoax. But why would Georgie go to such lengths merely to cause her a little inconvenience? No, that's nonsense, but then she begins to panic. What is she doing inviting this woman into her home? Yes, it's Georgie, Georgie who was so close that at one time she would have swapped her for both her sisters if anyone had offered her the chance. But this woman is a stranger. Sure, it is her, but fifty years have elapsed and she is clearly not the same person she was. Neither is Alice.

For the second time that day, she considers making a run for it. There is no sign of Georgie and it would be simple enough to drive away. She hasn't given her the address or even the name of her village. She's sure she could delete her from Facebook or do something to stop her making contact, it can't be that difficult. Scott will be able to tell her. Yes, that's what she'll do. This has got way out of control. She'll drive home, possibly even by a more circuitous route, and forget all about it. Leave the past in the past, that's the safest thing to do.

Her finger is poised above the ignition button when a battered old Volvo estate pulls up beside her. It is packed with bags and boxes and goodness knows what else and now it is too late. Again. She has missed her second opportunity to re-set her life back to normal. Georgie gets out with the nearest thing to a smile Alice has seen since they met this morning and walks across to where Alice is still sitting, her window wound down.

"Well, here I am. Sorry it took so long." Alice can't help but look at the jumble of possessions crammed into Georgie's car and Georgie notices. "Look, don't worry, I won't unpack all this. Just my overnight bag and my cameras. They're precious, but the rest of it - I doubt anyone would steal it even if I left it on the pavement."

Alice pushes aside a small worry about what the neighbours will think when they see Georgie's car parked on her drive. There's no denying it, it's a heap of junk even without the haphazard arrangement of its dubious contents. She has lived in her house for a little over one year. All that time, yet she has established nothing more than a nodding politely relationship with the thus far nameless neighbours. Will they ignore her now? She knows she shouldn't care if they do. She knows they aren't really worth the effort if they care so much about appearances, but she has been so much more lonely than she anticipated without John. She wants to be able to talk to the people who live nearby.

"It's fine. It's not a huge room but you're welcome to bring in whatever you like. Shall I give you the address?"

Georgie looks uncertain. "Um, it might be easier if I follow you," she says, and then Alice understands why. She has become so accustomed to the in-built satnav in this fancy car that it hasn't occurred to her that Georgie might have to rely on more primitive means of navigation. Satnavs probably didn't even exist when Georgie's car first rolled off the track.

"Of course, much easier," she says. "I'll watch out for you."

They set off, and Alice looks in the rear-view mirror every few seconds at first. She is careful to drive slowly, even when they leave town and join the de-restricted road out to her village. But she doesn't need to worry. Georgie drives like she used to climb trees – fast and with little thought of the consequences. She hurtles out of junctions and remains inches away from Alice's bumper even when they speed up. However fast Alice goes, Georgie matches it. Alice has never been more pleased to see a 30 mph speed limit and when she signals the final left turn into the crescent she realises she has been holding her breath.

The Volvo pulls up beside her with a rattle and a cough of blue smoke. Alice puts her fingers on the door handle but she is reluctant to open the door. What has she done?

OCTOBER 1963

That was not my last visit to Georgie's house that week. I practically lived up there, bolting down my breakfast, leaving as early as possible and only returning as the sun began to hover over the horizon. There were no lights on my bike so I was under strict instructions to return before dusk. Still, I think I would have stayed all night if anyone had suggested it, despite the fact that nobody seemed to bother much about food in Georgie's house. I was always starving when I returned.

By the time Friday came, we had made a huge dent in the unpacking. This had been my idea. The contents of the crates seemed mysterious to me. A house like this was bound to have all kinds of secret places and this seemed like an excellent excuse to explore them. Georgie had been reluctant at first, but we set aside a couple of hours each day and cleared all the crates in the hall. I had even had the opportunity to catch a glimpse of Hilary's room when one of the piles of books on the stairs was identified as his.

It was in complete chaos, with heaps of clothes on the huge double bed and cardboard boxes in various states of collapse covering most of the floor. Deep red, dusky damask curtains obscured at least half of the window, but they were far too long and lay bunched on the floor at each side. Against one wall there was an enormous oak wardrobe that could well have been a portal to Narnia or some other fantastic world. I longed to look inside.

"Shall we make a start on unpacking for him?" I suggested. What better way to learn more about this exotic creature, the Older Brother? But Georgie was adamant. Hilary's room was not to be touched. It was his mess and he could sort it out himself. She practically pushed me out and closed the door behind me with a force that implied I would be ill-advised to try opening it again. That didn't stop me another time, but I was braver by then and used to sneaking around.

Georgie's mother was wearing a silk dressing gown when I arrived that morning. She was sitting at the kitchen table with a cigarette, a mug of coffee and a faraway expression. There was no sign of the bust of Georgie, so I assumed that had met the same fate as its predecessors and was sitting scrunched up in the clay bin that was kept in the little scullery off the kitchen. Someone had given her end of the table a cursory wipe but it was still smeared with clay. She was using one fingernail to scratch a geometrical pattern into the fine dusty film that remained. She looked slightly grey, as if the black smudges around her eyes from yesterday's mascara had seeped into the surrounding flesh.

In contrast, Georgie was dressed and her skin glowed. She seemed fired with energy and enthusiasm for our task of the day, which was to sort out the kitchen. She bustled her mother out of the room as if she were nothing more significant than a stray cat that had wandered in out of the cold.

"Go and do some painting or something," she said. "It doesn't have to be clay every day, does it?"

I knew Georgie's mother painted as well as working in clay. Indeed there was far more evidence of this medium. I had found one bedroom practically full of canvasses, some framed but some obviously unfinished. Georgie hurried me out when I tried to look more closely, but not before I had caught a glimpse of a couple of very explicit nudes. The style was bold and colourful and the bodies were out of proportion, with tiny heads and oversized bottoms, but I thought they were wonderful – powerful and potent. They made me want to look closer and yet they disturbed me, provoking a strange feeling I could not describe, even with the help of my thesaurus. I crept in that room to steal another look whenever I had a few minutes away from Georgie's watchful eye.

We spent the whole morning in the kitchen. Half the cupboards and drawers were still empty, so we threw away the old, stained lining paper and wiped everything clean. We didn't have anything suitable with which to re-line them, but Georgie said that wouldn't matter so we started to unpack the crates of crockery that had been pushed under the table. I had never seen such a mishmash and jumble of different styles and services. In our house we had two sets of crockery, one for everyday use and one for best. There must have been the remnants of half a dozen services in those crates, to say nothing of all the pieces that seemed to belong to nothing at all.

Some of them were beautiful, though Georgie took no note of that. Delicate bone china cups with gold rims and ornate handles ended up next to chipped mugs. I was struck by a fine dish with a picture of a satyr chasing a girl. Her hair flowed out behind her and her diaphanous robes were tinted with some kind of silvery glaze. It was so realistic that you felt you would be able to pinch the fabric between your fingers if you tried.

"Look at this, Georgie. It's fabulous. Don't you think it should be in a dresser or something?" I said.

"We don't have a dresser. It was too big so we left it behind," said Georgie. Her face was inscrutable – a word I had borrowed from Sir Arthur Conan Doyle – but something told me not to pursue the matter.

Later, as I thought about it, I realised that there was not a lot of furniture downstairs – certainly not for the size of the house. Maybe there had been a dramatic midnight escape from the Russian agents when Georgie moved house. Maybe they could only take the bare minimum of possessions with them when they left. That was a tempting theory but it didn't fit in with the number of crates we had unpacked. It must have taken at least a week to fill them, so I found myself stumped. There was some kind of mystery about Georgie's move, and I would not be content until I knew what it was.

When we had finished unpacking and cleared most of the table, we ate toast and jam with a glass of milk and looked around at our handiwork. We had done a very good job and I was hoping Georgie's mother would come in and praise us. She could hardly fail to be impressed by the largely clean and empty surfaces and the cupboards neatly stacked and organised. There wasn't a lot of food in any of them, but Georgie assured me that they did their shopping on Saturdays so that accounted for that.

We rinsed and dried our plates and put them away, but still there was no sign of Georgie's mother.

"Come on, I've had enough of being inside for one day," said Georgie. "Let's go up to the hill."

Although I was very familiar with the woods and fields to the back of my house, I had never ventured as far as the North Downs. The hills were visible from our kitchen window, but I had no idea how to reach them and it had never occurred to me to try.

Georgie got our coats and we left by the front door. She didn't even try to tell her mother where we were going, but I said nothing. I didn't want her to think I was some kind of goody two-shoes and it wouldn't be me who got into trouble anyway. We turned left out of the drive and walked along the grass verge to the top of the road that led back into the village, but there we turned left again into a bridleway through the woods. This started to climb quite steeply after a few hundred yards and then, both of us puffing and panting, we emerged onto a wide, grassy area. I could just see a faint path winding its way to the top of the hill that loomed above us, topped with more trees.

A few minutes more and we were at the top of

the hill. I was speechless and this was only partly due to the exertions of the climb. When we turned round, laughing and holding our sides, there was what seemed to be the whole of Kent laid out before us, dressed in its best Autumn colours and only punctuated by the roofs and spires of its villages.

"It's a bit misty today," said Georgie, "but wait 'til you see it on a sunny day. You can see for miles and miles. Sometimes it feels like you are the only person in the whole world."

Suddenly, I was gripped by a wave of what I suppose was gratitude to Georgie. This was her special place, the place she came to when she wanted to feel like the only person in the world, and she had shared it with me. Not only that, her words implied that this would not be the last time. I would see it again when it was sunny and that would be even better. I wanted to do something to show how happy she'd made me. I couldn't think what else to do, so I deployed the best word in my mental dictionary.

"It's ravishing," I said.

I'm not sure what Georgie made of that adjective, but it wasn't long before she was restless again.

"Watch this," she said, then jumped up to catch the lowest branch of a pine tree and pulled herself up. Within minutes I could hardly see her, only catching glimpses of the blue of her jeans amongst the branches as she climbed higher and higher.

"Woo-hoo!" came her cry eventually. I stepped back until I could see the top of the tree. It was swaying wildly and there was Georgie, only a few feet from the very top, holding onto the spindly trunk with one hand and waving at me with the other.

"You should see the view from up here!" she called. I was terrified she would fall. What would I do if she crashed through the branches to lie lifeless at the foot of the tree? The grass up here was tight and bouncy, interspersed with patches of moss and other plants I didn't recognise, but it would hardly cushion a fall from such a height. What on earth would I tell her mother? I waved – a feeble little flap of one hand - but didn't reply in case our conversation caused her to lose concentration. Before long she gave one more whoop then disappeared back into the branches and I breathed a sigh of relief.

I watched Georgie's descent with my fingers tightly crossed on both hands. I couldn't see her, but the movement of the foliage indicated her progress. Soon I saw her legs dangling briefly before she dropped to the ground.

"That's better," she grinned. "I've been dying to get up there for days. You wait 'til you try it. There is absolutely no feeling like it, maybe apart from flying but I've never tried that!"

I said nothing in response. I was no stranger to tree-climbing, but I had always remained within a reasonably safe distance from the ground and the thought of swaying around at such a height made my palms tingle. Instead, I remarked on a bank of very dark clouds that was sweeping towards us on a freshening wind and we headed back. Georgie charged off down the hill at great speed and I followed more slowly, but it wouldn't have made any difference how fast we ran. The heavens opened before we even got back to the road and we were both drenched when we burst through the back door into the kitchen.

There was still no sign of Georgie's mother, nor any indication that she had even witnessed the kitchen's transformation. Georgie kicked off her shoes and draped her coat over a chair.

"Wait there," she said and left the room.

This was something that often happened with Georgie and usually I obeyed her. Normally, she would return within a couple of minutes and I would be released from this stasis by an explanation of where she had been. However, standing dripping onto the kitchen floor didn't seem like the most sensible option now and anyway I needed the toilet. I took off my coat, hung it over another chair and slipped off my shoes. I was just about to climb the stairs to the bathroom when I heard something. It sounded like somebody groaning and it was coming from the lounge.

Immediately, visions of Georgie's mother lying on the floor, a knife protruding from her chest or a single bullet wound in her forehead sprang into my mind. Of course! It was obvious! The Russians had caught up with her and attacked her. My heart pounding, I crept on damp tip-toe to the lounge door. It was partially open so I pushed it a little further and peeped inside, wincing as the hinges squeaked. It was indeed Georgie's mother who had made the groaning sound. I could see her sitting on the faded chintz sofa, leaning forward with her head in her hands. Her shoulders were shaking and she was rocking gently.

It took a moment for my brain to banish other explanations for what I could see and replace them with the one that was most obvious. No, she wasn't in the final stages of dying from poison administered via the half-empty cut glass tumbler on the table in front of her. She was simply crying. I stepped back, but then gasped and jumped as I felt a hand on my shoulder.

"What are you doing?" asked Georgie.

"I was, um, I was looking for you," I said.

An expression swept across Georgie's face in much the same way as the dark clouds had swept across the skies over the hill. She moved me to one side and gave the lounge door a shove that sent it flying open so quickly that it banged against the bookcase behind it.

"Oh, hello George," I heard her mother say. "My word, you're soaking. Is your friend still here?"

"Yes, she is, and her name's Alice. I keep telling you that."

"Well I'm afraid you'll have to make your own tea. I think I'm coming down with the 'flu," came the reply. Georgie stood back as her mother swept past us in a swirl of skirts and scarves and hurried up the stairs, a handkerchief pressed to her nose.

There was an uncomfortable silence broken at last by Georgie handing me a pair of jeans.

"Here, you can change into these before you go home," she said. "They're too short for me now."

I took the jeans but I knew I couldn't wear them. My parents were good people, but they had many strange prejudices and jeans were not allowed in our house. My mother insisted that they were 'common,' and that was something we had to strive against at all costs. It was common to eat in the street and common to say 'what?' instead of 'pardon?' There were so many ways to appear common that it was hard to remember them all, but I knew that if I arrived home wearing those jeans there was a chance that they would question my friendship with Georgie. Until now, the fact that she lived on Templars Way had guaranteed acceptance and I had told them nothing to change any assumptions they had made. There was no way I was going to risk all this.

Added to that, it was clear that Georgie was keen for me to leave. 'Before you go home,' she had said, although the sky had now cleared and it was still quite light outside. Every other day she had tried to persuade me to stay a little longer, so I took the hint.

"No, it's fine. I'll change when I get back," I said and handed the jeans back to her. They were real jeans, with orange stitching on the seams and a leather label on the waistband. What wouldn't I have given to have worn them? But it was not to be.

My mum was cooking when I arrived home, but she dropped everything when she saw the state of me. I had to have a bath even though it was not a bath day. She put a towel on the hot water tank and laid out a complete set of clean clothes on my bed. It was nice to be fussed over, although of course I complained. I thought sadly of Georgie up there in that big, often chilly house with a mother who had noticed how wet she was without doing anything about it. What would she be doing now? The smell of my dinner wafted upstairs but Georgie's mother had retired to her room. I knew there was nothing much in their cupboards. For the first time, I felt sorry for Georgie. True, her life was exciting and glamorous in so many ways, but would I swap with her now?

The downside of all this attention was that my mum insisted I went to bed early that night.

"We've hardly seen you this week, but I'm beginning to think you've been running wild. Didn't anyone notice how wet you were? I don't know about other people, but if Georgie had been in my house she wouldn't have gone home in that state!"

I tried to explain that Georgie's mother had been unwell and that Georgie had offered me a change of clothes. It was all to no avail. I needed to be taken in hand and a nice early night was the beginning of that process.

Of course I didn't admit it, but I was actually exhausted. I had cycled up to Georgie's for five days in a row and our activities had been almost exclusively physical. Neither of us were keen on sitting down for long, and that first day in her bedroom had been the only occasion we had spent any time relaxing. If we weren't unpacking and hauling wooden crates around we were slashing down the weeds in the garden or playing a strange version of cricket Georgie had invented, using a splintery wooden plank and a half-chewed sponge ball. The trip to Georgie's hill had just about finished me off. I sank into a deep sleep almost as soon as my head hit the pillow, despite my resolution to stay awake at least until my normal Friday bedtime.

I don't know what time it was when the sound of a cry awoke me. I sat up, sweating and breathing fast. Then the landing light went on and I saw the silhouette of my mum in the doorway.

"What's the matter, love?" she said. She was in her nightie and her voice was croaky with sleep. She sat down on the bed and put her arm around my shoulder.

"Good God, child, you're shaking!"

It was true, my teeth were chattering and my stomach was in knots. But I knew I wasn't ill. Flashes of a dream in which I was being pursued by Russian agents in huge, furry hats kept coming back to me and I knew that the cry I had heard was my own. I had been in Georgie's house, or a house that seemed like Georgie's. It had many extra rooms - secret rooms and tunnels I could hide in - but I was lost and they were just behind me with their guns.

My mother's hand on my forehead allayed her fears about a fever induced by my earlier soaking.

"You've had a bad dream, love. What was it about?"

I didn't want to tell her about Georgie's father, I really didn't, but somehow it all came out. It was just too hard to keep it all to myself when the panic was so close to the surface and the dream was still so real. I told her it was an absolute secret and we would all be in danger if she told anyone. I told her Georgie would not be my friend if she found out I had broken her trust. This thought made me cry; deep, heaving sobs that shook my body and replaced the fear.

"I doubt very much that the Russians are interested in us," said my mum, giving me a squeeze. "And I think your friend may have a bit of an over-active imagination. But don't worry, we won't tell anyone if you promise not to keep secrets from us."

This seemed like a reasonable arrangement so I agreed, but I was consumed with anxiety all through that weekend. Georgie had trusted me and I had betrayed her. Now there was a secret I was keeping from her, as well as the secret my parents were keeping on my behalf. Doubtless there were more secrets to come, secrets that had made Georgie's mother cry and secrets that explained their sudden appearance in our village. The very thought of what I may find out, and the decisions I would have to make about telling my parents, made me catch my breath. Nevertheless, I wouldn't have changed it for the world. How could I wish to go back to my old, dull life when every day held the promise of adventure? It was scary, but addictive and I was truly hooked.

DECEMBER 2016

Of course she can't sit there in the car for long. Actually, the time that passes while she composes herself could be measured probably in seconds, but time is funny like that. We have all sorts of ways of measuring it, but really it's a law unto itself. That's what she thinks as she opens the door and gets out. She has just about learned how to exit this low-slung automotive extravagance in an elegant fashion, and now she can't help but congratulate herself as her sensible shoes plant themselves firmly on the weed-free paving of the drive.

In contrast, Georgie erupts from the Volvo like someone being fired from a canon in an old movie.

"The door sticks," she says, patting herself down.

Alice tries really hard not to look across the neat shrubs of her garden to the house next door. She helps Georgie retrieve a couple of bags from the back of the Volvo and they go inside, but she can't help feel somebody in the crescent will have remarked on their arrival.

Once inside, she takes Georgie straight up to the guest bedroom. She can't find the words to ask her to remove her shoes, so she keeps hers on too and leads the way upstairs. The guest bedroom is in a pristine condition and has been since she moved in. No guests have enjoyed its anonymous charms. No-one has tested out the en-suite shower room or hung their coat on the handy hook on the back of the door.

When she first moved in, she imagined a succession of visitors and spent quite a lot of time and money ensuring this room had everything a guest could want. Matching towels on the heated towel rail, tasteful pictures on the walls, plenty of storage space. She even went to an up-market toiletries shop, bought a supply of miniature soaps and shower gel with exotic scents and arranged them on the window ledge. She could not have imagined that her first guest would dump a scruffy holdall and an Asda carrier bag on the white quilt before looking around at all her handiwork.

However, Georgie's reaction is all she could have

hoped for.

"What a lovely room!" she says, a real smile appearing for the first time and confirming that the old Georgie is concealed inside this careworn figure after all. "Are you absolutely sure this is ok? I mean ..." she gestures vaguely at her possessions, so incongruent on the bed.

Alice is pleased and uncomfortable at the same time, if that is possible. It is nice to be helping someone less fortunate than herself, nice to be appreciated. But this is Georgie. This is not how things were and it all feels strange. Although their relationship became more equal as time went on, it never swung completely in her favour and she always felt diminished by her class. Now the pendulum seems to have gone mad - as far as material possessions are concerned, anyway.

"Don't be silly," she says. "I've got an empty room and you need somewhere to stay. It was always intended for guests. I live alone and I'm not expecting anyone else, so of course it's fine."

She tells Georgie to make herself comfortable and goes downstairs. Somehow, the afternoon has disappeared and she is starving. She rejects the siren calls of a packet of chocolate brownies, somehow knowing that she will feel awkward if Georgie comes downstairs and catches her eating one. Ridiculous, but there it is. Instead, she makes a couple of rounds of sandwiches and eats one of them while she looks in the freezer. If she'd known she was entertaining she would have included a trip to the supermarket in her morning's itinerary. Now they will have to make do with whatever she has in the house. She can't really work out why, but something tells her not to risk leaving Georgie in the house alone.

She has finished eating and has drunk half of her coffee by the time she hears Georgie's feet on the stairs.

"In here," she calls, so Georgie won't have to go looking for her.

Georgie has the Asda carrier bag with her when she enters the kitchen. She looks sheepish.

"I don't suppose ..." she starts. She has flushed a deep red and suddenly Alice feels terribly sorry for her and yet much more relaxed. Poor Georgie. How awful this must be for her. To be reduced to such circumstances when you've been used to such a different way of life. At least she can look after her for a couple of days. She leaps up and takes the carrier bag before Georgie has time to protest.

"No problem at all! Here, give it to me. I'll pop it in now. What temperature? Forty degrees ok?"

The washing machine is in a utility room just off the kitchen. She is in there, reaching up for the box of washing tablets when she realises Georgie has followed her.

"Do you mind if I do it?" Georgie says. Alice turns. Georgie's face is a picture of despair and her hands are clasped firmly together, knuckles white. Alice has not really looked at the contents of the carrier bag, but now she sees underwear, not very new underwear at that, amongst the garments.

"Of course! Here, let me just show you ..."

The washing machine is a top of the range model with more programmes than anyone could ever want, but Alice has worked out the two or three she is ever likely to use. Washing is an intermittent chore these days, with no shirts for John, no school uniforms or PE kits for the kids. She shows Georgie how to get it started, then squeezes past her. She busies herself re-filling the kettle although it is still half full, humming a little tune to herself to lighten the mood.

It does not take Georgie long to load the machine, and soon it is swishing away in the background. Alice makes Georgie a mug of tea and watches while she eats one of the remaining sandwiches. She nearly gets out the brownies, but decides against it.

"I thought I'd defrost a couple of steaks for dinner," she says when it is clear Georgie is not going to eat the last sandwich. "Would that suit you?"

There is a pause.

"Um, sorry," says Georgie, "but I'm vegetarian."

NOVEMBER 1963

Everything returned more or less to normal when we went back to school. Georgie sat with Caroline and me from time to time but not very often. Not often enough for anyone to notice. I don't think this was part of any plan, it was just the way she was, but it suited me. I kept my secret friendship close, like a little charm in the corner of a pocket. I could look across the classroom and be certain that I knew more about Georgie than anyone else in the class. I knew how she lived and I knew her secrets. She had shared them with me, so they were my secrets too.

At the same time, I tried not to talk about her too much at home. I even invented little stories about Caroline to throw my parents off the scent. I began to think I had got away with it. Georgie was unaware that my parents knew her secret and, in turn, they hardly mentioned her. With a little more time they might forget about her altogether. That's what I thought. True, it was a short-term strategy, as I was already looking forward to the next holiday and the opportunity of having Georgie all to myself again. However, I would have to worry about that later.

That's why it was quite a shock when my mother raised it, out of the blue, one morning before school a couple of weeks later. I was eating my cornflakes and it was fortunate that I had just swallowed a mouthful when she spoke.

"Alice, would you like to invite Georgie to come for tea one day after school?"

"Um, no, I don't think so. She has to do homework as soon as she gets in, and she wouldn't be able to get home afterwards."

"Well, we'll make it a Friday then, so she has the weekend to do her homework. Dad will run her home. You could even do your homework together while she's here."

Desperately, I ransacked my mind for another excuse. This was terrible. There were so many reasons why Georgie should never come to my house. First, and most terrifying, was the possibility that one of my parents would say something stupid about her father and give the game away. Then she would know that I couldn't keep a secret. She would know that I was a great big baby who got scared by bad dreams and spilled the beans. But that wasn't the only reason. As I concealed my second-hand bike in the bushes and stood at the end of the drive, I'd vowed Georgie would never come to my house.

There was no getting away from it. I was embarrassed. Ashamed. My house was perfectly nice but it was so … so ordinary. I couldn't think of another word and I could hardly run upstairs in order to look one up. What I was unable to articulate then, was how conventional, how aspirational working-class my home seemed in comparison to Georgie's. Why did everything have to be so neat? Why did the ornaments on the mantelpiece have to be arranged like that, with such petty-minded symmetry? Why was there no chaos or artistic disarray to greet Georgie as she walked through the door? She would think my parents were boring and, by association, I must be boring too. This was a nightmare.

"Well, maybe after Christmas," I said, hoping to buy some time. "I know they're very busy at the moment, with all the unpacking and that."

"Don't be silly, Alice, they can't still be unpacking now," snorted my mother, hands on hips. She would have had those crates unpacked and their contents stashed away within a week. Of course, I had never told her about the state of Georgie's house. "Anyway, you can't keep taking their hospitality without returning it. It's rude. I won't have her mother thinking we have no manners until after Christmas! You do as you're told and invite her. I'm telling you, there'll be no more going up there to play until you do."

I knew when I was beaten. There was nothing my mother hated more than somebody thinking she was rude. Unless it was that she was common. I wasn't sure which would be worse. It was clear that she meant what she said. If I wanted to go to Georgie's house in the Christmas holidays, Georgie would have to come here first.

It was two days before I summoned up the courage to ask her. Part of me wanted her to say no she couldn't come, but that would cause as many problems as it would solve. My mum would either not believe I had asked her, or she would think Georgie was ill-mannered and snobbish. I could just imagine her response: *'Oh, so we're not good enough for the high-and-mighty Georgie, is that it? Just because you live on Templars Way, doesn't make you better than everyone else!'*

She was such a strange contradiction, my mum. Part of her believed it - that she was as good as anyone and that money was no indication of worth - but another part of her would have been desperate for acceptance by a family like Georgie's. Well, not a family like Georgie's, clearly. The family she had visualised when I told her about the size of the house, the wood-panelled hall and that Georgie's bedroom was in the former servants' quarters.

However, as it happened, she never had to wonder at Georgie's motives for refusing her kind invitation. Georgie accepted immediately, with every indication of pleasure.

"I suppose I'll have to check with my mother," she said, "but it'll be fine. She probably wouldn't notice if I didn't come home at all. Next Friday then! Thanks! I can't wait to see your house."

I'm sure Georgie didn't notice my lack of enthusiasm. We were on the bus, and I had left the invitation late enough for there to be little time for awkwardness if she said no. In any case, my powers of deception were increasing almost on a daily basis. She stood up as the bus approached her stop and gave me gave me her customary broad smile.

"I'll ask now, as soon as I get in. See you tomorrow!"

I wandered home miserably, trying to remember what I had said about my house. Had I exaggerated its size? Had I painted a picture in Georgie's mind that would be contradicted by the sad truth as she walked through the door? Well, it was too late to do anything about it now. I resigned myself to a shift in my relationship with Georgie. There would be another dimension to her opinion of me. I wouldn't be the Alice she thought I was. I would be the Alice who lived in a house that was everything hers wasn't. A house that was a boring representation of my boring little family who never did anything exciting or risky.

And so the day of Georgie's visit arrived. It was Friday, 22nd November, a day I had been dreading for nearly a week. I had underlined the date in my diary and written 'Georgie' beside it. Otherwise, the page was still blank, but I had already composed the first sentences of what I would write later. 'I will never forget the expression on Georgie's face. All her expectations dashed, destroyed and ruined by harsh reality. Our friendship in tatters on the floor. Dead, expired, lifeless.'

I was quite proud of these words, despite the sad circumstances of their composition. I had recently learned about the power of three and used it whenever I could, regardless of whether it was appropriate and certainly more often than was wise within one paragraph. Unfortunately, I had yet to learn the term hyperbole as that may have helped. As it happened, these somewhat hysterical sentences were destined never to appear on paper. They were consigned to a literary dustbin somewhere in my head the moment Georgie followed me through the back door and into the kitchen. She grinned and held out her hand to my mum.

"Thank you so much for inviting me," she said. "What a lovely house!"

Was there something else there? Was she being ironic or simply polite? I didn't think so. If anything her expression contained a hint of sadness, but she continued to exclaim as we went into the lounge.

"Oh, how cosy!" she said. "I've always wanted to live in a cottage. You're so lucky."

My house was not a cottage. It possessed none of the features of a cottage apart from being quite small – at least in comparison to Georgie's house. It was a mid- 20th century semi with not an exposed beam or brick fireplace to be seen. All the same, it was warm and comfortable. I tried to look at it through Georgie's eyes. Yes, I could see how different it must seem to the cavernous lounge in her house. That was sparsely furnished and the single radiator's valiant attempts to heat such a large space seemed doomed to failure.

"Well, you sit down and make yourself comfortable," said my mum, taking Georgie's coat and shooing my desperately curious sisters away with a vigorous flap of her hands and a fierce expression that scared no-one. "Alice, hang this up then come into the kitchen."

I did as I was told. There on the worktop was a plate of biscuits – two bourbon, two custard creams and two chocolate fingers. Two glasses of squash were also ready so I carried everything through to Georgie. I was filled with pleasure and pride at my mum's hospitality. Georgie was both delighted and hungry and gobbled up her share of the biscuits so quickly that I offered her my chocolate finger. This was despite the fact that it was my favourite and I had been saving it until last. It was only then that I started to feel a hint of embarrassment mixed in with the pride. What a contrast to the first time I had met Georgie's mother. What would Georgie feel like if she remembered it too?

The rest of the visit was equally successful. Georgie declared my bedroom to be 'sweet' and she loved my sisters. She spent ages with them, far too long for my liking, admiring their toys and helping them with jigsaws. I became so jealous that I was actually relieved when we were called to eat, although I had been dreading this part of the visit. My mum was of the old school where food was concerned, which meant there was no tolerance of fussy eating. You ate what you were given, certainly unless you had tried something many times and still hated it, and you were thankful for it. Anyone showing signs of flagging before their plate was cleared would be reminded of all the starving children in the world who would surely be grateful for that bit of gristly meat or that forkful of lumpy mashed potato. What would Georgie make of this?

Although I had eaten at her house many times, I

had yet to sit down to a cooked meal there. We tended to fend for ourselves and I hadn't a clue about Georgie's mother's cooking or attitude to eating. Indeed it was hard to imagine how they would even sit down to a meal together. The table was always so cluttered. But I needn't have worried. Georgie loved my mum's steak and kidney pudding. If she hated kidney – as I did – she hid it well. She ate every morsel on her plate and accepted seconds with alacrity. I had rarely seen anyone eat with such gusto and in such quantities. A large bowl of banana custard disappeared just as quickly and at last she sat back in her chair with a satisfied sigh.

"That was the best dinner I've ever had," she announced, causing my mum to flutter a little.

"Oh, thank you dear. You're very kind. It's only plain food here I'm afraid, but I'm glad you enjoyed it."

I think my mum had been entertaining a vision of Georgie and her mother sitting down to fancy three-course meals every evening. She probably imagined a white tablecloth and silver cutlery, with maybe candlesticks or red roses in a crystal vase. If only she knew! I noticed that she had gone to a little more trouble than usual today – a clean tablecloth and glasses for our drinks instead of plastic beakers – but actually this was how we ate every day. She was a competent but plain cook and she ensured that we ate a healthy and balanced diet. I had never remarked on this before, it was simply the ways things were. Neither had it occurred to me that other people might not be so lucky, apart from the starving children in some far-flung corner of the world, of course. Could it be that Georgie didn't have a proper meal when she got home? Could it be that I was luckier than her in this respect?

Georgie's offer of help with the washing up was refused, gratefully but firmly. No, she was a guest and she certainly wouldn't be doing any domestic chores. We watched tv for a while and then my dad came home and was introduced. Georgie was very polite and reiterated her compliments about the house and the meal, but it was almost time for her to leave. We had only the short time it would take for my dad to eat his evening meal before he would drive her home, so we went into the lounge. Georgie had promised to teach me how to play chess and we would be uninterrupted in there. My sisters were getting ready for bed and the tv was in the other room.

"Why isn't your telly in here?" asked Georgie as she arranged the pieces on the board.

"My parents thought it would stop us talking or listening to music in here," I said. "Actually it just means we spend most of the time in the other room crammed onto that tiny sofa or sitting on hard chairs, but there you go."

Georgie looked thoughtful, and I think she was about to say something when we heard my mother's cry.

"Oh, my God!"

It was not the sort of cry you could ignore. I hadn't heard the telephone so it couldn't be bad news delivered that way, but clearly something had happened.

"Wait there," I said and hurried into the other room.

Both my parents were sitting bolt upright, their eyes fixed on the tv. They looked up as I came in.

"President Kennedy's been shot," said my mum. She looked as if it wouldn't take much for her to cry.

I didn't know what to say, or what to make of this. Of course I knew who he was, but I had little idea about what he stood for or what an impact this event would have. I was still a child, my head full of stories and my life full of little triumphs and disasters quite unconnected to the world stage. Apart from my brush with the Russians, that was.

"Oh. I'd better go and tell Georgie," was all I could think of to say.

So we sat, a sombre little foursome, while my

dad picked at the remains of his dinner and the BBC tried to cope with this apparently earth-shattering event. It was about half past seven, the time that Georgie was supposed to be returning home, when the news came through that Kennedy had been shot in the head and then, shortly after that, we heard that he had died. My mum dabbed at her eyes with her handkerchief and my dad's face assumed a colour similar to that of the tablecloth.

"Come on, young lady," he said to Georgie. "Let's get you home. Your mum will be wondering where you are."

When we got back, the television had reverted to its normal programmes. It was Harry Worth, a comedy programme we usually watched together on Friday evenings.

"I can't believe they're still showing this," said my mum and she switched it off. "That poor man. And his wife, and all those beautiful little children. How could anybody do such a thing?"

"It's the bloody Russians, you mark my words," said my dad. "When it all comes out, they'll be behind it."

A great wave of fear swept over me as I heard these words. I felt as if I'd been punched in the stomach. If the Russians could do this, if they could kill a man as important as President Kennedy, they could wipe out the whole of Georgie's family – and mine if it came to it – with no trouble. What had I got myself into?

DECEMBER 2016

She makes a macaroni cheese instead. It's nothing wonderful, especially as she has to leave out the pancetta that John used to like so much, but Georgie can't stop praising it. Even though she has eaten a tiny portion compared to Alice, she leans back in her chair with her hands resting on her stomach as though she has come to the end of a seven course banquet. Alice isn't quite sure how to take all this fuss over a relatively simple meal, but assumes it is genuine.

She loads the dishwasher, refusing all Georgie's offers of help, then takes her glass and the bottle of red through to the lounge, inviting Georgie to follow. They sit in the matching armchairs on either side of the fake coal gas fire. Alice turns it on. It's not a patch on a real coal fire, she tells Georgie, but it's better than nothing and there's no mess. Georgie looks round the room, her eyes taking in the generous proportions, the smooth plaster, the deep pile of the carpet.

"This is a lovely house," she says.

"Thanks," says Alice, topping up both their glasses.

"Oh, I'm not sure ..." begins Georgie but Alice doesn't stop until Georgie's glass is full.

"Oh, come on. A couple of glasses won't hurt you. You're not driving, are you? Look what a funny day it's been for you. It'll help you relax."

Alice takes silence to mean consent, and this seems to be confirmed when Georgie picks up her glass and drinks about a third of it almost without stopping.

"Would you like the tv on?" asks Alice, but Georgie is non-committal on that. Indeed it is hard to get any conversation out of her at all. Alice wonders why she bothered making contact with her in the first place if she has so little to say for herself. She doesn't even seem interested in asking about Alice's life. But then she reconsiders. Georgie is probably exhausted. She is just about to ask if her guest would like a nice hot bath and an early night, when Georgie sits up straight in her chair.

"I suppose I'd better tell you," she says.

Alice's heart misses a beat and suddenly she is eleven again. Is this something to worry about, just when she has started to relax, to believe she hasn't made a monumental mistake after all?

"Tell me what?" she says, hoping her voice does not betray her.

"Why I'm living like this," says Georgie. "Like some kind of mobile bag lady. You must've been wondering."

"Well ..." says Alice.

"It's alright. Anybody would. Especially anybody who knew me before." She picks up her glass and takes another mouthful. "I used to have a house, you know. A nice house – not new and smart like this one, but nice."

"What happened?"

"Gordon. Gordon happened," says Georgie and her eyes fill with tears.

It takes Georgie a few minutes and another swig of her wine to compose herself enough to speak again. Alice suggests she stops there, thinks about something else, but there seems to be no stopping her now she has made up her mind.

"I'm a photographer, you know," she starts. "I bet you never thought that was how it would turn out, but I was good at it. I probably still could be, if

I could only get myself sorted out. I worked for magazines mostly, but I did some freelancing work from time to time. I had a picture in The Guardian once, and a couple in The Times. Arty kind of takes on popular stories, you know the kind of thing."

Alice doesn't, not really, but she nods encouragingly and tries to look impressed.

"Anyway, I was working on this lifestyle mag. It's gone out of publication now and you probably never heard of it – it doesn't matter. The thing was, that's when I met Gordon. I'd been a widow for over a year and I was just about back on my feet, but I was vulnerable I suppose. Or maybe I simply didn't like being alone. I never have. I've made some really bad choices in my life, and nearly always because I would rather be with someone unsuitable than be on my own.

This is a lot to take in. A lot of information compressed into a few sentences.

"What happened to your husband?" asks Alice. 'If you don't mind me ..."

"No, I don't mind. It's a long time ago now. Water under the bridge and all that. He got cancer and he died. That's the short version. The long version might have to wait for another day, or maybe stay untold, as it doesn't make easy listening. Lots of pain, lots of treatment, lots of hope, lots of despair. You know the story."

Alice nods. She gets that little ache in her stomach that she always thinks has gone until something reawakens it. She sees her father in his hospital gown, shrunk to less than half his previous size, his face collapsed inwards and his eyes huge and shining. Oh, those disproportionate eyes. She wishes she could get them out of her head.

"Yes," she says. "I know that story. My dad died of stomach cancer about four years ago, but you never forget how horrible it is."

Georgie's hands fly to her mouth. There is genuine dismay on her face. "Oh, I'm so sorry to hear that! Your dad! He was so lovely. I had such a crush on him, you'd never believe. Of course I never told you, but I thought he was perfect!"

"Well, he wasn't perfect, but he was pretty good," says Alice, knowing that her voice is a bit shaky but not really caring now. "Luckily it was all pretty quick, and he'd been in really good shape until then, but still."

They are both quiet, both thinking their own thoughts and filing away their sad memories. Alice looks across at Georgie and a warm feeling replaces the little pain in her stomach. This is her friend. She's been absent for such a long time, but now it seems she is back.

DECEMBER 1963

It was almost Christmas before I could wake up in the morning without being greeted by a surge of stomach-churning anxiety. There was still some media coverage of the assassination and the search for the truth about Lee Harvey Oswald, but it was less intensive by that time. My parents were quite impressed by my sudden interest in world affairs and remarked upon how grown up I was becoming. They couldn't know that I was interested in only one thing. I watched the news on tv and perused the newspapers as if my life depended on it. Then, if there was nothing on Kennedy or the Russians, I would breathe an inner sigh of relief and try to go back to being a child. It never happened, not completely. Nothing would ever be quite the same again, but I didn't know that then.

If I hadn't already been a very self-sufficient and

sometimes solitary child, maybe my parents would have remarked upon the change in me during those weeks. I would spend hours in my room completing imaginary homework. At weekends, I would take the dog for long walks around the fields unless it was absolutely too wet to do so. I was on high alert, waiting for something to happen, although I struggled to imagine what it might be. Maybe they did notice, and put my behaviour down to incipient puberty or the start of teenage angst. They could hardly have guessed the real reason for my behaviour.

It was strange, given that Georgie should have had more to worry about than me, that she was apparently perfectly sanguine about the death of President Kennedy. We still spent little time together during the school day but always sat together on the bus. That was where I tried to raise it, several times.

"My dad says it was the Russians behind it."

"Behind what?"

"You know, President Kennedy. He says the Russians paid Lee Harvey Oswald to kill him, or else he was one of their agents, then they paid that other man to kill him so he couldn't talk."

"Really? I don't know. Anyway, I was going to ask you something. What was it? Oh, yes, I remember. It's my birthday on Saturday and I wondered if you'd like to come and stay the night. I'm not having a party or anything but ..."

This wasn't the first time she had changed the subject. I had no idea whether it was because she was hiding something or simply not interested. However, on this occasion I didn't even stop to consider her motives. Staying the night at Georgie's! It was a notion that was both wonderful and terrifying. I pictured us in her room, chatting away in the dark when we should have been asleep, and I knew that I really wanted to agree. Ok, there was a chance that enemy agents would choose that day to call on her mother for whatever reason they might have, but surely it wasn't that likely? I put my over-blown fears about the secrets behind Georgie's father's disappearance to one side. This was an an opportunity I couldn't miss.

"That would be lovely! I'll have to ask my parents, but I'm sure it'll be ok. Thanks!"

Was I really sure it would be ok? I had hardly ever slept away from home and never with anyone unconnected to my family. There was an unmarried aunt in London who liked me to spend a night or two with her from time to time and I had stayed with my cousins from Hastings, but that was about it. Nobody had invited me for a sleep-over, if such a thing even existed back then. This would be a first.

I walked home slowly, trying to phrase the question in such a way that it could not lead to a refusal. Should I play it down, as if it were an everyday occurrence – *Oh, by the way, Georgie's asked me to stay at hers on Saturday. That's ok isn't it?* Or should I make more of the compliment we were being paid? *You'll never believe this! Georgie's only allowed one friend to stay for her birthday and guess who they've chosen?*

In the event, I was so excited by the time I arrived home that I've no idea what I said. It all came spilling out, like water breaching a dam. I jumped up and down, trying to gain my mum's attention. She was engaged in sorting out a dispute between my sisters and was quite immune to my pleas.

"Alice, for goodness sake, stop it!" she said as I tugged on her arm in desperation. "Whatever is the matter with you?"

"I'm trying to tell you! It's Georgie! It's her birthday on Saturday and she wants me to stay at hers. I can, can't I?"

Of course she didn't agree. She would talk about it with my dad but she wouldn't make any promises. The reasonable part of me knew this would be the case, but there was another part of me that couldn't bear the wait.

"But it will be alright, won't it? I will be allowed?"

"I've told you, Alice. I'll talk to Dad about it. I'm not saying 'no' but I'm not saying 'yes' either. We've never met Georgie's mother. I know you've spent a lot of time up there, but sleeping over is another matter. You'll just have to be patient."

Looking back, I can see that I was lucky I didn't blow my chances altogether. I stomped around in a ridiculous display of pre-adolescent moodiness and hardly spoke to anyone. Fortunately, my mum was much too sensible to pay any attention to that. Then, when my dad came home, it occurred to me that this might be a poor strategy so I washed up without being asked and played the part of a sensible and dutiful daughter until he had finished eating. That was when I could stand it no longer.

"Alice, upstairs!" shouted my mum. She very rarely raised her voice but we all knew to take notice when she did. "I told you I would speak to Dad about it and I had every intention of doing so, but now I'm beginning to change my mind. Early night for you. Go!"

I scuttled upstairs and resisted the temptation to creep back and try to listen. They probably wouldn't discuss it straight away anyway, and if I were discovered half way down the stairs with my face pressed between the bannisters that would be the end of it. I tried to read my book but none of the words would sink in. Even my thesaurus game couldn't stop my mind wandering. It was hours before I fell asleep, or at least it felt like that, and then my dreams were redolent with wish-fulfilled scenarios, all set in Georgie's house.

The answer, when at last my mum delivered it, was good news and bad. I would be allowed to stay over, but only if the invitation were confirmed in person. No, a phone call would not be enough; they wanted to talk to Georgie's mother directly. No, it wasn't that they didn't trust me and it wasn't that they didn't trust Georgie. Georgie was a very nice girl. It was simply that they hadn't met her mother and it was apparently standard practice that they should. Unfortunately, I had no evidence that would contradict this. I was sure Georgie's mother would have allowed her to stay at my house with no such formalities, but you could hardly call her a standard mother. There was nothing I could do about it. I would have to tell Georgie or it would all be off.

"Did you ask?" It was practically the first thing she said to me the next morning. There was no putting it off.

"Yes, I'm allowed, but there's one thing." I paused. Swallowed.

"Well, what is it?"

"They want to meet your mum first."

"Bloody hell!" Georgie didn't swear very often, but this did seem like an appropriate occasion. Then she laughed. "Don't worry, she can come over as quite normal when she wants to. It'll be fine."

I tried to persuade Georgie that I hadn't been worrying about her mother – it was my parents I was worried about – but she didn't seem to care that much anyway. She said she would talk about it when she got home and suggest my dad's idea. This was that he should call in on his way home from work, just to introduce himself. She was sure it would all work out.

Of course Georgie was right. It was her mother who really concerned me. Much as I admired her, I wasn't sure what my parents would make of her unconventionality. Suppose she opened the door in her dressing gown, a cigarette in one hand and a paintbrush in the other? It wasn't unknown for her to get so involved in some artistic endeavour that she forgot to get dressed all day. Suppose she invited my dad into the kitchen rather than keeping him in the relative magnificence of the hall? What would he make of the pervading untidiness and disrepair that actually seemed to be getting worse rather than better?

I was in a state of total anxiety by the time it had all been arranged and we waited for my dad to come home. It was now the day before Georgie's birthday and time was running out. By then, I had more or less persuaded myself that the whole thing was doomed and I even had some good words to use in anticipation of completing my diary later. I would be desolate, despondent and disconsolate – a triple with the added benefit of alliteration – but I was also quite impressed by the visual strength of crestfallen and wanted to try to fit that in too.

It took an enormous amount of will-power to refrain from pouncing on my dad the minute he walked through the door. I watched him put down his briefcase and take off his raincoat. I waited while he gave it a shake and took it through to the hall to hang it up. I held my breath as he gave my mum her obligatory kiss on the cheek and they conducted their usual 'how was your day?' exchange. All this seemed to take place in slow motion, or as if I were viewing it from a position miles away. I was just about ready to spontaneously combust by the time he turned and saw me sitting at the dining room table with my untouched homework in front of me.

"She's a very charming woman," he said with a smile. There was even the hint of a twinkle in his eye.

"Oh, you went then?" said my mum, as if she had somehow managed to completely forget about the most important thing to happen to me in my whole life.

"Yes, I went, and I don't see any reason why Alice shouldn't stay. Stella was very keen – she says Georgie gets quite lonely up there with just the two of them. It must be tough, looking after that big house on her own. As I say, she's charming."

"Did you go inside?" asked my mum. I thought I could detect a slight edge to her voice. Maybe she had seen that twinkle too.

"Yes, yes. Pretty amazing place, but needs a lot of work. No man about the place and you can see that. There's a son at Cambridge – did you know that? Yes, he's due back tomorrow as it happens, but I don't suppose he's there enough to be much help. Pity really."

Stella! I didn't even know that was Georgie's mother's name and yet there was my dad, slipping it into conversation as if he'd known her for years. Adults were such strange creatures I thought, but actually none of that mattered. Now that my dad had approved, it would follow that my mum would too. I would be going to stay at Georgie's and, better and better, I would be meeting the elusive Hilary. Older brothers were like creatures from another planet to me, exotic and mysterious. Girls who had them moaned about the teasing, the mess, the smelly socks, but I would have given anything to change places with them. Despite what Georgie said about him, I was sure that Hilary would be perfect. My happiness was complete. My diary entry for that day shows that I was filled with tumultuous, ecstatic pleasure and relief. I'm certain that was true.

The next day, my dad drove me up to Georgie's house after lunch. My overnight things were packed neatly into a duffel bag together with all the spare excitement that wouldn't fit into my body. I hugged it tightly to me as we made the five minute journey. We pulled into Georgie's drive, stopped in front of the house and he turned off the engine. Heavy clouds hung low in the sky and the place looked dark and delightfully creepy.

"Shall I come in with you?"

"No!" I said, opening the door and scrambling out as if the car were in danger of exploding. "I'm not a baby, I'll be fine. You go. See you tomorrow."

Just then, the front door opened, casting a shaft of golden light onto the drive. Georgie skipped out, her mother behind her. They were both smiling and I noticed that Georgie's mother had done something to her hair. She was wearing a neat fitted dress too and looked completely different. She raised her hand in greeting and my dad wound down his window and leaned out, his elbow resting on the glass.

"One child, delivered as promised, in full working order," he said.

Oh, for God's sake! Why did parents have to be so embarrassing? Not only was he referring to me as a child, but he was putting on some kind of a stupid act for Georgie's mother. He never spoke like that in normal circumstances. He was entirely down to earth. If anyone was likely to put on airs and graces it was my mum, but here he was, employing irony - or was it some kind of extended metaphor - in order to impress her. I scowled at him, my face reddening, but he was all smiles.

"Come on," said Georgie with a sideways look at her mother. "Let's take this upstairs." She took my duffel bag, swung it over her shoulder and marched inside.

We went straight up to her bedroom, where a narrow mattress had been placed on the floor beside her bed. A pillow and some blankets were in a heap at one end.

"Don't worry, it's more comfortable than it looks," said Georgie, but I wasn't worried. I would have been quite happy to sleep on the bare floor if it meant staying with Georgie. She dumped my duffel bag beside the bedding and flopped onto her bed. "What do you want to do?"

This threw me completely. Georgie tended to be

in control of our activities and it had not occurred to me to plan anything.

"Um, go up to the hill?" I said. It was the first thing that came into my head. We hadn't returned since that day when Georgie had scared me half to death with her tree-climbing. Doubtless some part of me recalled how I'd felt about being taken to her special place. There was such a mis-match between Georgie's casual acceptance of my presence today and my overwhelming excitement at being there. Maybe I thought this would help to even it out.

Suddenly, I remembered why I'd been invited. It was Georgie's birthday and I hadn't even remarked on it! Neither had my dad. He'd been too busy trying to be amusing. I rummaged around in my bag and brought out Georgie's card and present.

"Happy birthday!"

Georgie looked surprised, but thanked me and opened the card. She placed it on the window ledge. I assumed all the others were downstairs. Then she opened her present. It was a wooden box for pens and pencils, with a sliding lid decorated with oriental-looking patterns. There was a second section underneath, which could be accessed by twisting it round. Georgie didn't notice this at first.

"Here," I said, taking it from her and demonstrating. "This can be a secret compartment."

"Thank you!" she said. "That's fabulous! I don't know what to say." She put it on the bed beside her then stood and grabbed me in an awkward, brief embrace. This was a complete surprise, as we had hardly touched before. I was not the kind of girl who went around with my arm draped over somebody's shoulders or wrapped around their waist. There was plenty of that kind of behaviour at school but the height difference between me and Caroline would have made it difficult even if we had been inclined.

"Right, come on then. Let's go," she said. The moment had passed. She left both the card and the gift in her room. We headed off to the hill without another mention of her birthday, but I felt as if the imprint of her body was still there on mine. There was nothing sexual about it, of that I am sure. It was, though, an indication of acceptance – affection even – that I had never dared to hope for. It was the kind of thing that friends did and I had been very wary about referring to Georgie as a friend. Friendship was supposed to be equal, reciprocal, but I was always in Georgie's thrall. Always waiting for her to become tired of me. Maybe I could hope for something more and now the hill, with its symbolic importance in my mind, was waiting.

In the event, nothing much happened when we got there. Georgie tried to encourage me to have a go at tree climbing but I was wearing my best slacks. I knew what trouble I'd be in if I ripped them. She climbed to the top of the same tree and down again, but there was none of the exuberance of last time. Many of the trees were bare, the grass was thin and muddy and the view had lost its sparkle. It was as if someone had painted a thin, grey wash over everything including us. Still, there remained the prospect of meeting Hilary to look forward to. There had been no sign of him when I arrived, but Cambridge sounded as if it might be a long way away. There was plenty of time.

D'you think your brother will be home yet?" I asked. I had intended the words to float across the intervening space in an apparently indifferent manner but they seemed to have ideas of their own. I was sure they'd given the game away when Georgie looked up sharply.

"No, and he won't be, thank God!" she said. "He's decided to go and stay with some friends, although it's a mystery to me how he ever got any. Seems like they're more interesting than us, but good riddance, I say."

"Oh. But he will be coming for Christmas, surely?" My heart plummeted but my mind was racing, trying to work out if there would be another opportunity to meet him. How long were the holidays for students at Cambridge University?

They were a breed of which I had absolutely no experience and now it looked as if that would remain the case.

"I suppose so. I can't see anyone wanting him that long," was all Georgie would say on the subject. I could always tell when a conversation was over. The muscles in her jaw would tighten and experience told me there was no point pursuing it further.

Later, we watched tv while dinner was being prepared. Georgie and I sat together on the lumpy sofa while her mother wandered in and out, sometimes with a cigarette, sometimes with a glass and sometimes with both. It was the night of the first Doctor Who episode to feature the daleks. We were gripped, although we didn't watch from behind the sofa. I am sure Georgie would never have admitted to being scared, but when a metallic arm reached out and grabbed the Doctor's companion, we both shrieked and held onto each other for a second or two. It was wonderful, an echo of the earlier moment of intimacy. I glowed with pleasure. This was perfect, beyond anything I could have imagined, and the evening was not yet over.

That's what I thought as Georgie's mother came in and announced that dinner was ready. Georgie must have told her about eating at my house. One end of the kitchen table had been cleared and wiped and three place settings had been laid with table mats and ornate, if assorted, cutlery. Georgie's mother flitted around in front of the stove, giving the pans an occasional stir. Then she disappeared again, returning after a few minutes with a smudge of paint across her cheek.

At last, there was a flurry of activity. She brought two steaming plates to the table and placed them in front of us.

"What's this?" asked Georgie.

"Spaghetti Bolognese," was the reply. "You remember, we had it in Venice. You said it was the best thing you'd ever eaten so I thought I'd make it for your birthday."

"Mother, that was four years ago," said Georgie, picking up a fork and dipping it into the mound of what appeared to be mince and carrots on her plate.

"Yes, I know, but it's a fairly simple dish. I read the recipe in a magazine when I was at the doctor's and I thought at the time, I could easily do that. I just needed an occasion and here it is! Your birthday, with your friend here to help you celebrate." She fetched her own plate and sat down, still smiling.

I had never tried Spaghetti Bolognese. The only pasta I knew was macaroni. That appeared in my mother's repertoire solely in the form of a milky and somewhat slimy pudding, edible only because of the amount of sugar I heaped upon it when she wasn't looking. Doubtless some foreign influences were creeping into the English diet by that time, but not in our house. We had never taken holidays abroad and my experience of eating out was limited to a cafe on the way to Hastings. The menu may have been extensive for all I know, but we invariably ate beans on toast followed by a slice of cake if we'd been well-behaved in the car.

So, not only was spaghetti a new gastronomic experience for me, but it was a complete nightmare to eat. I watched Georgie's mother twirl it round her fork and tried to emulate this, but with no success whatsoever. The spaghetti remained stubbornly on my plate. That meant I had to eat as much of the mince as I could, but there was a different challenge there. It was lumpy and parts of it had obviously caught on the bottom of the pan as they were a much darker brown and tasted bitter. It was pretty revolting. Georgie must have agreed as, suddenly, my plate was whisked away.

"Massive portions, mother," said Georgie, "but thanks for that."

I echoed Georgie's words. I said how much I had enjoyed the meal and explained I had never tried it before. Georgie was backing away towards the door by then, but I heard what she said.

"Doubt you'll ever want to try it again, either."

I managed to get out before laughter overcame me but then I felt terrible. It was fine to laugh at your own parents, but you wouldn't want other people to join in.

"Don't worry," said Georgie. "She's a hopeless cook. Always has been, but it's not always quite that bad. You're so lucky having a mum like yours."

I don't know what I said then. I was assailed by conflicting emotions – pride, embarrassment and sadness too. It was hard to reconcile myself to the idea of Georgie envying my life when I envied hers with such intensity. I popped my head back round the kitchen door and offered to help with the washing up but Georgie's mother said she would do it later and we should enjoy ourselves. We went back into the lounge. That was when I noticed the solitary birthday card on a bookcase. It was hand-painted and I guessed it was from Georgie's mother. Was this the only other card Georgie had received? Was it something to do with her birthday being so close to Christmas or did nobody know where they lived?

We watched tv again for a while, but I could tell Georgie was restless. At last, she jumped up and announced it was time to go up to her room. I think she would have gone straight there without saying a word to her mother, but I insisted on saying 'goodnight' first. We found her in the kitchen. She wasn't bustling around washing up or mopping the floor as my mum would have been. There was no evidence of anything having been started in that respect. Instead, she was rooting around in one of the cupboards, her back to us. She jumped when Georgie announced that we were going to bed and her expression said something I didn't understand.

"Oh, right you are, darling. Have you made sure your friend has everything she needs?"

Georgie rolled her eyes and assured her that all was well. Then she practically dragged me out of the kitchen. There were no good-night hugs or kisses. How grown-up Georgie was in comparison to me, I realised yet again. I decided that I would tolerate no more babyish behaviour when I returned home. I would drift casually off to bed like Georgie. Thank goodness she hadn't come to stay with me! Suppose my mum had tried to kiss her when she kissed me! By the time we reached Georgie's room I was so engaged with exploring the embarrassment I had avoided, that I didn't take much notice of what she was doing.

"Here we are," she said, tipping the contents of a carrier bag onto the bed. "Midnight feast!"

As an avid reader of adventure stories, I knew all about midnight feasts. Until then, my experience had been limited to the written word, but now, it seemed, life was set to be more perfect still. There on the bed were a packet of cheese and onion crisps, a bar of Cadbury's Dairy Milk, a packet of Rolos, a can of Pepsi Cola and some iced fancy biscuits. It was as if Georgie had somehow read my mind and provided all the things I loved best but experienced rarely. I was hardly ever allowed any of these delicacies, even one at a time. The prospect of consuming them all together was enough to strike me dumb.

"What's the time?" Georgie asked. It took me a moment to recover my composure, but then I looked at my watch. It wasn't much after ten. I assumed we would go to sleep and somehow wake ourselves at midnight in order to enjoy these illicit goodies at the correct time.

"Oh, never mind," said Georgie. "We'll call it a ten o'clock feast instead. I can't wait another two hours, especially after that disaster my mother produced. I'm starving!"

It was true, my stomach had been complaining about lack of attention to its needs for a while. I pushed aside my disappointment at losing out on the magical midnight element of this experience and helped myself to some crisps.

It didn't take long to polish off the contents of Georgie's carrier bag. We giggled and snorted as one wrapper after another fell to the floor. We floated on a fluffy sugar and caffeine cloud. When everything was gone, we collapsed onto our respective beds and lay there in the darkness, full and slightly queasy. Something about the dark seemed to relax Georgie's tongue and she chatted as she never had before. She told me about her old house. It had eight bedrooms, three bathrooms and a tree house in the garden. She told me about her father's Bentley, with its soft leather seats that smelled of tobacco and aftershave. This didn't sound very attractive to me, but she assured me it was a heady combination recalling all the important people who had sat there in the past.

At last Georgie's words ran out, leaving a space that didn't ask to be filled. Her breathing told me she was asleep. I dozed for a while too, but then I awoke from a troubled dream that slipped through my fingers when I tried to remember it. Try as I might, I could not get back to sleep. I was terribly thirsty. My brain was still buzzing from the sweets and the fizzy drink, to say nothing of the fact that the mattress was hard and the blankets were thin. What on earth would my mum say if she could see me now? She had probably imagined me tucked up in a stately four-poster under a mound of eiderdowns, like a princess in a fairytale. Reluctantly, I decided I would have to go to the bathroom for a drink. I pushed off the blankets and tip-toed to the door.

I managed to open the door without disturbing Georgie. I left it slightly ajar and felt my way down the steep stairs onto the landing, my heart pounding. I had not thought of it until now, but what if the house were haunted? Was that sound I'd heard earlier really the wind rattling the window, or had it been something more sinister? The fact that I didn't believe in ghosts seemed quite irrelevant as my feet sought out the safety of each stair and the boards groaned and squeaked in response. Luckily, I could see much better when I reached the landing, as someone had left a light on downstairs. That was something that would never happen in my house, but I had learned not to worry too much about such things while at Georgie's. They did things differently, that was all.

There was a toilet on a little half-landing so I headed there. I would be less likely to disturb Georgie's mother as the bathroom was next to her room. It was also lighter, and a much more attractive proposition than venturing into the gloom of the corridor. Suddenly, the house had assumed a new and slightly menacing air and I was desperate to return to my uncomfortable bed.

I had almost reached the top of the main staircase when I heard a crash. My heart, already in overdrive, began to thump harder. I was just about to run back and call for help when I saw that it was neither burglars nor the Russians stumbling around at the foot of the stairs. It was Georgie's mother. She looked very unsteady on her feet. At first I thought she must be unwell so I hurried down the first few steps to help her. Then I saw the broken glass on the floor and the glazed look in her eyes and understood.

"Ah, Georgie's friend," she slurred as she shuffled past me. "I do apologise for waking you. Bit wobbly I'm afraid."

DECEMBER 2016

Both their glasses are empty now, but so is the bottle. Something tells Alice that a second bottle would be ill-advised. She has no idea how alcohol affects Georgie, nor does she want to be any less in control of her own faculties than at present. Instead, she rises to her feet and picks up both the glasses in one hand and the bottle in the other.

"Tea or coffee?" she asks. "Or I have hot chocolate if you prefer?"

Georgie's face lights up at the mention of chocolate, so Alice makes two mugs. She has a momentary twinge of sadness, or possibly regret, as she remembers the routine they had in the old house. The ritual bickering about whose turn it was, followed by one of them giving in and stomping off to make it. John never stirred it properly and she would complain about the lumps of congealed chocolate powder at the bottom of the mug.

Alice gives herself a little shake. No point in dwelling on the past. She puts the mugs on a little silver tray and brings them through. Georgie's eyes are closed and Alice takes a moment to observe her. She is stick thin, but not attractively so. This is not the slim absence of fat to which Alice has aspired at the start of her many abortive diets. Now the heat of the room has provoked her into removing the bulky cardigan she arrived in, Alice can see her collar bones and the deep hollows behind them. Her arms make Alice think of photographs of famine. They make her wince. She puts the mugs on the coffee table and creeps to her own chair, but the tiny sound is enough, and Georgie's eyes fly open.

"Oh, sorry!" she says.

Alice reassures her it is fine for her to have a little doze if she wants, but Georgie sits bolt upright and sips her chocolate.

"Shall I tell you the rest of it?" she asks after a while.

The combined effect of the wine and the hot drink is making Alice drowsy. She tries to find a polite way of suggesting that they leave it until tomorrow, but she is too slow. Georgie puts her mug back on the coffee table and clasps her hands together in her lap.

"I was going to tell you about Gordon, wasn't I?"

"Yes, you met him at work," says Alice, to show she has been listening.

"He was one of those people. You know - you must have met them - people who occupy every room they walk into?"

Alice nods. There were times when Georgie herself was a lot like that, but there was someone else, too. Someone she has no intention of mentioning.

"Like I say, I must've been vulnerable. I couldn't stop looking at him. It wasn't even that he was all that good-looking, but he had something I couldn't resist. I didn't know he was married then, and by the time I did know it was too late. I'm not proud of myself but it was so easy to believe him when he said they had separate lives. I wanted to believe it, so I did. Do you think that's terrible?"

Alice doesn't know what to say. Georgie's words seem to have reacted with the wine and chocolate in her stomach and turned them to acid. Did John say something like that to *her*? She swallows down her bile and pulls herself together.

"It's not up to me to judge you, Georgie," she says. "Like you said, you were vulnerable and he didn't tell you at the beginning when it would've been easier to get out of it. These things are messy. They're never simple."

Georgie seems completely unaware that she is in difficult territory. She is utterly absorbed in her own story, but then that was often the case when they were children. Alice regularly found herself wondering if Georgie was listening to her at all.

"No, it certainly wasn't simple," she says. "We started having an affair – you'll have worked that out – but it didn't stop there. It progressed to him staying two or three nights at a time and then, eventually, he moved in. He left her. Well, that's what he said, anyway. I'd always known he was a drinker – it's a big problem in journalism, you know – but I hadn't realised quite how bad it was until then and it was a long time before I found out about the gambling. Years. Enough time for him to use up all the equity in the house. It was easier to let it go in the end."

Alice is about to say something sympathetic, but Georgie has not finished. Her cheeks are flushed.

"He would go on these terrific benders for days at a time and he was impossible then. Violent, pig-headed, obsessively jealous. It would all come to a head and I'd boot him out. I wouldn't see him for days, sometimes longer, then he'd be back on the doorstep. He'd be devastated, promise it would never happen again. I'd take him back and he'd stop drinking for weeks, months even, and everything would be fine. It's not a new story, I suppose."

She stops. She reaches out for her mug but it's empty. Alice wonders how she should respond. Is this the sort of occasion that demands a hug? But then they never had that kind of relationship before and it could be awkward. She decides against it.

"That must've been horrible," she says, wishing at once that she'd chosen a better word. You might use 'horrible' to describe a minor break-in. What Georgie has told her deserves a better word than that. But there is a part of her that thinks maybe she deserved it. After all, she took a man away from his wife. She could have stopped it when she discovered he was married. Maybe she deserved everything she got.

DECEMBER 1963

I doubt I'd ever had such a poor night's sleep. I've had worse since, many times, but I'd never been so troubled by disturbing dreams, discomfort and cold in my protected little life. It was still early when I awoke for the final time, my hips aching from the lumpy surface of the mattress and my whole body tense with cold. I even considered sneaking into the bottom of Georgie's bed and curling up at her feet, but I couldn't imagine how I would explain my presence when she awoke. I wrapped my thin blankets around me and tried to sleep again.

It didn't happen. I lay there, watching the light creep between the curtains to reveal the now familiar features of Georgie's bedroom. The house was utterly still. Whereas there had been all sorts of creaks and clanks earlier in the night, it seemed to have settled down for its own slumber now. This made my own state of alertness even more frustrating.

At last, I could stand it no longer. I crept down to the bathroom and ran my hands and lower arms under the warm tap which, mercifully, was working well for a change. There was little I could do about my feet, though. Despite the fact that I had remained fully dressed all night, they were frozen. I sat on the toilet and rubbed them until some of the feeling returned.

When I got back, Georgie was awake, stretching and yawning.

"God, it's freezing in here," she said, lying back and pulling the covers up to her chin. "Did you sleep ok?"

"Yes, fine thanks," I lied, but I doubt she believed me. She jumped out of bed and pulled me to my feet.

"Come on, let's go downstairs and see if we can get the fire going. There's crumpets."

So we did, and there followed the best meal I ever ate at Georgie's house. I hadn't even realised there was a working open fire, as it was hidden behind an ornate screen decorated with pictures of fire-breathing dragons and delicate ladies with parasols. Certainly nobody had ever lit it when I'd been there. Georgie asked me to help her move the screen to one side, then we dashed out to get handfuls of twigs from the garden. We laid them in the grate with scrunched up newspaper. There was half a scuttle of coal so we piled this on top and watched as the wet twigs hissed and spat before flaring up. The coal began to glow red, and I showed Georgie how to hold a sheet of newspaper in front of the fire to help it draw.

I can picture us now. We sat cross-legged on the rug, a packet of crumpets and a slab of rapidly-melting butter on the hearth in front of us. Our cheeks were rosy from the heat. We speared crumpets onto a carving fork, held them over the coals until they were brown and smoky, then covered them with a thick layer of butter. The result was heavenly. I have no idea how much carbon I consumed that morning. We somehow demolished the whole packet of crumpets between us, but I didn't care. If I'd been at my house, we would have been sitting politely around the table eating cereal or toast. My dad would be enjoying his weekly fry-up and my mum would be politely dabbing at a boiled egg with a geometrically regular rectangle of toast. That was the thing I was beginning to hate about my family. We were always so sensible. We were always so dull.

When the last crumpet had gone, we flopped into

two armchairs and bemoaned our bloated stomachs. I was in paradise. If the Beatles themselves had walked in and set up their equipment in front of the fire it could not have made me happier. It would have been exciting, but the feeling I had then was beyond excitement. It was something about belonging. I thought then that Georgie's family was where I belonged. I loved my own family and I didn't want to leave them, but I felt an almost spiritual connection with Georgie and her strange and random lifestyle. I thought it would last for ever. I thought I had achieved my goal. I was wrong about that, but I couldn't have known it then.

I don't remember how long we stayed like that, chatting in a desultory way from time to time. We had reached that stage where silences didn't need to be filled. I was deep in my own thoughts when the door opened. We looked up and there was Georgie's mother, some sort of silky robe only partially concealing the fact that she, too, appeared to have slept in the clothes she was wearing the day before.

Slowly, she raised one hand and pinched her forehead. She swayed a little, like a sapling in a light breeze.

"George, be a darling and make me a coffee will you?" she said. Her voice was raspy with sleep and smoke.

"Not feeling too good, mother?" said Georgie,

raising one eyebrow in a way I had tried to emulate many times without success.

"No, not brilliant, darling."

"Wonder why that might be?" muttered Georgie darkly as she swung her legs to the floor and went out to the kitchen. Her mother shuffled over to the sofa and lay full length along it, looking like a cross between some sort of pre-Raphaelite painting and a day-old corpse. That was a comparison I made much later. At the time I simply remarked on the waxy pallor of her skin and wondered if she would ever be able to get those knots out of her hair.

I followed Georgie out to the kitchen and watched while she made a mug of extremely strong, black coffee. Outside, the sky was so dark that it appeared almost like night. Squally rain hammered against the windows and the wind whistled and moaned around the house. I shivered, possibly due to the fact that the kitchen was anything but warm, but was that another kind of chill creeping around my shoulders? The room seemed to be nursing its own kind of grudge and felt nothing like the sun-lit space I'd entered all those weeks ago. It was fanciful to imagine that a house could reflect the mood of its occupants, but the atmosphere here varied in a way that was never the case in my own house. I looked across at Georgie, but she was subdued and hardly spoke. I guessed she was embarrassed that I'd seen her mother in such a condition. She had no idea that this only added to the charm.

We took the coffee through, but Georgie remained dispirited and she couldn't seem to settle. The bubble had burst and I began to look at my watch from time to time. My dad was collecting me at one, in time for lunch, and I was actually quite pleased to see the car pull up outside as we waited in the hall.

Georgie handed me my coat and my duffel bag.

"Look, I'm sorry about ..." she started, but I had to stop her.

"I've had a phenomenal time," I said. Although this was a word I had spent some time researching, it was no less true for that. "Honestly, the best time ever." I poked my head round the lounge door. Georgie's mother appeared to have fallen asleep, but I called out a cheerful 'goodbye and thanks' anyway and hurried out of the open door before my dad had a chance to come in and see what had been going on.

I climbed into the car and gave him a nod and a smile in response to his query. I'd had an amazing time, a brilliant time, but it would be unwise to say too much. The more I said, the more questions would be asked. I'd had the sense to change my clothes before he arrived and now I had only one problem to face. How on earth was I going to eat any lunch?

Of course I saw Georgie at school during what remained of the term and we still sat together on the bus, but there was no suggestion that we should meet up during the Christmas holiday. My parents had made it clear that Christmas was a time for family and I should be grateful that I had one. I was grateful I suppose, but I couldn't help feeling a desperate sense of loss as school ended. It would be more than two weeks until I saw Georgie again. Added to that, it was possible that Hilary would have left again by the next time I visited and I would have missed out on meeting him at all.

Normally, as soon as school finished, I would be consumed with excitement at the approach of Christmas. Everything would be as it always was. We would be practically hysterical with joy when my dad came home with the Christmas tree sticking out of the boot of the car. There would follow the tension of locating the one defective light bulb that was causing the complete malfunction of the whole set of tree lights, the arguing over the position of the baubles and chocolates and finally, the ceremonial placing of the angel. Janey was the only one of us still light enough to be held aloft by my dad. There would be no point in fighting over that, but somehow I found I didn't care much anyway. I found myself looking at my family Christmas through an outsider's eyes and judging what I saw. It all looked a bit tame to me.

Nevertheless, my mood lightened as the big day approached and I had a good time. I recorded the presents I received but added little information other than that as I wrote my diary that night. The day had followed the same pattern as always, and did not stand out from any of the other Christmases I had experienced. There was a lot of fun, at least one argument between me and one of my sisters and a few tears. It was just what a family Christmas should be.

It was the day after Boxing Day and we were playing jumping off the stairs onto a heap of cushions when the post rattled through the letter box right where we were playing. There was one brown envelope and what looked like a couple of belated Christmas cards so I sent Janey to take them through to my mum. She was in the kitchen, turning a blind eye to our somewhat dangerous game. We had loads of energy but it was freezing cold outside and we felt cheated by the fact that no snow had fallen. This time last year the snow had just started and although it would last for weeks, it had been a novelty at that stage.

I had just leapt from the fifth stair and I was

daring Angie, my middle sister, to match my feat when my mum appeared. I expected an immediate instruction to replace the cushions and 'play nicely,' but she hardly appeared to notice what we had been doing. She was holding a Christmas card.

"Alice, listen to this," she said. "It's from Georgie's mother." I wasn't remotely surprised that Georgie's card to us was late. I was amazed that her mother had actually organised the writing and posting of a card at all. However, the words my mum read out left me speechless.

"Dear Frank, Marjorie and family. Hilary, Georgia and I cordially invite you to share some drinks and refreshments next Tuesday (31st) to celebrate the coming of the New Year. We would be delighted to see you at about 7pm. Yours sincerely, Stella May. RSVP. Dress informal."

"What about that then?" said my mum. "That's a turn up for the books, isn't it? Wait 'til I show your dad."

Suddenly, the game we'd been playing lost all attraction. My heart pounded and I could do nothing to stop myself smiling. I was going to Georgie's! I was going to meet Hilary! I ran upstairs so I could enjoy this moment alone but then it hit me. The invitation had been to everyone. My parents would see the true state of Georgie's house. Georgie's mother might decide to have another try at cooking spaghetti Bolognese. Even worse, they would spend hours in each other's company. Surely the subject of Georgie's father would be raised. They would give the game away, I knew it. All was lost.

I was astonished at how quickly delight could turn to despair. I poured my heart out as I wrote my diary that evening. I was so miserable that I needed to sequester the next day's page to fully express my morbid predictions. Even the promise of meeting Hilary was ruined by my conviction that it would be the first and last time. Now I would have the added misery of knowing what I was missing after I had been banished forever for my loose tongue. I cried many tears into my pillow that night and my wretchedness was only slightly tempered by the wonderful range of synonyms for sorrow the English language provides.

DECEMBER 2016

They go to bed then. Alice knows Georgie's story is unfinished, but she also knows she needs time in which to process what she has told her thus far. She is a little disappointed with herself, at how raw it still feels after nearly two years. But, more importantly, she can't risk losing control and saying something sharp or unsympathetic. It would be awkward. Whatever she thinks of Georgie's behaviour as the other woman, it is clear that there is a lot more to this than meets the eye. Life has not been kind to Georgie. She just needs a little space so she can compose herself and maintain her kindly persona. The chances are Georgie will only stay a couple of nights and they will probably never see each other again. That might even be best, now that she knows what she knows, and then Alice's life can return to normal.

Georgie looks a little surprised as Alice stands and whisks the mugs off the coffee table. She may or may not be taken in by Alice's exaggerated yawn, but she follows her upstairs and says goodnight with more expressions of gratitude before closing the guest room door behind her. Alice goes into her own bedroom and breathes out. Well, at least they've got through the first evening with no major difficulties. She is grateful for all the en-suite bathrooms in this house, as that means there will be no uncomfortable meetings on the landing. Yes, it will all be fine.

It is only when Alice is in bed that she realises she does not feel fine at all. She knows it is ludicrous, but suddenly she is unsettled, scared even. There are no locks on any of the bedroom doors and that means Georgie could walk in at any time and … And what? What is she thinking? This is Georgie, not some waif she has picked up off the street, someone with God knows what issues. No, this is Georgie, who she'd loved as much as her own family. Sometimes more. Why would she want to hurt her? There was never any animosity, even after it happened. She never knew a thing.

She knows all this is true, but the absurd thoughts will not go away. Even though she does fall asleep eventually, they insinuate themselves into her dreams. At one time she is overwhelmed with relief at finding a previously unknown lock on the door and then she is in a different house altogether, the first one she lived in with John, explaining to someone that there really is no spare room. It was all a mistake and she's sorry.

She is awoken very early by the heating coming on. She is normally a sound sleeper, and has never been aware of the rush of water into the radiator before, but now her eyes fly open and her heart pounds. What was she dreaming of then? The dream is lurking in the background, just out of reach, but the anxiety it has caused remains.

Alice forces herself to lie down again. She tries to remember some of the exercises she learnt at a yoga class she attended for a few months after the accident. She didn't enjoy it, so she stopped going, but sometimes she wishes she had persevered. She breathes in slowly, counts, breathes out again. No, it's no good. She will have to get up. But then, if she does, she might wake Georgie. She longs to have the kitchen to herself, to enjoy her morning routine with no interruption, but the guest room is directly above the kitchen and the slightest noise carries in this house. It might be new-looking and smart but it's basically a brick-built box divided up by plasterboard.

She decides to shower and dress before

breakfast. At least that will pass some time and she won't be sitting around looking ten years older than she did yesterday when Georgie comes downstairs. So that's what she does. Then she closes the bedroom door quietly and creeps downstairs.

She jumps visibly when she sees Georgie sitting at the kitchen table with a mug of tea. It's almost like coming down to find an intruder in the house. Georgie is swathed in a pale blue towelling robe but there are dark streaks on the shoulders and down the back, as if she has been wearing this garment while dying her hair. She remembers noticing Georgie's grey roots yesterday and wonders what has happened. Her own blonde highlights and tinted roots are maintained on a strict timetable, but Georgie appears to pay little attention to her appearance. The clothes Alice has seen so far are shapeless and worn and she certainly wasn't wearing any make-up yesterday. Georgie swivels round.

"Oh, I'm sorry! I hope you don't mind. I tend to wake up so early these days and I was gasping."

Alice assures Georgie she is very welcome to help herself. She must make herself at home. She puts the coffee machine on and bustles around making toast, finding jam and marmalade, but she can't help feeling secretly that Georgie has overstepped the mark. On the rare occasions she has been invited to stay with friends or relations, she has always remained in her room until she is sure her hosts are up and about. Even with the kids, when they lived within travelling distance, she always tried to respect their privacy.

She offers Georgie a variety of breakfast options but she will accept only a single slice of toast. She smears it with a thin layer of butter and nibbles her way through it without enthusiasm. Alice feels obliged to forego her usual hearty breakfast and makes do with a small bowl of cereal. She will be starving later, she thinks, but maybe Georgie will go out. Maybe she will start her search for somewhere else to stay.

It is not long before it becomes apparent that Georgie has no plans to go anywhere that day. She asks Alice if she can bring in another couple of bags, so of course Alice has no choice but to agree. All the same, her heart sinks as Georgie struggles upstairs with a huge suitcase then returns to the car only to reappear with a carry box full of camera equipment.

"That's it, I promise," she says. "It's so nice to have a bit of space. I'll be able to do a bit of sorting out and it'll be so much easier when I move on."

Alice is somewhat placated by this, but then Georgie disappears for a while and reappears with the Asda shopping bag which she takes straight into the utility room. She has already taken one full load back to her room and now this is another. How many dirty clothes can one person accumulate? Did she have nowhere to do any laundry before?

Next, Alice begins to worry about food. Her repertoire of vegetarian meals is small and she knows she will have to visit the supermarket today even without that consideration. There is very little milk and there is a long list of items on the handy white-board beside the fridge. But how can she possibly insist that Georgie comes with her? She knows she is being unkind and that Georgie would be terribly hurt if she knew what she was thinking, but she feels no better about leaving her alone in the house than she did yesterday. There is no justification for it. It simply doesn't feel right.

In the event, she has no choice. Even the offer of a visit to the in-store cafe does nothing to persuade Georgie.

"No, it's fine, really," she says, completely oblivious to the fact that it is not fine, not for Alice. "You go ahead, you don't need to worry about me. I've got all these clothes to sort out and then I want to make a start on … Anyway, I'd only slow you down and I'm not a great fan of supermarkets. You go. Take as long as you want!"

So Alice leaves the house. She drives to the supermarket and dashes around the aisles as if the house is likely to burn down if she leaves it too long. That isn't what she thinks, but there is some other kind of nebulous fear that urges her on. She hops from foot to foot in the queue and only narrowly avoids crashing her trolley into that of a slow and elderly woman as she approaches the sliding doors of the exit.

She apologises and almost runs across the car park, her breath coming in painful gasps. She hasn't moved this fast for years. Stop it! She tells herself. You're going to give yourself a heart attack and all for nothing. Georgie isn't going to do anything stupid. Why should she?

Nevertheless, she feels a huge wave of relief as she pulls into the crescent and sees the house standing, just as it was before. The dilapidated Volvo is in the same position on the drive. She lets herself in. Everything is the same inside too. Georgie has transferred her load of washing to the tumble drier but there is no other evidence that she is even here.

Alice places the bags of shopping on the table and puts everything away. She feels her shoulders relax. She has bought the ingredients for a mushroom risotto and is almost looking forward to cooking for Georgie again. She realises with a pang that this is one of the most difficult aspects of suddenly becoming single. There is nobody to plan meals with. Nobody to cook for, nobody to cook for you. She has grown used to it, and it is certainly easier to think only of yourself, but it is nice to eat together and even nicer when somebody appreciates your food. She remembers when the kids were little and she made sausages and cheesy mash. The look on Scott's little face.

She puts the kettle on and gets out two mugs. Everything is ok after all. She doesn't know what's been wrong with her, getting into such a state with absolutely no cause. She reaches into the cupboard and locates the chocolate brownies. She'll have one, even if Georgie does persist in being so abstemious. Why shouldn't she?

She puts everything on a tray and takes it into the hall. She stands at the bottom of the stairs and calls.

"Georgie, I'm back! I've made some tea if you'd like to join me." There is a muffled thump from above, then Georgie opens the guest room door.

"Lovely, thanks. I'll be right down."

Alice enters the lounge, her mood lighter than it has been all day. Possibly lighter than at any time since Georgie's arrival. She is going to concentrate on being a good hostess and stop being so stupid. She puts the tray on the coffee table and straightens up. She is about to sit down when something catches her eye. There is something different about the fireplace. She looks again and then she sees what it is. There, at one end of the fake marble mantlepiece, is a small photo in a silver frame. It is a photo of a man and a woman holding hands. The man is looking sideways at the woman but she is looking straight ahead, her head thrown back slightly. They are both smiling – no, more than that, they are laughing. She has no idea who the man is, but she would know the woman anywhere. It is Georgie.

DECEMBER 1963

Nothing much happened in the days leading up to New Year. There was little of interest to record in my diary. If I wrote anything at all, it amounted to hardly more than a few lines of semi-coherent, self-pitying ramblings. We ate a fair bit of turkey in various re-hashed forms and played with our presents, but I was too fixated on the impending disaster to notice much. Then, on the day before the visit, my mum got into a mad panic that no-one could ignore.

"But what does 'dress informal' mean?" she cried. My dad had only just got home and had barely sat down. Added to that, he was probably less equipped to answer that question than my little sister. Still, ignoring my mum when her voice had risen to this pitch was not an option, even for him.

"Um, I suppose it means … well, you know what informal means, Marj. It means, it means not formal, not … oh, I don't know!"

Clearly I had not inherited my love of words from my dad. Luckily for him though, I was there with my trusty thesaurus. Even my state of advanced depression could not deter me from helping to solve a lexicological problem.

"It means casual, relaxed, comfortable, everyday," I pronounced. Sadly, a range of synonyms was not, it seemed, what my mum had been seeking. She rounded on me.

"Do you think I'm stupid?" she cried. "I know what informal means, you silly girl! But what does it mean to them? What's their idea of informal? Alice, you spend half your life up there so stop trying to show everyone how clever you are and tell me something useful for a change!"

I tried, but it really was difficult to describe how Georgie's mother dressed. The truth was that her attire varied enormously from day to day but there seemed to be no rhyme nor reason to her choices. One day she might be floating around the house in flowing skirts and the next she might be wearing paint-spattered overalls. This would have been reasonable if the overalls had coincided with the days on which she was painting, but that was not always the case. She was just as likely to be seen wearing silk culottes while sporting a paintbrush behind one ear.

My mum declared me to be useless and stomped off to her bedroom where she covered the bed with practically everything in her wardrobe. I kept well out of the way from that point. She was normally the most sensible, level-headed of people but this was about maintaining face in a situation in which she felt at a disadvantage. That always rattled her.

Somehow, we all managed to get into the car just before seven on New Year's Eve. I was wearing my new blue trousers. They were made of stretchy fabric and had elasticated strips that sat under the arches of my feet. I suppose they were very like ski pants, but no-one I knew went skiing so any resemblance was lost on me. I loved them. I had matched them with a sloppy jumper with wide blue and white stripes and I thought I looked pretty good.

My sisters were both wearing party dresses and my dad was wearing his suit. This didn't seem to be very informal to me but I had extended my embargo on fashion advice to the whole family. That left my mum. To be fair, she didn't have that many clothes to choose from. Not like Georgie's mother, who had a wardrobe crammed with all sorts of evening gowns and other sparkly creations. I had crept into her room one afternoon when she and Georgie and her mother were arguing in the kitchen. It was the one room I had yet to see, and I couldn't resist it.

Anyway, my mum had made her choice and I certainly wasn't about to remark on it. Not when she'd been so unfair to me. She was wearing the skirt part of her only suit – the one she had worn to my grandmother's funeral - and a peach-coloured twin-set. She looked dowdy and conservative; older than her years. I knew I would be embarrassed when she took off her coat.

The house was flooded with light as we pulled into the drive. Even the upstairs rooms were lit and for a moment I panicked. What if this were a big party, not the little get-together we had all assumed we were attending? But there were no other cars in the drive and when Georgie opened the door wearing jeans and a polo neck sweater I breathed a sigh of relief.

I relaxed even more as we went inside. Somebody had been very busy in Georgie's house. The hall was tidy and the floor had been swept. There was no sign of the shoes and boots that normally lay scattered by the front door. Each internal door was simply decorated with a sprig of real holly, complete with red berries, and a single candle flickered on the window ledge, its flame caught by the draught from the ill-fitting frame.

The lounge was even more improved. There was

a lovely real Christmas tree, and a log fire that danced and lent a warm glow to the room. Some of the furniture had been moved closer to the fireplace, so everyone would have a warm place to sit. The understated decorations continued in this room, too, with a garland of holly and other evergreens strung beneath the oak mantelpiece and fat, white candles encircled by a simple red ribbons on many of the surfaces. A coffee table I had never seen before stood in front of the sofa, and on it were a number of glass dishes containing all sorts of snacks. In addition to the usual crisps and tiny cheese biscuits there were some strange green things sitting in a puddle of oil with cocktail sticks in a glass beside them. I filled with pride on Georgie's behalf and gave thanks for the knowledge that neither she nor her mother would ever see our Christmas decorations.

What a contrast that would have been. Our lounge was positively festooned with a canopy of gaudy crepe paper garlands and three-dimensional paper bells and balls that hung from the ceiling like strange, deformed fruit. Added to that, my sisters had made yards of paper-chains that had started to become un-stuck and now drooped sadly and brushed the heads of anyone taller than five foot. It was a riot of colour and, now I realised, utterly tasteless. What had possessed my parents? Had they no restraint, no idea of style?

Georgie took our coats with solemn formality and invited us to sit down. Then she carried them upstairs, leaving us alone. I looked at my mum's face and saw her eyes flitting around the room, taking it all in.

"Where's Georgie's mum then?" she whispered. She steadfastly refused to refer to her by her first name, however many times my dad reminded her of it.

"How am I supposed to know?" I said, somewhat emboldened by my position. I received a glare in return, but was saved from further retribution by Georgie's reappearance, closely followed by her mother. My parents stood as one, as if royalty had made an unexpected appearance. Both my sisters gasped audibly.

"Ah, hello, Happy New Year!" said Georgie's mother, advancing towards my dad and proffering a cheek to be kissed. Unfortunately, he had never been greeted in this way before and there followed an awkward shuffle leading to the eventual shaking of hands. My mother followed suit, sticking her hand out rigidly before there could be any further confusion.

"I'm so sorry I wasn't here to greet you," said Georgie's mother, giving me a brief hug and smiling at my sisters who appeared to have turned to stone. "I'm plagued by malfunctioning zips," she said, looking at my mum for sympathy. My mum offered only a weak smile in response and there was another painful silence.

I looked at our two mothers, standing side by side and wondered how it was that two people who were as close as Georgie and I could come from such different stock. There was my mum, plain and also apparently rooted to the spot and there was Georgie's. She was dressed in skin-tight black trousers and a bright red silky top with a plunging neckline that left very little to the imagination. She had pulled her hair back and tied it with a matching red chiffon scarf and she looked … well she looked stunning. There was no other word for it. I looked it up later. Yes, she was gorgeous, dazzling, sensational and many of the other adjectives I found, but stunning remained the best.

And, indeed, we were all stunned. I had never noticed the fine line of her jaw or the high, prominent cheek-bones before. There were little spots of colour on her cheeks which may or may not have been natural, but she wore no obvious make-up otherwise. Georgie's mother was a beauty, and mine, well, she wasn't.

Eventually we were encouraged to sit down, but I was the only one to lean back in my chair. The rest of my family perched on the edge of their seats as if they were afraid of being swallowed up by the upholstery. Georgie passed around the little glass dishes. I noticed that her mother was alone in spearing any of the green things with a cocktail stick.

"Where's your brother?" I asked Georgie quietly.

"Out, thank God," she replied, creating a surge of disappointment. But I wasn't surprised. Everything had seemed destined to go wrong recently and this was just part of the pattern.

"Well, this is nice," said my dad, rubbing his hands together completely unnecessarily.

"Yes, thank you so much for inviting us," added my mum. "This is such a lovely house."

"Oh, it's a nightmare," said Georgie's mother. "You can't imagine how much it costs to keep warm. And there are so many things that need doing all the time."

There followed a very dull exchange about house maintenance. Georgie looked at me and rolled her eyes, so I had to suppress a giggle. My sisters had demolished all the crisps and cheesy biscuits when no-one was looking, and they each had a fine layer of crumbs on their party dresses. I watched as Janey, the younger, tried to brush them off without being seen and glared at her when I managed to catch her eye. It didn't matter that Georgie and I routinely ate toast in this room and brushed the crumbs to the floor with impunity. This was different.

The conversation had ground to a halt again and I could see the adults weighing up other options. Although less anxious than before, I was still terrified that the subject of Georgie's father would come up and I was on permanent alert. Suddenly, Georgie's mother jumped up as if somebody had attacked her from behind with a cattle prod.

"Oh, my goodness! What must you think of us? We've been sitting here all this time and we haven't offered you a drink! Georgie, why didn't you remind me?"

Georgie rolled her eyes again and proceeded to ask me and my sisters what we would like. Her mother asked my parents, then she ushered Georgie into the kitchen. We could hear her continuing to remonstrate with Georgie on the subject of her poor hostessing skills. I thought that was highly unfair. We could also hear a lot of Georgie's animated response, which caused my parents to look at each other and raise their eyebrows.

At last they re-appeared with drinks on a silver tray. I remembered unpacking that tray, all those weeks ago. I could never have imagined sitting here like this. My dad had asked for a small glass of beer, and my mum had a glass of sherry. They were not great drinkers at the best of times. In contrast,

Georgie's mother had a substantial cut glass tumbler of something brown that I took to be a spirit. I had seen empty whiskey and brandy bottles in their bin on many an occasion. She took one long mouthful and sat back, cradling the glass in her hands.

"Ah, I've been looking forward to that all day," she said.

Georgie looked as if she might be about to say something out loud but instead she leaned in close and whispered in my ear.

"That's a joke. It's at least her second."

"Georgie, it's rude to whisper," said her mother. "Come on, if you've something to say, you can say it out loud."

"It was private," said Georgie, looking embarrassed and cross at the same time. "I'm sorry if that was rude," she added, looking at my parents.

Of course they both said it was fine, but then there was yet another silence filled only by the sound of the ticking of the huge clock on the mantelpiece. This was punctuated by the occasional clearing of throats and the sound of glasses being picked up and replaced. I had never seen that clock working before and I wondered who had found the key. I was trying to work out how to use this as a conversation opener when, suddenly, we heard a noise coming from the hall. Everyone turned to look as the lounge door flew open and there stood a tall young man. His hair was as dark as Georgie's and hung in waves around his face, almost below his collar. He was dressed in a long dark gaberdine mackintosh. He was wet through.

"Hilary!" said Georgie's mother. "I thought you were out for the whole evening."

"Change of plan, Mother," said Hilary, his eyes sweeping round the room. "Forgot you were entertaining."

"Well, at least come in and let me introduce you," she continued. "Frank, Marjorie - this is Hilary, my son. Hilary, these are Alice's parents. You've heard George talk about Alice? Well, here she is and these are her sisters ... you'll have to help me out here, George."

So Georgie stood and completed the introductions. I was in something of a daze, as I had more or less given up all hope of meeting Hilary and now here he was, large as life and even more handsome and singular than I had dared imagine. Then, to complete my delight, he approached my parents and shook their hands, declaring himself charmed to meet them. I assumed that would be the end of it, that he would go upstairs to change out of his wet clothes, but no. He stood in the small space between the coffee table and the sofa where Georgie and I were sitting and held out his hand to me.

"Alice. George's friend from the village," he said, pronouncing the word 'village' as if it were some faraway place of which he had no knowledge or experience. "Did you know, she does nothing but talk about you? I'm delighted to make your acquaintance." I held out my hand, expecting him to shake it, but he took my fingers, bent low, and raised my hand to his lips. They were soft, but I could also feel the faint scratch of his whiskers, as if he needed a shave. A shiver went right through my body.

He stood up and excused himself while I tried to process what had happened. I could still feel the faint imprint of his lips on my hand and I vowed never to wash it again. I glanced across at my sisters, who were unable to stop giggling, and then at Georgie. She was scowling. If I had made a face like that in company I would have experienced the full force of my mother's wrath at some point, but Georgie's mother didn't appear to notice. She was re-filling her glass from a decanter on a side table and she sat down again with an expression I couldn't fathom.

Although I was floating on a little fluffy cloud of ecstasy that hovered just above the assembled group, I was not immune to the fact that the evening began to go downhill fast from that point. The gaps between the conversational forays became longer and more painful and my sisters became increasingly restless. Eventually, Georgie suggested taking them into the kitchen to help her re-fill the little glass dishes, and we all leapt on that opportunity as if we'd been invited to a private showing of the Christmas pantomime.

Georgie and I appeared to have an unspoken agreement that we would take as long as possible over this apparently simple task. We sat my sisters at the kitchen table and gave them strict instructions about quantities. If the dishes were a fraction too empty or too full, we poured the whole lot back into the packets and made them start again. We also gave them a couple of plates with their own little picnic and Georgie poured more glasses of lemonade to quench their salt-induced thirst.

At last, when we could string it out no longer, we gave each of them a dish to carry and made our way back to the lounge. At first, I didn't register that anything had changed. My parents praised their younger daughters for helping nicely and took polite handfuls of crisps and biscuits from the bowls. Georgie and I sat down, prepared to listen to whatever boring conversation would follow. It was only when I looked across at Georgie's mother that I saw the awful truth. I had seen her like this before and I knew what it meant.

"Nice children," she said, rousing herself a little.

"I keep telling George. Alice is a nice girl. I bet she doesn't cheek her mother."

I could feel Georgie stiffen beside me. I felt terrible for her but there was nothing I could do. Not so my mum. Clearly she had underestimated the effect of spirits or maybe she hadn't counted her hostess's re-fills. In any case, she liked Georgie and I guess she didn't like to see her publicly humiliated.

"Oh, don't you believe it! Alice is no angel, I can assure you. I think Georgie is a lovely girl. Such good manners! And then there's your son. University! My goodness, you must be very proud."

There was a pause, but no-one can have been in any doubt about who would fill it. Georgie's mother picked up her glass, discovered it to be empty, and replaced it on the table with a force that would have cracked anything less well-made. A large proportion of her breasts was visible as she leant forward and I watched my dad turn his eyes away. She took a deep breath.

"Ah, yes. My son. The venerable Hilary," she slurred. "Yes, he's well on the way to becoming just like his father. What more could a mother want?"

My heart leapt into my mouth at that, but I needn't have worried. As if they had been communicating by telepathy, my parents rose in unison and declared that their younger children were very tired and they really must be going. There were no protests. Not from me, not from my sisters and certainly not from Georgie. Only her mother struggled to get to her feet but Georgie stepped in.

"Don't bother, Mother," she said, a quiver in her voice. "I'll see them out."

She ran upstairs and returned almost immediately, dropping some of our coats on the way. We had drifted into the hall by then, so I retrieved them. We put them on as quickly as we could, my mother chiding my sisters in an unnaturally high voice. My dad repeatedly cleared his throat and walked back and forth between my mother and the front door as if someone had asked him to measure the distance in paces and he kept losing his place. I looked at Georgie. If a massive hole had appeared in the middle of the impressive wood floor I'm pretty sure she would have jumped into it, however cliched that may have seemed. I wouldn't have blamed her at all.

DECEMBER 2016

Alice stretches out her hand to the photo but withdraws it quickly, guiltily, at the last moment. Suddenly, she is dispossessed. This feels like somebody else's mantelpiece in somebody else's house. What right has she to touch things? She knows this is ridiculous, but she sits down without any further attempt. She has a strange feeling in her stomach. It isn't fear, but she can't think of an appropriate word to describe it. If anything, it's a bit like being lost.

She occupies herself with the chocolate brownies and they don't disappoint. Pretty soon the rush of sugar and fat has replaced that other, nameless, feeling with a comfortable queasiness that is familiar if nothing else. She considers taking a third but decides to wait. She can hear Georgie's footsteps on the wooden floor of the hall so she fixes her face in a smile.

"Oh, thanks!" says Georgie. She sits in what seems to have become her chair and takes the second mug.

"Brownie?"

"No, I won't, thanks. It'll spoil my dinner."

Alice sighs inwardly. Now she will have to make do with what she has already had. She finishes her tea and tries really hard not to let her eyes creep to the mantelpiece. Sadly, they seem to have a mind of their own.

"Ah, there it is!" says Georgie. She stands and takes the photo from its place. "I left it in here to remind me to show you."

She sits down again, looks at it briefly, then holds it out, waiting for Alice to take it. Their hands hover in the space above the chocolate brownies, not quite able to touch. For a moment, they look like a banal parody of God creating Adam, on the ceiling of the Sistine Chapel. Alice leans a little further forward and takes the photo. She looks at the image, then at Georgie.

"And this is …?"

"It's Matthew; Matt. My husband. I thought you might like ..."

"He looks really nice," says Alice. "And it's easy to see you were in love. You look really happy."

"Yes, we were." Somehow, Georgie has retrieved the photo and is studying it. "This was taken shortly after we met. It was pretty well love at first sight. For him, too. He was the only one. The only one who loved me the same as I loved him."

There is a silence then. Georgie seems lost in her own memories and Alice finds she is able to relax. There, she has been silly again. Georgie wasn't making some kind of territorial claim on her house. She wonders what's wrong with her at the moment. Why is she constantly teetering on the verge of panic? Nearly fifty years have passed. Nothing is going to happen now.

Later, after they have eaten the risotto, they sit in the lounge once more. This time, Alice doesn't wait to ask Georgie, but switches on the tv. They watch the Channel Four news for nearly an hour, but there is little to lighten the mood. They see people trying to survive the bombardment of Aleppo. There is travel chaos and yet more news about Donald Trump. At last, Alice reduces the volume until there is little more than a murmur coming from the set.

"Do you have any plans for tomorrow?" she asks.

"Not really," says Georgie. "Actually, it's my

birthday, but I tend not to celebrate that these days."

Alice's hands fly to her mouth. "Oh, my God! Is it really? I remember it being in December, but I'd forgotten … How awful of me. I haven't even got you a card."

Georgie laughs and tells Alice not to be so silly. How could she possibly have remembered after all these years? She says she regrets saying anything about it, but Alice will not let it pass. Now there is an excuse for her to do what she's been thinking about for the last day or so. She hasn't been able to find a way to achieve it without an embarrassing discussion about money, but Georgie's birthday has provided the answer. She can have a break from vegetarian food and she won't need to cook.

"Right, that's it," she says. "Tomorrow we're going out for a nice lunch. My treat!"

Georgie protests for a while but she is no match for Alice, whose carnivorous instincts appear to be more powerful than she thought. Alice fetches her laptop and Googles places to eat nearby. She is surprisingly excited by the prospect of dining out, then she realises why. This will be the first time she has shared a proper meal out since Scott went back. That was months ago. She is turning into a hermit.

She finds three possibilities and reads the reviews. One is a restaurant in town and the other two are country pubs. The restaurant is rather smart, so she discounts that. Then she looks at the menus of the two pubs to find only one of them has much choice of vegetarian dishes. She knows this pub. She stands and puts the laptop on the coffee table in front of Georgie.

"How does this look?" she says. "The last time I went here was with my son and his girlfriend. It was nice, but none of us are veggies."

Georgie doesn't look at the screen. She looks at Alice.

"Oh, you have a son! I didn't know. How old is he? Does he live round here?"

Alice explains that Scott has moved to Canada to be with his girlfriend. It seems likely they will stay there.

"I have a daughter, too," she adds. She can't mention Scott without mentioning Lucy. "Would you believe it? She's in New Zealand. It was supposed to be a sabbatical, but it's been two years now. It seems my children can't get far enough away from me!"

Georgie laughs. "I'm sure that's not true. Young people these days, they don't see distance as any kind of barrier. You must miss them though. Do you have any pics?"

Alice looks around. It hasn't occurred to her

before, but no, there isn't a single photo in this room. It is entirely anonymous. She changed everything when she moved, even the mirrors. Although of course they had no means of retaining their short history of unhappy reflections, they all ended up in the Oxfam shop, along with boxes and boxes of perfectly good household goods. The staff must have thought it was Christmas.

"Um, not handy, no," she says. "I'll dig some out later."

SPRING 1964

There was such a lot to think about. I hardly knew where to begin. Should I concentrate on re-living that magical moment when Hilary, the embodiment of all my chaste and girlish dreams, had lifted my hand to his lips like a prince from a fairytale? Or should I worry about what seemed to be a real and present danger: Georgie's mother's behaviour and my parents' obvious disapproval. Would they stop me visiting now they had caught a glimpse of the cracks in the fabric of Georgie's apparently enviable life? With no way of resolving this problem, my thoughts veered wildly from one extreme to the other.

Still, at least one mystery seemed to be solved. Now I understood why Georgie's mother appeared tearful from time to time. It probably also explained the drinking. If Hilary was following in his father's footsteps as she'd said, he must be planning to join the Secret Service. It was obvious. It was equally obvious that Georgie's mother was unhappy about that. Who wouldn't be? Her husband had been captured by the Russians and now her son was about to put himself in the same kind of danger. I wondered how old you had to be before you could start such a career. Was I going to lose Hilary so soon?

I was almost relieved to go back to school. There was less time for thinking. Nobody, not even Georgie, mentioned the way New Year's Eve had ended and I began to entertain the hope that it had all been forgotten. This was partly because I had caught a few words of a conversation between my parents. "I'd want to let my hair down if I ..." my mum had said, before she saw me lurking by the lounge door and clamped her lips shut. I found it hard to envisage a scenario in which my mum's hair would be anything but under strict control, but it gave me some cause for optimism.

An opportunity to test this theory arose within a week or two of term starting, when Georgie made an unexpected suggestion. We were on the bus, talking about the Maths homework we'd been set that day. I was actually quite good at Maths, whereas it was not Georgie's strongest subject.

Although I was doing reasonably well at school, Georgie was ahead of me in most lessons and it always felt good when I received better marks.

"My mother says I can invite you over to do homework once a week," she said. "I absolutely understand if you don't want to, and it would mean your dad picking you up I suppose, but I thought I'd ask. Don't worry if ..."

"No, I mean yes, that would be great," I said. Something to break the monotony of weekdays, each following exactly the same pattern as the one before, would be very welcome. "I'll have to ask, though," I added.

"Yes, I know. And they might say 'no.' It's a school night, and after the ... Anyway. If it's ok, I thought Wednesdays would be good, as you could help me with Maths and I could ... well, if you needed any help with French ..."

Georgie was being tactful. I was pretty hopeless at French. It was as if all my language skills were already employed by my obsessive interest in English.

"I always need help with French!" I laughed and Georgie laughed too.

As I walked home from the bus stop, I planned my strategy for putting this proposal to my parents. I didn't want to repeat my previous mistakes and go charging in with desperation written all over my face. This time, it would be different.

It took every ounce of self-control I could muster to wait until my dad returned from work. I acted as if everything were normal. I was neither overly well-behaved nor particularly difficult. I sat down and opened my French book with every apparent intention of getting on with my homework as usual. I let a few minutes or so elapse, then sighed and allowed my pencil to drop. There was no sign that anyone had noticed. My dad continued to eat his dinner while my mum started the bedtime routine for my sisters.

"Dad," I said, trying to sound a little anxious without over-doing it.

"Hmm?"

"When you've finished, can you help me with this French homework?"

My dad looked up in alarm. I knew he'd forgotten any French he'd ever known.

"You'd be better off asking your mum," he said.

So I waited. I huffed and puffed, wrote a few words then rubbed them out vigorously. Wrote a few more and repeated the process. I always completed my French homework in pencil first, but I made sure my dad could not ignore the amount of rubbing out I found necessary.

At last, I heard my mum's footsteps and leapt up as she entered the dining room.

"Mum, can you help me with this? It's French, and Dad says I have to ask you."

"Oh, he does, does he?"

My mum sat down beside me and, to be fair, she did try. She may even have been helpful on a different occasion. But I confused her with inaccurate explanations of the behaviour of verbs and generally sabotaged her attempts until she had to admit defeat.

"I'll write you a note," she said. "I'll tell them it's too difficult."

That was when I played my final card. I shed a few tears and then I appeared to hide them.

"It's not usually this hard," I sniffed. "I don't want to be put down a group. Georgie's mum asked her to invite me up there on Wednesdays to help with her Maths, but I thought you'd say 'no' so I didn't ask. But if I did, she could help me with French too."

I saw my parents look at each other and I knew I'd won. What a brilliant little tactician I was. Of course there were conditions and caveats. I understood that adults needed to assert themselves and show who was boss. But actually I was in control that evening. It was the first time I could say that, and I liked it. I liked it very much.

So that was the start of my weekly visits to Georgie's house. Hilary was not at home by then, so it was not exciting as such, but something else happened. As the weeks passed, I became assimilated into Georgie's household until it felt almost as familiar as my own. I could walk from room to room without invitation, without having to follow Georgie around and do as she did. If I became thirsty, I could help myself to a drink. If I needed a break from homework I could turn on the tv and nobody thought anything of it. Georgie's mother took little notice of us, but supplied us with an unpredictable and eclectic selection of evening meals ranging from beans on toast to beef bourguinon depending on her mood. We dreaded the days we arrived to find her in the kitchen though. Beans on toast was always a safer bet.

At last, Spring began to arrive and the days lengthened. That meant homework could be supplemented by some time in the garden. We had more or less taken over the area furthest from the house, and now we were able to continue making our den. It had started last Autumn with a couple of corrugated sheets and some broken fence panels, but now we began to hatch more ambitious plans. Nobody else seemed to venture this far and we were quite undisturbed as our structure grew.

It was amazing what we found in that garden. There was a shed containing quite a few rusty but serviceable tools and there were all sorts of potential building materials. A semi-demolished wall yielded bricks. The skeleton of a fruit cage yielded steel poles and brackets. The old greenhouse lost quite of few of its remaining glass panes to provide us with a skylight. Our den grew in size and complexity as the hours of daylight increased and it was a wonder we ever completed any homework at all.

It was early April when Hilary returned, just after the Easter weekend and one of the few times I saw Georgie that holiday. I had guessed he would be back at some point, but Georgie was so reluctant to talk about him I didn't like to raise the issue. I certainly wouldn't have asked her mother. How awful it would have been if she'd started to cry. We had been watching Newsround that afternoon. I remember it clearly, as there had been fights between mods and rockers somewhere on the coast and we were fascinated. Some of the older girls in school had begun to ally themselves to one or the other faction and it was all very exciting.

I left Georgie watching the next item and went into the kitchen. Her mother had bought a cake mix for us, and twelve little sponge cakes were in the oven in their paper cases. Goodness knows what my mum would have said if she had seen this culinary travesty, but it seemed like a perfect solution to me. Very little effort and more or less guaranteed results. I opened the oven door and placed a careful finger on one of the cakes. Yes, it sprang back up again when I pushed it, so they were done. I turned to find something to protect my hands and there was Hilary, right in front of me. I started, and narrowly avoided falling back against the open oven.

Hilary was smiling. His hair was even longer now, almost down to his shoulders, but he wore the same black raincoat.

"George's little friend!" he said. "Well, well. Something around here smells very nice. It looks as if you have hidden talents. What do you have to say for yourself?"

I had nothing to say for myself, not one word. Nobody had ever spoken to me like this. There was a kind of mockery in his voice that I found unsettling, yet his smile was very friendly. I was trapped between him and the cooker, the backs of my legs were becoming hot and the cakes would burn if I didn't get them out. I needed to act, but somehow I seemed to have lost the power of movement as well as speech.

I was saved by Georgie.

"Are they ready?" she asked, marching in and completely ignoring her brother. She picked up a tea towel from the back of a chair.

I stammered something, I don't remember what. Before I knew it, Georgie was right beside me, nudging me to one side and carrying the tray of cakes over to the table. Hilary left without a word and I didn't see him again that day. By the time my dad arrived to pick me up we had eaten most of the cakes and I felt a bit sick but I didn't tell him that. I didn't tell him about Hilary either, nor the fact that Georgie had been grumpy and out of sorts from the moment she laid eyes on him.

The first incident in school was soon after we returned. I had been up to Georgie's house only once in the interim although that had not been my choice. My parents had made it clear there would be no more 'living up there' as they put it, and Georgie made no attempt to contact me. The holiday dragged terribly, despite the pleasure of consuming large amounts of chocolate. I was quite pleased when it ended.

I could hardly wait to see Georgie, but soon it became clear that there was something different about her. Something different I couldn't define, even later, with the help of my thesaurus. She seemed brittle and edgy but she laughed a lot, at things she wouldn't normally have found funny. A few weeks ago, before the holiday, I would have broached this without a qualm. 'You're in a funny mood,' I would have said, and she would have told me why, or laughed and given me a playful punch. Now, something stopped me and I felt bereft at the lost easiness between us.

When I say 'incident', that makes what happened seem very serious, but of course it wasn't. However, it was the beginning of another change, and I suppose that's why it stands out in my mind. We were in English, my favourite subject of course. My fear of Mrs Hunt had grown into respect and now I felt able to exchange a few words with her after lessons. Once, I showed her a poem I had written and was shocked at how her eyes misted up, so I didn't show her any more.

However, there is no denying that the lesson that day was very dull. We were identifying the subject and object of sentences, a concept that both Georgie and I had grasped about three lessons before. Not so some of our class-mates. Thus, we were ploughing through it yet again with an ever-more-desperate Mrs Hunt trying to think of new ways to explain an apparently simple idea.

Georgie always sat beside me in English, and now she leaned across and whispered in my ear.

"Pretend there's something funny about Mrs Hunt. Pass it on." As soon as she'd finished speaking, she nudged me and made a small gesture towards Mrs Hunt, smiling as she did. Mrs Hunt didn't notice and I pretended not to have heard.

"Go on," urged Georgie. "It'll be fun."

I really didn't want to, but it was like that sometimes with Georgie. There were times when I just didn't feel able to say 'no' to her. This was especially the case then, when I was desperate to regain the closeness I felt I had lost.

I nudged the girl next to me and repeated Georgie's words. Meanwhile, she had sent the message the other way too. Soon, a substantial number of our classmates were nudging each other, pointing and grinning at some invisible cause of merriment about poor Mrs Hunt's person. Dedicated teacher though she was, she could not remain immune to this for long. She began to check her clothes and pass her hand over her face. This provoked more merriment from the class. Next, she disappeared into the stock cupboard for a minute or two and there were audible snorts of amusement as she re-appeared. At last, she excused herself and left the room, but she can't have failed to hear the explosion of laughter as she closed the door and hurried off down the corridor.

I imagine she went to the staffroom and asked colleagues to check her physical appearance. I imagine she was both mystified and hurt. I felt no joy as she returned and abandoned the rest of the lesson, instructing us to read quietly until the bell rang and we filed out. Many of the girls were still in high spirits and Georgie was the heroine of the hour, but I could only wonder what had happened here. The girl I knew was spirited and independent of mind but she wasn't mean. I didn't like the idea of having to get used to a new Georgie. I was perfectly happy with the one I had.

Nevertheless, Georgie was still full of it when we caught the bus home.

"Did you see her face?" she crowed.

I tried to strike a balance somewhere between kill-joy and accomplice but this was not very successful. I could tell Georgie was seeking more approval than I was willing to give but there was a limit to what I would do for her. If my parents found out I was involved in any kind of misbehaviour in school they would be shocked, angry, heart-broken. The list of potential verbs was long, but, more than that, my relationship with Georgie was also at risk. It was not only that she was behaving strangely. If my parents thought she was becoming a bad influence they would have no hesitation in stopping my visits altogether. Then I would lose Georgie and Hilary at once. I would lose the freedom of her house and her garden. I would lose my entire social life and all hope of Hilary talking to me again. I had spent hours imagining conversations in which I didn't stand there dumb and idiotic. I craved the chance to redeem myself in his eyes and that was at risk too.

Unfortunately, it didn't stop there. There was no repeat of the Mrs Hunt trick, but Georgie surprised us all in Maths about a week later. She wasn't sitting with me, but I could see her clearly from my seat about two rows behind. Her desk was next to the central gangway. All heads turned as she stood abruptly, took a couple of steps forward then collapsed in front of Miss Nugent's desk. There were gasps of dismay as Miss Nugent hurried round to tend to her.

"Go and get help!" she shouted to the girl nearest the door. I was horrified, consumed with anxiety. What had happened to Georgie? I wanted to go and kneel beside her, to do something, anything, to help, but Miss Nugent had told us all to remain seated.

It was only a matter of minutes before help arrived in the form of the Deputy Head and the school nurse. By that time, Georgie was sitting up and declaring herself to be fine, but she was taken down to the sick room where she remained until lunch time.

She came and found me as I left the sandwich room. She was smiling a huge smile, but I was still concerned.

"Oh, my God! Are you ok?" I said.

"Course I am. You didn't believe all that did you? Got me out of Maths, though."

I could hardly believe what she had said. It had all looked so real. She had disrupted the lesson, but that was of little consequence. She had also scared me half to death. I had to tell her how I'd felt as she lay there on the floor, but she seemed to think it was all part of the joke.

"Anyway, you'll know next time," she said.

DECEMBER 2016

Alice waits until Georgie goes up to bed then searches the desk. She knows there are some cards somewhere. Most of them prove to be unsuitable – a condolence card she never sent, a humorous thirtieth birthday card she bought for Scott before changing her mind about it. A couple of characterless, flowery designs she bought for emergencies. They won't do. Then she comes across a small, hand-made card. It has a silk flower in the centre, held in place by a tiny bow. She can't remember buying it, but it will be fine.

She writes a cheery message, signs it, then takes it up to her room. At least Georgie will have something to open on her birthday. Nobody else knows she's here. She's sixty-five and apparently alone in the world. How sad. But then she wonders how many cards she'll receive when her birthday comes. How many did she get last year?

This train of thought is leading in only one direction and Alice decides to put a stop to it. She will enjoy tomorrow. Then, surely, Georgie will start to think about moving on. It was only supposed to be a stop-gap. It was only supposed to be a few days. Once she has the place to herself, she can start to sort out her life. This has been a wake-up call. She has drifted into a series of solitary routines since Scott left. Coffee shops, aimless wandering around town, daytime tv. What happened to all those things she vowed to do as soon as she had time? Where is the novel she was always going to write? What about the trips to all the places she's never seen?

The fact is, her life has no focus, no meaning. Yes, as soon as Georgie leaves, she will start making some changes. Maybe some voluntary work, or a class. There may even be a writers' group in town. She has hardly written a word since she retired and now she realises what a gap this has created in her life. Travel may be less easy to fix – it's no fun going on holiday alone – but she may meet other single people. There are always chances, if only you're willing to take them.

The next morning, Alice awakes very early. She puts on her dressing gown, creeps downstairs and is relieved to find the kitchen empty. She puts a mug of tea and a slice of toast on a tray, together with the little card. She looks forward to seeing the smile of gratitude on Georgie's face.

Upstairs, she taps on Georgie's door but there is no answer. She puts the tray on the floor and tries again. She puts her ear to the door and listens. Maybe Georgie is in the shower. Alice thinks about opening the door but rejects that idea. Georgie could wander out of the en-suite in the nude and that would be beyond embarrassing. But still, the tea and toast will get cold and Georgie could just as easily be lying in bed. Alice taps once more, then opens the door a crack. She can't see the bed, but she can see the open door of the en-suite. Georgie must have raised the blind, as a shaft of light falls onto the soft grey tones of the bedroom carpet. There's nobody in there.

She opens the door a little wider and looks across to the bed. The curtains are still drawn but there is enough light to make it out. Her brain has loaded up a picture of Georgie asleep, curled up. She always slept like that, with one hand clenched, the thumb against her lips. Now she has to erase that image. The bed is empty. The quilt is thrown back and the pillows are in disarray. There is no sign of Georgie.

Alice steps into the room and looks all around, but it is a rectangular box like every other room in this house. There's nowhere to hide, even if Georgie wanted to. Then something makes her hurry to the window. The guest room, like the kitchen, is at the front of the house. She parts the curtains and looks down. There is her car, sleek and shiny as always, but Georgie's car has gone. There is nothing but an area of dry paving where it stood.

Alice whirls around. Has Georgie left without saying anything? Surely she wouldn't? But then she sees that the room is full of her possessions. Clothes are draped over the chair and there is a clutter of shoes in one corner. The carry box of camera equipment is on the chest of drawers. Alice breathes out. She retrieves the tray and takes it back to the kitchen, where she disposes of the tea and toast. She puts the card on the table, propped up against the tasteful vase of dried lavender. For some reason, she feels cheated.

It's only another five minutes or so before Alice hears the rattle and growl of the Volvo outside. It's enough to wake the whole street, she thinks. She jumps up, expecting to have to let Georgie in, but the front door opens. Georgie has a carrier bag in one hand and Alice's keys in the other.

"Oh, you're up!" says Georgie. "I was hoping to surprise you. I wanted to thank you for being so kind to me and, as you're buying lunch, I thought I'd do breakfast. I took your keys in case you were still asleep. Hope you don't mind."

Alice does mind, a little, but she assures Georgie it's fine. They go into the kitchen, where Georgie instructs her to sit down.

"I'm going to wait on you for a change," she says.

So Alice has to sit on her hands while Georgie rummages around in her cupboards for plates, for the cafetière, for the coffee. She has to watch as Georgie fiddles with the cooker, trying to work out which knob controls the grill. She has to wait while the croissants and pain-au-chocolate warm up in a glass dish she would never have used for that purpose. It doesn't matter, she tells herself.

Eventually, coffee and pastries are assembled on the table. By this time, Alice has secreted the little card in her dressing gown pocket. She wants to wait for the right moment.

"This is lovely," she says. "What a treat! You can't imagine how much I love pain-au-chocolate."

Georgie passes her the plate with a smile. Everything is back to front. Alice was supposed to be the one receiving the thanks, but she tells herself to stop fussing. This is Georgie's birthday. She has gained pleasure from providing breakfast. In a way, Alice is doing her a favour by accepting her hospitality despite the fact that they are in Alice's house.

"Here you are," she says, holding out the card. "Happy birthday!

MAY 1964

Of course it couldn't go on forever, despite what Georgie seemed to think. She threw herself on the floor in an ever-increasing number of lessons, to the consternation of the teachers and amusement of our class-mates. They had worked it out after the first few times, but the tone of the letters Georgie was given to take home to her mother became more and more alarmed. Georgie would open them on the bus and read them with a strange smile, before crumpling them up and pushing them into the deepest recesses of her school bag. To begin with, she would let me read them too, but I could never provide her with the response she was looking for. By the time it ended she barely read them herself.

It seems strange that it never occurred to her that the school would not be content with her assurance that she had visited the doctor and been given a clean bill of health. I had tried to warn her at first, but she had cut me off so sharply that I decided to leave well alone. I couldn't risk losing our Wednesdays together, especially as these were the only times that the old Georgie showed herself. It was as if some kind of weight was removed from her shoulders the minute we packed our books away and headed off to the garden. The world we had constructed for ourselves, out of sight of the house, appeared to exist in a wonderful, protected bubble. I had no idea what had changed Georgie's behaviour in school but I hung on to the magic of our dens and tunnels and tried not to think about what it might mean.

It was a Wednesday when the end came. It was a lovely day and I was looking forward to completing the new section of our construction we had started the week before. This was the furthest outpost, nestling up against the rickety back fence and providing a view of the area of woodland behind the house. This, I had decided, was the most likely place for spies to be hiding in order to gain access to the house, but I never spoke of this to Georgie. Instead, I pointed out the advantages of having a den behind the apple trees and thus almost invisible until you were right upon it.

Georgie appeared to agree and I put her apparent lack of enthusiasm to one side in my own passion for this new project.

My head was full of plans as we walked the short distance along the Templars Way to Georgie's house. The new den was almost complete, but how to join it to the rest of the structure? The other three dens were connected by tunnels constructed from a series of rusty metal arcs that must have formed some kind of protective structure for vegetables. They were draped with bedding from one of the remaining unpacked crates and an old stair carpet we had found in the shed. Now, however, we were fast running out of materials. I barely noticed Georgie's mother standing in the open doorway as we walked up the drive.

"Ah, Alice," she said as we approached. Her expression was grim and her arms were folded. "Of course, it's Wednesday. I'm sorry, but I'm afraid Georgie will be staying in today. Are you ok to get yourself home? It's still early."

My heart thumping, I assured her it would be perfectly fine to walk home. It would be light for hours and there were plenty of people around. I started to say goodbye to Georgie, but she was already in the house by then and the words faded on my lips. The door closed with an ominous thud before I had taken more than a few steps. It was then that I realised what had happened. Of course I had to wait until the next morning to hear the details from Georgie, but I knew it was not the kind of bad news I had feared at first. Nobody had died, nobody had been captured. Georgie's mother was angry, not sad, and it was pretty obvious what she was angry about.

My next problem was how to explain my unexpected appearance to my mother. I decided to buy some time by inventing a headache that had affected Georgie so badly that I'd needed to walk her home. This worked at the time, but proved to be a mistake later, when Georgie informed me that our Wednesday sessions were cancelled for the foreseeable future.

"I'm in such trouble, you wouldn't believe," she moaned, on the bus the next morning. "I've never seen my mother in such a state. She's been summoned into school to discuss my medical condition and she's going to tell them it was all fake."

I tried to be suitably sympathetic, but actually I was angry with Georgie. What did she expect? Even a mother as relaxed as hers could hardly be expected to see the joke and try to explain it all away. No, Georgie had messed everything up and for no apparent reason. She was banned from having friends around – that meant me, as I'm sure nobody else came – and the punishment would affect me the most even though I was entirely innocent. Added to that, I had to lie to my parents about Wednesdays in case they decided to stop me seeing Georgie even when her punishment expired. I told them a complicated story about Georgie's mother and an unspecified after school commitment but I doubt they believed it. I expect they thought we had fallen out.

So that was that. My whole social life ended, suddenly and completely. But that was not all. What of my dreams and fantasies? What were the chances of seeing Hilary now? How could I engage in that imagined conversation in which I was both clever and amusing? How could I undo the damage caused by my pathetic behaviour the last time we'd met? Now Hilary would never look at me with admiration from under his floppy fringe and marvel at how mature I seemed. I was doomed to remain Georgie's unremarkable and awkward little friend from the village and it wasn't fair.

Georgie and I continued to sit together on the bus, but relations were strained on both our parts. She was moody and quiet and I was angry, but my anger remained unspoken. I still hung on to the possibility, however remote it seemed, that things might somehow return to how they had been. Georgie's mother would relent at some point and I would step back into Georgie's world as if I had never been absent. That was the dream that I rehearsed every night before I slept, and I enacted it so often that I could have quoted each person's lines if requested.

The house would be bathed in a rosy glow as I walked up the drive. The door would open, just as it had that first time, to reveal Georgie and her mother, wreathed in smiles.

"Alice! How lovely to see you! We've missed you so much," Georgie's mother would say. Then we'd go into the garden, where the sun would be busy baking the ground until it was warm and dry, and we'd walk through the long grass. Bees would be buzzing, birds would be singing and we'd stand there, looking at our dens. Then, without a word, but as if we simultaneously responded to some unheard call, we'd run right up to the end of the garden. We'd sprint past the apple trees, where the sun had to fight its way through the leaves and immature fruit to dapple the grass. Then, back in the glare of the sun, we'd crawl into our shady final den and lie back, laughing.

I never got further than that. Either I would fall asleep, lulled by the joy of it, or the bubble would burst as I began to doubt whether it was possible to go back in that way. Would the old Georgie still inhabit that space as before? Could she? Had I lost the only part of my life I really cared about?

To make matters even worse, the Whitsun break was approaching and this was when we took our annual holiday. For weeks I had been trying to work out how Georgie could come with us, but now it was a waste of time. It is extremely unlikely that it would have happened anyway, as our car only had seats for five and the flat we rented was very small. But that wasn't the point. All the time the question remained unasked, there was still a chance, still a hope. Now there was no point in mentioning it to my parents, as Georgie wouldn't be allowed even if they agreed. For the first time, I found myself dreading a week at the sea-side. A week with only my parents and my sisters for company. Part of me felt cheated at the loss of my friend but another part of me felt cheated at the loss of something else. I couldn't express what it was, but I knew it had gone.

In the event, I had a good time. It was hard to be miserable when the beach, with its endless rock pools and fine sand, was only a few minutes' walk away. How could an eleven year old girl fail to join in with the construction of elaborate castles and walls against the in-coming tide? How could she fail to savour ice-creams sitting on the sea wall or fish and chips straight from the paper? I enjoyed myself, there is no doubt about that, but it was a slightly muted enjoyment. Sometimes I would see Georgie, just at the edge of my field of vision. Then my heart would lurch and I would turn, but of course she wouldn't be there. It would either be another girl, nothing like Georgie, or there would be nobody there at all. It was as if she were hovering, always just out of reach, waiting to join us if only we would let her.

Despite this, and despite the fact that my thoughts often turned to the future and all its uncertainties, the week passed quickly enough. I stopped counting the days almost as soon as we arrived and then, before I knew it, it was nearly time to return. We were leaving on the Friday as my dad was not a confident driver and believed the traffic would be easier then. My sisters were outraged and begged him to give us one more day, but I said nothing. A plan was beginning to hatch in my mind.

On the afternoon of our final day, I asked my mum for an advance on my next week's pocket money.

"I want to buy Georgie a little present," I said in answer to her query. "I don't think she's been anywhere and I feel sorry for her."

My mum was obviously surprised, having considered the friendship over, but there was no reason to refuse so I took my two shillings down to the little shop by the sea and bought Georgie a bag of sweets shaped like colourful pebbles. They were in clear polythene, tied up with a red ribbon. I thought they were perfect.

The journey back from Devon took all day. Our car wouldn't have driven very fast even if my dad's caution and the roads had allowed it and we stopped several times en route. Despite leaving early, it was past seven by the time we got home, tired and fractious. My sisters had bickered for the final few hours and even my dad, normally the calmest man you could hope to meet, had snapped at my mum when she sent us the wrong way at a junction.

I had remained aloof from all this nonsense. I had my mind on one thing and one thing only: tomorrow we would be home and it would only be Saturday. Georgie was not allowed to have friends to play, or to do homework, but I had a present for her. Nobody could argue against a quick visit to deliver a present, and who could tell where that would lead?

The next morning I awoke early and scrabbled around trying to find something suitable to wear for what I was hoping would turn into an afternoon in Georgie's garden. It looked like being another sunny day, but all my summer clothes were still packed away, waiting to be washed. Eventually, I dug out a scruffy pair of shorts and a faded T-shirt. At least I didn't have to worry about being smart at Georgie's house, however grand it might appear.

I ate breakfast quickly and put the present for Georgie in my saddle bag. I was itching to cycle up to Templars Way straight away, but there were many chores to do and my parents were adamant that I should share them. I was hugely frustrated, but I could foresee a scenario in which bad behaviour would lead to a ban on going to Georgie's house at all. So I bit my lip and helped to wash and stow away the sandy buckets and spades. I hung washing on the line and brushed sand out of the dog's fur. This was a pointless exercise surely designed to delay me as long as possible, but I carried it out without complaint.

"Can I go now?" I asked.

My mum looked around but seemed unable to invent any more tasks for me to perform. She also had no idea about Georgie's extended punishment, so imposed no restrictions on my visit, other than that I must be home in time for tea.

I don't think I ever completed the journey to

Georgie's house in less time than I did that day. The muscles in my calves were burning by the time I reached the junction with the Templars Way and sweat was pouring down my face. I stopped for a few minutes to get my breath back, then cycled the last few hundred yards at a more leisurely pace in case anyone was watching. I didn't want to appear desperate, even if I was.

I don't know if my face was still red as I stood on Georgie's doorstep clutching the bag of sweets. Maybe it was, maybe it was streaked with dust or maybe my hair had escaped from its plait. Normally, none of these things would have mattered, but today was different. The door opened and there stood Georgie, but I had to look twice to confirm it was her. Her hair was tied back and she was wearing a dress of all things. She didn't smile but looked confused; surprised.

"Oh," she said. "We weren't … I'm not sure ..."

"Who is it, George?" came her mother's voice from within. Georgie turned away, leaving the door only partially open, and I heard fragments of a whispered conversation before it opened again.

"Alice," said Georgie's mother. "Please come in. Georgie's cousins are here and we're having some lunch, but you're very welcome to join us."

If my life had been an animation, the cartoon

figure of me would have shrunk to something around knee height at that point, like my namesake when she ate the mushroom. I must have made a peculiar picture, my skinny legs protruding from scruffy shorts and my hand held out to offer the sweets that nobody seemed to have noticed. Suddenly, I wished I could be back at home.

"Um, it's ok. I'm sorry. I'll come back another time ..." I stammered, but Georgie's mother was having none of it. I believe she was quite fond of me by that time, or maybe it was just that it was the polite thing to do. In any case, I was ushered through the remarkably tidy kitchen into the garden, but it was not the garden I knew so well and had longed for so intensely. To begin with, somebody had mowed the grass near the house. True, it would have made a very poor cricket pitch, as some areas were still straggly and others were bare, but it was a kind of transformation all the same.

A long table covered with a white tablecloth sat on what was now a lawn rather than a meadow. Four pairs of eyes surveyed me from chairs around this table and I felt myself blush a deep red. What on earth had happened to Georgie's family? I had been gone only a week, and yet everything had changed. Georgie and her mother were both dressed as I had never seen them before, and who were these stuck-up looking people in their garden, the remains of a feast spread out before them?

"Have you eaten, darling?" asked Georgie's mother.

"Yes," I lied, cringing at the thought of sitting down with these people who were staring at me with such unconcealed disapproval.

"Very well, if you're sure. Everybody, this is Alice, Georgia's friend from the … from school. Alice, this is my brother, Georgia's uncle Edward, and this is her Aunt Elizabeth. George, perhaps you'd like to introduce Alice to your cousins, then you can go and play."

Georgie's cousins were a boy and girl around the same age we were. The boy was called Theo and I took an instant dislike to him. He was tall and gangly with sandy hair and a crop of fierce-looking acne. He barely deigned to nod as Georgie introduced us, his eyes sweeping over me then flicking away as if I were some kind of urchin. His sister was also much taller than me, but she, at least, smiled and took my hand. She was blonde and looked a lot like the haughty woman sitting at the table. If she felt any distaste at taking my sweaty fingers in her own cool palm she was much too well-bred to show it.

Introductions over, we had been instructed to play so play we must, but the atmosphere was beyond awkward. If I hadn't been feeling so sorry for myself I might have felt bad for Georgie, who had the unenviable task of bringing together two apparently incompatible facets of her social life. Clearly it would have been impossible to explore the dens, even if I had wanted these interlopers to get anywhere near them. The cousins might have snagged their smart clothes on the many nails that protruded from the fence panels or scraped their shiny shoes on the bricks that held some sections aloft.

We played a version of tennis with an assortment of bats and no net, but I couldn't stand it for long. I wish I could say that I had Georgie's obvious discomfit in mind as I pretended I had to return home by two-thirty, but actually I was thinking only of myself. It was torture to be in my magical place with these insufferable people. It was torture to be dressed for fun and adventure when everybody else looked as if they had just returned from church. It was torture to have looked forward to something so much, to have dreamed such happy and soft-filtered dreams, only to have them dashed by a bunch of people from a different world.

I remembered my manners enough to say

goodbye to Georgie's mother and her guests, who were now lounging around the table smoking and drinking wine like something out of a film. Georgie's mother was wearing a floppy, straw hat and tendrils of her hair escaped to form a dark halo around her face. She rose as if to see me out, but I said it was fine, that I would let myself out. After all, this was my second home. There were times when I practically lived here. Did she want to make me feel like a guest? Did she want to destroy that too?

I was seething as I dragged my bike out of the bushes and jumped on. My eyes were stinging with angry tears and I was lucky not to be mown down by a passing car as I pulled out of the drive without really looking. Shaken, I walked my bike to the top of the lane then sat down on the grass by the bridleway that led to the hill. Part of me knew that it was perfectly normal for Georgie to have a family and for them to visit, to be a part of her life. But part of me feared this was another indication of the fragility of my hold on everything that house contained, on everything it meant. I don't know how long I sat there, waiting until I was composed enough to return home, but it felt like hours.

DECEMBER 2016

Georgie insists on clearing away after breakfast. She sends Alice out of her own kitchen. She piles the crockery in the sink, despite the fact that there is a perfectly good dish-washer. Alice hopes she will at least leave everything on the drainer. She imagines having to re-arrange the whole lot afterwards, without Georgie noticing.

Later, Georgie comes into the lounge where Alice is walking up and down, pushing the vacuum cleaner. She stands there, so Alice feels obliged to switch it off.

"You know this pub we're going to?"

"Yes, The Minstrel," says Alice.

"Did I see something about it being good for walking?'

Alice thinks. Walking isn't one of her regular pastimes. Maybe it should be, but she always feels self-conscious walking through woods or parks without a dog. Round here, the dog walkers seem to form an impenetrable clique. She has never walked anywhere near The Minstrel, but she has certainly seen people in walking gear there.

"I believe it is," she says.

"Only I was thinking, as it's not a bad day today, maybe we could combine lunch with a little walk? I love the light on days like this, and I'd like to take a few shots. What do you think?"

Alice agrees. She can hardly do otherwise. This is Georgie's birthday treat, after all. At least it will solve one problem that's been troubling her. If they both look like people out for a walk, there will be no uncomfortable contrast between her clothes and Georgie's.

So Alice dresses down. Her jeans are designer, but nobody would know. She wears a fairly plain top with a thin fleece and a warm jacket. That should cover all eventualities. She finds her wellies in the conservatory at the back and waits patiently while Georgie covers half the drive with the contents of the back of the Volvo in the search for hers.

When they arrive at the pub it is nearly an hour before they are due to sit down. They park in the pub car park, change into their wellies and head off to the lake. Alice soon finds it impossible to keep up with Georgie, who strides off as if five, not fifty years have elapsed since they last walked anywhere together.

The lake is not very big. It is really only the widening out of the river that feeds it, but it is busy with small boats in the summer. Not so now. The water looks dark and freezing cold. Only a few sad-looking moorhens lurk about in the reeds at the edge. Georgie takes out her camera and clicks away for a few minutes while Alice gets her breath back. She sneaks a look at her watch.

"Ok to try the woods?" says Georgie.

"Yes, fine," says Alice. She wonders if Georgie will notice she's struggling and slow down. Somehow, that doesn't seem likely.

It is gloomy in the woods. Georgie takes some shots through the trees then suddenly she turns and points the lens at Alice. "Stay like that!" she commands. She clicks away. "Now turn a bit – no, to your left – that's right. Fantastic!"

Alice is hugely uncomfortable. It is many years

since she has enjoyed having her photograph taken. There is so much more of her to photograph now and she hates to see it. In one part of her mind she is still slim. She still has a neck rather than a fatty extension of her jowls below her chin. She can cope with her reflection, but photographs are another matter. They are a permanent reminder of how she looks to other people and she'd rather not see them.

Back at the car park, they change out of their muddy boots and Georgie puts her camera case in the boot.

"We'll have a look at those later," she says with a smile.

They are shown to their table and Alice assumes control, for the first time today. She tells Georgie she must have anything she wants and reminds her there will be no cooked meal tonight. This might be Georgie's treat, but she intends to benefit too. It takes them no time to choose as they have both seen the menu online. They order, then sit back to wait.

After a few standard remarks about the cosy décor and the nice real fire, they seem to struggle to find anything to say. Alice feels obliged to break the silence.

"So, do you have any children, Georgie?"

"No," says Georgie. "By the time I met Matt it was a bit late. But anyway, I'm not sure I would've made a very good parent. I was very unsettled as a young woman and probably a bit selfish. I'd had a poor role-model, I suppose."

Alice doesn't know how to respond. "Oh, don't say that! I really liked your mum," she says at last. "I know she wasn't your average mother, but at least she was interesting. Is she still alive?"

"Yes, she's in a nursing home. She's losing it now, I'm afraid. I haven't seen her for weeks. The last time I went, she got so agitated the staff suggested I leave it for a bit."

Alice says how awful that must be. "You wouldn't have wanted her to be different though, would you? I always envied you. My family were so dull compared to yours."

Georgie puts down her glass and fixes Alice with a steely look.

"With respect, Alice, you don't know what you're saying," she says.

Alice nearly chokes on her mouthful of orange juice. She has no idea how to respond. But, luckily, their food arrives just at the right time and this disperses the tension. Alice attacks her steak and kidney pie as if it is the last decent food she will eat for a while, which indeed it might be. She decides she may have just experienced a lucky escape. Clearly Georgie is sensitive about the past and she will have to be careful what she says. However, she seems to have been right in her assumption. Georgie appears to have very few people in her life. Alice decides that Georgie's visit has done her a favour: it has made her grateful for what she has. Her children may be far away, but at least she has them. Who would miss Georgie if she died?

JUNE 1964

At least there was one positive to arise from my angst-filled afternoon at Georgie's. The ice was broken and her mother appeared to forget about Georgie's misdemeanours the previous term. In fact, everything reverted more or less to how it had been, at least on the surface. Our Wednesday homework sessions resumed and we spent as much time as possible in the garden. Even more surprising was the fact that Georgie increasingly hung around with me in school. This was a little awkward at first, as we often talked about the dens or what we had done out of school. Caroline found it hard to participate but, after a week or two, she drifted off and joined another group, so that problem was solved without too much trouble.

I hadn't forgotten that afternoon though. It was as if an imprint of that scene in the garden had been superimposed on the real thing. The anxiety this provoked was not helped either by subtle changes in Georgie's house. The cheerful chaos of the kitchen never really reappeared, and there was much more food in the cupboards. This should have been a good thing and it was certainly better for Georgie who must have been on the verge of being neglected at times. However, it was another crack in the facade as far as I was concerned, another reminder that things could change at any moment. I yearned for the days when Georgie's mother would not appear to cook us dinner and we would create something bizarre from whatever tins we could find in the cupboard. Sadly, they seemed to have gone for good.

A couple of weeks after we returned to school, we were on the bus returning home when a buzz of excitement went around the few remaining passengers.

"Look, it's the fair!" I told Georgie. "It comes every year about this time. It's brilliant!"

It was true. In a village where hardly anything ever happened, the annual visit of the travelling fair was something extremely exciting. It was only a small concern, but it had a few rides including dodgems, roundabouts and revolving swings that sent you spinning high and fast. There were also a number of stalls and an arcade of slot machines. Loud music competed with the noisy generators, and the intoxicating smell of fried food and candy floss greeted visitors as they passed into the field normally occupied by sheep. It would stay for two or three days and everyone loved it.

We soon found out it was due to open on Saturday afternoon, so I arranged to meet Georgie there. My parents would be bringing my sisters, but I had no intention of spending any time with them. I had all my pocket money plus an extra two shillings to spend, and I knew exactly how I was going to spend it. One turn on the swings, one turn on the dodgems and the rest for the slot machines. My favourite was a machine that allowed you to bet on the apparently random selection of one of four pop stars. Elvis Presley was worth four pence if his light came on, whereas Adam Faith was worth only two. I was convinced that there must be some kind of sequence involved, and that I could win a fortune if only I could work it out, but of course I never did.

Georgie and I had a brilliant afternoon and spent all our money. We were hanging around, watching other people spend theirs, when my parents approached us.

"We're off now," said my dad. "You may as well walk back with us."

There followed a tense and highly embarrassing negotiation. Georgie shuffled around from foot to foot trying not to appear to be listening, and I sent out death rays to my parents for treating me like a baby. Eventually they agreed that I could stay for a while, but I must walk back to the crossroads with Georgie and I must be back by six-thirty. I was not at all happy with this, but I did manage to beg a few more pennies from my dad before they left, my sisters squealing at the unfairness of it.

We decided to invest this unexpected bounty in the slot machines and, this time, good old Elvis came up trumps. That meant we now had enough money for one more ride on the dodgems. It was Georgie's turn to drive and we were sailing round the outside when we felt a sudden bump that sent the car lurching to one side. Georgie righted it quickly, but before we could get going again another crash sent us into the side bumper. We both turned round and there were a couple of boys in the car behind us, laughing their heads off. I knew them from primary school, but we hadn't spoken a word since we left.

Georgie gave me a funny little smile and pressed the pedal hard. We hurtled round, weaving from one side to the other, the car containing the boys on our tail the whole time. We were doing quite well until one of the fairground lads jumped onto the back of our car and leant between us. He grabbed the steering wheel and guided us round in a manner more decorous and befitting our age and gender, until our time was up and we drifted to the side. The boys behind had backed off, but they were still laughing as we all jumped down onto the grass. It was not long before they approached us.

My instant reaction was to treat these boys with the contempt they deserved. They had spoilt our last ride. I summoned up my best disdainful expression and prepared to stalk away with Georgie at my side, but, it appeared, she had other ideas.

"Hello, girls," said one of the boys. His name was Tommy Webb and he had been in the year above me at school. He had a shiny leather belt holding up his jeans and he hooked his thumbs into it as he spoke.

"Hello, yourself," said Georgie.

"Who's your friend, Alice?" asked the other boy, Nigel Watson. He had been in my year and was notorious for being the class clown. I had always thought he was stupid so I didn't bother to reply.

Georgie pulled down her top and tossed her hair.

"Actually, I can speak," she said. "My name's Georgia. And you are …?"

I think I had forgotten about the Georgie who had surprised us all on that first day in school. The Georgie with the painted nails and the sophisticated air. I had become so accustomed to seeing her in jeans, climbing trees and hauling junk around the garden, that I had forgotten how grown up she could be. And how attractive. Both Tommy and Nigel were clearly only too aware of this, and they were soon larking about trying to impress her.

I can't imagine that Georgie was very impressed by their antics but she did nothing to discourage them. Instead, she teased them, pretending to forget their names and reaching out as if to touch them before withdrawing her hand at the last minute. She batted her eyelashes and employed all sorts of coquettish expressions until I could stand it no longer. I looked at my watch.

"Georgie," I said, taking her arm. "It's nearly time to go. Shall we have a last look round?"

"I think I'll stay for a bit," said Georgie, barely

looking in my direction. "You go if you like."

I opened my mouth to remind her that we were supposed to walk back to the crossroads together, but I swallowed my words. I didn't want to look like a baby, needing to be walked home. I said goodbye and told her I'd see her at school on Monday, but I doubt she even heard.

They were still together as I reached the entrance to the field and risked a brief glance over my shoulder. There wasn't any point in waving or waiting for Georgie to catch me up, that was crystal clear. I had plenty of time to walk home and still arrive before six thirty, but instead I ran. I ran as if my life depended on it. I ran until my breath seared my chest and I could run no more. I don't even know why I did this, but at least the physical exertion helped to explain my red face and watery eyes. I told my parents I had a headache due to too much sun, and went up to my room where I threw myself onto the bed.

I suppose I must have fallen asleep. It was still just about light when I rolled off my bed, walked over to the window and opened it wide. I could hear the sound of the fair if I listened carefully, the chug of the generators and little bursts of music carried across on the breeze. I dragged a chair across and knelt on it, leaning out of the window as far as I dared. A strange yearning feeling swept over me. Everything was still happening just a short distance away, and I wasn't part of it. My stomach felt empty, but it was nothing to do with food. Would Georgie still be there, chatting to the boys and riding on the dodgems with them?

It was strange, but we didn't discuss the fair or the boys at school the next week. It was as if we had come to a mutual agreement to put it to one side. As usual, I was too concerned with maintaining access to Georgie's house and all it contained to risk upsetting the apple cart. I'm not sure if Georgie even realised she had hurt me.

In any case, it was only the following Wednesday that something happened to push all thoughts of the fair out of my mind. We were in Georgie's room finishing off our Maths homework when her mother called from the bottom of the stairs.

"George! I need you to try those clothes on. Mrs Mills is here."

I knew Georgie sometimes wore second-hand clothes. I had seen a label with somebody else's name in her blazer. It was something my parents would never have entertained, but it didn't seem to bother Georgie.

"Wait there," she said, but I had no intention of doing that. I gave her enough time to get downstairs then crept down to the landing and leaned over the bannister. Muffled voices came from the kitchen, so I should be safe for a few minutes.

My first stop was Hilary's bedroom. This was normally a scene of great fascination, as it was full things he had touched, things he had worn. It even smelled of him – a musty aroma I would have found unpleasant in any other circumstance. I loved to stand just inside the room and imagine he was asleep in the huge bed. However, today it was locked, so I hurried along the corridor to the room where the paintings were stored.

I knew exactly where I was going to look. The paintings nearest the door were fairly tame – some semi abstract landscapes and a few self-portraits in dark colours. These were of no interest, but those at the back were a different matter. This was where the nudes were stacked. They were mostly very large canvasses, three or four feet square, and they never failed to excite me. Having been brought up in a household where the human body was always kept well covered, the sensual abandon of these figures felt like forbidden fruit. It was a peek into an adult world that was alarming and enticing at once.

I opened the door carefully and left it wide so I could hear anyone approaching. I picked my way to the back, and that was when I saw another door. I hadn't noticed it before. It was shaped to fit in the space where the ceiling sloped down towards the floor and it was painted the same muted green as the walls. I moved a couple of paintings to one side and pulled the handle. Nothing. This was very annoying, so I pulled harder and nearly fell as the door flew open. The space behind it was dark and festooned with cobwebs, but I could see that there were more canvasses stacked inside. Carefully, I pulled out the first and stood it up. What I saw made me jump and stagger back into the stack of larger paintings. What if somebody had heard? Quickly, I replaced the painting and closed the door, my hands shaking. I crept back up to Georgie's room and tried to calm my breathing, but I could do nothing about the thumping of my heart.

The painting I had seen was not a nude and it was not like anything else I had seen in that room. It was a wild swirl of colours that were entirely abstract at the margins but gradually resolved themselves into hundreds of knives, or daggers, revolving around a central figure. This was a man lying slumped on his side in a pool of red that crept outwards and matched the blades of many of the knives. He looked very like an older version of Hilary, and I assumed it must be Georgie's father. I could hardly begin to work out what this might mean and I certainly couldn't ask Georgie. I closed my eyes and tried to imprint the painting onto my memory. I would have to think about this later.

For once, I was glad when my dad came to collect me. I had no space in my mind for further architectural innovation. I had even found myself agreeing when Georgie suggested that we had done enough building for now and perhaps we should spend the rest of the summer enjoying what we had made.

Back home, I went up to my room as soon as I could without drawing attention to myself. I lay on my bed and tried to recall every detail of that painting. What was it telling me? I mulled it over for ages, but there seemed to be no other possible conclusion. The figure in the middle was Georgie's father and he had been stabbed to death. Georgie's mother must have found him lying in a pool of blood and this was her way of dealing with that experience. It made sense so far, but then there were all sorts of problems. For a start, how could this have happened without Georgie knowing? He must have been murdered somewhere other than their house, but it was still hard to see how it had been kept from her.

Surely the police would have been involved? Surely it would have been in the newspapers and she would have found out that way? But then I remembered that the Russians were involved, and the Secret Service. Obviously it had all been hushed up, and Georgie had been told a pack of lies to avoid her finding out and spilling the beans. I shivered and my stomach cramped. This was even more serious than I thought, but it was also the solution to Georgie's behaviour. No wonder she had started playing up at school. All these months believing her father had been captured, waking up every morning to wonder if he was alive or dead.

I sat up. Enough is enough, I told myself. Georgie deserves to know the truth. How can she ever come to terms with the loss of her father if she is held in this limbo? How can she return to her former carefree state? Still, clearly there were risks associated with telling her my theory without proof. If I showed her the painting I would have to admit to sneaking around the house whenever an opportunity presented itself. No, I would have to do this properly. I would find more evidence – it must be there in the house somewhere – and then I would find a way to let Georgie know the truth. I wasn't at all sure about this last part, but I could work that out later.

I slept remarkably well given the import of my decision. It was as if everything was beginning to fall into place. It would become obvious that I had an understanding well beyond my years. I would become indispensable as Georgie's support as well as her friend. Hilary would find out about it when he next returned and he would thank me. Clearly he already knew the awful truth – after all, he was being prepared for a life in the Secret Service, despite the dangers. He would take my hand as he had before and tell me what a good thing I'd done. How stupid they'd been to keep the truth from Georgie.

I couldn't wait until the next Wednesday so I more or less invited myself to Georgie's house on Saturday. Unfortunately, it was hopeless. I tried to manufacture all sorts of reasons to be in the house alone, but I became sure Georgie was suspicious so I had to stop. There was one small opportunity when we returned to the house for a drink and her mother called her. I darted to the big old oak desk at the back of the lounge and opened the front, but it was bulging with papers that threatened to fall in chaos to the floor. I closed it again and only just got back to my seat by the tv as the door opened. No, this would not do. I would need uninterrupted time to find what I was looking for – most likely a death certificate – and that was not going to happen without a plan.

The plan presented itself to me on Monday. If I hadn't been such a logical child I might have thought I was in receipt of some kind of celestial support for my enterprise. As it was, I saw it as an indication that fate was on my side.

"You'll never believe what I've been dragged into," said Georgie as the bus set off from school.

"What?"

"Bloody debating society," she sighed. "Every Thursday after school. I tried to get out of it but Mrs Hunt phoned my mother. Then it was all 'oh, George, you know how good you were at Hawfield, it's such a useful skill, blah, blah, blah.' Bloody Hawfield, she's obsessed with it, but I just want to forget all about it!"

My ears pricked up. Georgie had never spoken about her old school. This was a part of her past that was completely unknown to me.

"Why, what was wrong with it?" I asked.

"It was in the middle of bloody nowhere and we weren't allowed out," said Georgie, her arms folded across her chest.

"There aren't many schools that let you out during the day," I said. I had rarely heard Georgie swear so much within a few sentences.

"No, not during the day, stupid," she said. "I was a boarder. I was stuck there for weeks at a time unless mother and … unless anyone visited me. And then it was a quick drive into a poxy little town, a cream tea and back again. I tell you, I've never been so glad to move."

I tried to continue the conversation but that was Georgie's first – and last – exploration of her life at boarding school. That didn't matter though. Although it might have been interesting to hear more, she had told me enough. Now I knew how her family had managed to keep her in the dark so effectively. She wasn't in the family home when her mother made the terrible discovery. That meant the murder could have happened there. She wasn't there when her mother was stricken with initial shock and grief, nor when the British Secret Service came to sort it all out and cover it up. It could have been weeks before anyone told poor Georgie anything.

By the time I got home I was buzzing. Not only had I solved one of the most intractable problems of the mystery, but I also had the beginnings of a new plan.

"Mum, I'm going up to revise," I said, as soon as I'd had a drink and a biscuit. "We've got a science test tomorrow."

My mother smiled fondly at her dutiful daughter. If only she knew the truth. I had promised not to keep secrets from her, but what was I to do? These events were too big for little promises to interfere with them.

I sat in my room with a science book open on my lap, but I didn't look at it. My eyes were wide but they registered nothing. Georgie's enforced participation in the debating society had provided an unexpected opportunity but I would only have one shot at my target. I had to get it right.

DECEMBER 2016

Alice half expects Georgie to suggest another walk, but they have taken their time over this meal and it is nearly dusk by the time they leave. Having managed to persuade Georgie to share a desert with her, she feels full and content. The excursion has been a complete success, apart from that one moment of awkwardness.

"Thank you so much," says Georgie for at least the fifth time. Alice doesn't know why, but this is beginning to irritate her. Why can't Georgie accept her generosity, say thanks and then leave it at that? Every time she thanks her, Alice has to say how pleased she is to do it, or that it's nothing, don't mention it. Or that she enjoyed it too. She might run out of suitable responses at this rate, or her irritation will show and the happy mood she has nurtured will be lost.

Back home, Alice experiences a sudden and overwhelming urge to be alone. She feels as if she can't breathe. She pretends to remember an email she has to send and excuses herself, taking the laptop with her.

"Make yourself at home," she says, gesturing vaguely. "Help yourself to a drink, watch tv, anything you like. I won't be long."

She closes the bedroom door after her and leans against it. She looks like someone being pursued in a tense tv drama. She puts the laptop on the dressing table and flops onto the bed. Clearly, she has become far too used to being on her own. She has a tight feeling all around her head, as if it is constricted by a heavy-duty elastic band. This is entirely due to the extended period of considering the needs of somebody else, she thinks. She knows there are many, many people who do this all the time, but she is not one of them and she is totally out of practice. If she's honest, it has never been her strongest suit. Right now, the thought of Georgie packing up all her junk and driving off seems very attractive. She hasn't been difficult, she hasn't been demanding, but she is occupying Alice's precious space.

She awakes with a start to find the room completely dark. How long has she been asleep? What will Georgie think? A quick look at the bedside clock shows it is past six. She has slept for nearly two hours. Should she admit to this, or try to think of a task that could take that length of time on a Saturday afternoon?

In the end, she decides not to lie. She tries not to, these days. Her brain isn't as agile as it was, and she is much more likely to give herself away. She hurries downstairs rubbing her eyes, apologies on her lips. But she needn't have worried. Georgie is half lying on the sofa with her feet curled under her and her scruffy old slippers on the floor. There is a plate containing a few crumbs on the coffee table and the aroma of toast in the air. The tv is showing something anodyne. She looks perfectly content.

"I'm so sorry," says Alice. It feels like the right thing to say. "Can you believe it? I sent my email, felt a bit sleepy and next thing I know it's evening. Must be getting old!"

Georgie looks concerned. She hopes she hasn't worn Alice out with all that walking. Alice returns this conversational serve with a firm denial and eventually wins the rally. It is her house, after all. However, there is one difficulty to overcome. Georgie has swung her legs round and assumed a more formal position, but there is still the issue of the tv. Alice decides she can't bear another round of 'who can be the most polite?' right now. She says she needs something to eat and leaves the tv to Alice.

Strangely though, she is not at all hungry. She opens and closes cupboard doors half-heartedly. There are the crumpets she had intended to make for Georgie's tea, but there's no point getting them out now. Georgie's toast will be enough to keep her going until morning. She brushes aside the picture of the two of them sitting either side of the fire with plates on their knees and butter running down their chins. Maybe another time.

Eventually, she discovers the last few chocolate brownies. She knows they are a very poor choice, especially as Georgie's idea of sharing a desert is to eat two mouthfuls then put her spoon down with a finality that brooks no argument. She eats two, feels slightly sick then looks in the fridge. Ah, yes, there it is. A bottle of Prosecco. She hasn't liked to open it until now, as she knew it would either go flat or she would drink too much of it. It will provide a fitting finale to Georgie's birthday.

She opens the bottle and pours two glasses. That way, there is less chance of Georgie refusing. She returns to the lounge, puts one on the coffee table beside Georgie's still unwashed plate and raises the other in salute.

"Cheers! Happy birthday!" she says.

Georgie accepts the drink with apparent pleasure and more thanks. She drinks quite a lot of it within the first five minutes. Then she puts her glass back on the table.

"I don't suppose I could borrow your laptop for a minute?" she says. "I'd like to see how those photos came out, and mine is so slow it's just about useless."

Alice agrees of course. She says how much she would like to see the photos. Minutes later, Georgie has put the card from her camera into a slot in her laptop Alice didn't even know existed, and the first of the photos appears on the screen.

There is no denying it. Georgie is good. Somehow, she has transformed the dull, bleak lake into a moody and atmospheric landscape. A jagged divide splits the water in two, one half almost black with the reflection of the trees on the far side and the other half silvery white in the winter sun. Alice hadn't even noticed this phenomenon at the time. She was expecting some pretty shots of the moorhens in the reeds.

It is the same when the images of the woods appear. Georgie hasn't said much so far, apart from to tut when something hasn't worked out as she intended. Now she flicks past the first two or three images and pauses on a shot of the light forcing its way between the trees and illuminating a small clearing with a beam like a searchlight.

"Ah, that's the one I was hopeful of," she says.

"It's brilliant," says Alice. She really means it. The background is dark and grainy while everything in the centre stands out in sharp relief. Even the sad winter foliage looks splendid, as if it is basking in its few minutes of fame.

Georgie clicks again, and there is Alice in the woods. The first two or three shots are nothing spectacular. It could be anyone really, swathed in winter clothes and standing against a backdrop of trees. But then Georgie clicks the touch pad again and there is a close up. Alice is bathed in the light that Georgie seems to be able to harness at will. Her face is glowing and she looks … well, she looks beautiful. It's not the face of a young woman, there are some lines, the flesh isn't firm. But Georgie has used her skill to create a picture Alice can look at without getting the usual sinking feeling. She'd be proud to display this on a wall.

"There," says Georgie. "That's my favourite. I knew that one would be good."

JULY 1964

The first stage of my plan went like clockwork. It was no problem to tuck my Maths book under

Georgie's bed before I left on Wednesday. Neither was it a problem to make a show of discovering the book was missing the next day in school and suggest coming home with her to retrieve it. Then I put on a pretty good display of frustration when she reminded me she had to stay after school for debating. Oh, dear. I would have to go to Georgie's house without her. What a nuisance. What a shame it couldn't have been another day.

I felt a little guilty at including Georgie in the list of people I had lied to, but it was for her own good. It was also quite satisfying that she obviously believed everything I said. I was getting pretty good at this. Perhaps I could join Hilary in the Secret Service and forget about being a famous author.

So I took the bus alone and got off at Georgie's stop. I knew my mother would worry when I didn't arrive home at the normal time, so I asked a girl who lived on my estate to drop a note through the door as she passed my house. I couldn't afford to have people out looking for me. That would draw attention to my activities.

Georgie's mother was surprised to see me but quite happy for me to go up to Georgie's room. It felt strange to climb those narrow stairs alone. I felt a little shiver of anxiety as I pushed the bedroom door, as if Georgie would somehow be in there and would demand to know what I was doing. However, I pulled myself together, recovered the book and put it in my bag. I sat on Georgie's bed to wait until for a suitable length of time to elapse, but the hands on her sunshine yellow alarm clock were moving far too slowly and I couldn't stand it for long.

I went into the kitchen where Georgie's mother was sitting at the table, hunched over a large sheet of paper. She was alternately scratching at it with a stick of charcoal then smudging what she had drawn and it looked a complete mess from where I stood. Her face and hands were streaked with black.

"Did you find it, sweetie?" she asked, glancing up at me with a smile.

"No, I couldn't see it. Would you mind if I checked in the lounge?"

"Of course! Don't be silly, Alice. You can look anywhere you like. You go ahead."

I mumbled my thanks and headed for the lounge, almost closing the door after me. I made sure she hadn't followed, then took the Maths book and put it with some magazines on the window ledge. I crept to the door and peeped out. The coast was still clear, so I hurried to the desk and pulled out the top drawer. It was rammed with envelopes, some of them old and stained, some of them bulging with papers and some of them thinner. None of them was labelled, although some had old addresses on the front. It would take hours to go through this lot, so I decided to try another drawer.

But the drawer would not close. I re-arranged the envelopes, making sure they were not sticking up at the back, but still it stuck. This was a nightmare. Any minute now, Georgie's mother might come in to see how I was getting on. What possible reason could I have for searching her desk for my Maths book?

I pushed the drawer hard and it shifted slightly on one side, so then I tried the other and at last I managed to close it, a fraction at a time, by applying pressure on alternate sides until the last few inches slid into place. Sweat was beading on my forehead and I'm sure my face was beetroot red. I ran to pick up my Maths book and headed out to the hall.

"Found it!" I called through the open kitchen door.

"Well done, see you soon," said Georgie's mother. Quite probably it would have been an hour or even longer before she came to investigate what I was up to. It is possible she had already forgotten I was there. However, the incident with the drawer was enough to deter me from any further illicit searches of the desk. That, and the fact that its contents were obviously completely disorganised and I might never find what I was looking for. I had envisaged something like the cupboard in our house where all important papers were stored in a selection of tins and boxes, neatly labelled in my dad's block capitals. I should have known this would not be the case. Now I was back to square one.

It was so annoying. People on tv always found important things really quickly. Although they made a great show of haste and frustration, it was always just a matter of pulling out a couple of drawers, rummaging around for a while and there it would be. The passport, the gun, the diary. The heroes I had watched never had to deal with desks that were so full they were likely to explode papers everywhere or drawers that stuck when you needed them to close.

Still, I wasn't depressed for long. My birthday was imminent and my parents shocked me by suggesting I was getting too grown up for parties. Would I like to take Georgie to see the new Beatles film instead? There were no words to express how much I liked this idea, and I was practically bursting with excitement by the next morning as I waited for the bus. We were to go to the Saturday matinee performance and then my dad would pick us up and take us back for a birthday tea. I wasn't so sure about the tea, but I was so happy about the film I decided to keep quiet. I didn't like to seem ungrateful.

Of course Georgie was as delighted as me and we talked of nothing else all that week. Term was drawing to a close and there was a nice atmosphere in school. The teachers were relaxed and set us easy work or gave us jobs such as prising drawing pins out of the walls with scissors, or sharpening pencils. This provided endless opportunities for talking about The Beatles and which one we liked best.

It is unlikely that A Hard Day's Night will be remembered as one of the great films of the twentieth century, or even 1964. I have actually no idea what it was about, but it showcased The Beatles and their songs and that was enough for us. There was such a lot of screaming it was quite hard to hear the music, but none of that mattered. I don't think I had been happier in my entire life. I had my friend by my side and she was grinning from ear to ear too. I had the whole summer to look forward to, and I guessed a lot of that would be spent in her garden. True, I had failed in the task I'd set myself, but Georgie hardly mentioned her father now. Maybe she had got used to living without him. Maybe I could let things lie for a while. After all, there was plenty of time.

But that was not the case. I didn't know it then, or as we streamed out of the cinema blinking and disorientated. I didn't know that decisions were being made – had already been made – that would change everything. For now, it all seemed perfect. We found my dad and tumbled into the car, talking non-stop the whole journey.

"And what about the bit where Paul ..."

"And when that man came up to John and he ..."

There was too much, and the music sailed around in my head until I thought it would burst. Angie was outraged at not being included, but Georgie was kind to her and gave her a badge with Paul's face on it. The tea was lovely and Georgie, as usual, complimented my mum until her ears glowed.

Later, after my dad had driven Georgie home and my sisters were in bed, the three of us were curled up on the sofa watching tv. I had to swallow a lump in my throat.

"I've had a fab day," I told my parents. "Thanks for everything." I nearly added something about them being the best mum and dad ever, but I didn't. They were happy enough with what I'd said and I didn't want to provoke too much in the way of hugs.

So the last Wednesday of term arrived. We didn't have any homework, but I went back with Georgie anyway. We hadn't spent much time in the garden recently and now I wanted to do what Georgie had suggested: enjoy what we had constructed. The weather was warm and humid and I saw a bank of angry-looking clouds creeping over the hills, but we should have an hour or two before it rained. Georgie's cousin Camilla had left a copy of Jackie magazine the last time she'd visited, containing pages of Beatles photos and information. I wanted to take it down to the original den and read it with Georgie. It didn't matter that the den wasn't very comfortable, or that it smelled of damp grass and old carpet, with undertones of something sharp and pungent. It was quiet and private and it was ours.

I had noticed that Georgie was very quiet on the way home. I had not forgotten either, that she had wondered aloud whether I still wanted to come to her house, given that we had no homework. But I did want to come. I wanted to come really badly. I pushed these worries to the back of my mind and assured myself everything would be fine once we got out into the garden. After all, this had always been the case before. Even in the days when Georgie had been acting strangely, the garden seemed to have a transformative effect on her. I had employed that word to great effect in a diary entry at the time, so I knew it to be true.

We let ourselves in, as Georgie had been given her own front door key. My parents had received my request for the same privilege with bewilderment, as they could think of no reason I could possibly need it. Surely Georgie's mother wouldn't let her come into the house by herself? I'd had to back-track madly then, in case they stopped me visiting, but the truth was that Georgie did come home to an empty house from time to time.

Not this time though. We had hardly kicked off our shoes before the lounge door opened and Georgie's mother appeared.

"Ah, there you are. Come in here and sit down. Alice, George and I have something we need to tell you."

Immediately, my heart began to pound and the blood rushed in my ears. What could it be? Was it something about her father? But Georgie's mother had never spoken of him and Georgie had sworn me to secrecy. It couldn't be that. I had no time to explore my fears further as, before I knew it, we were sitting on the threadbare chaise longue with Georgie's mother opposite. I noticed the familiar cut glass tumbler containing half an inch of brown liquid on the coffee table in front of her.

I glanced at Georgie beside me. She looked stricken. Her back was straight and rigid and her hands were two tight fists on her thighs.

"Don't look so worried Alice, nobody's died!" said Georgie's mother with a half-hearted smile. "Georgie is very unhappy about this, which is why she didn't want to tell you herself. You can't imagine how many arguments we've had or all the shouting that's gone on in this room. Anyway, here it is. Georgie is starting a new school in September. She's going to St. Anne's."

I said nothing and nor did Georgie. She looked as if she might cry if she so much as opened her mouth. I was truly lost for words. How could this be? Georgie had to wear second hand clothes. The house was falling apart. How could they possibly afford it?

"I know that's a big surprise, Alice," said Georgie's mother. For a minute I thought she was about to get up and hug me, but she was only reaching out for her glass. "But look, I want you to know – we both want you to know – that it doesn't mean the end of your friendship. I know how

much it means to you. You can still come and play
– well, maybe you're getting too big for playing,
but you know what I mean. You're always
welcome here Alice, and I really mean that."

There was another silence, broken eventually
by Georgie who stood and gave her mother a
withering glare.

"Thanks, mother. Thanks for ruining my life,"
she said and stalked out. I followed, with only a
brief backward glance. Georgie's mother had her
head in her hands.

Georgie stomped into the garden and marched
right up to the furthest boundary. She didn't crawl
into the den, but occupied herself by kicking an
already unstable fence post until I felt I had to stop
her.

"It's alright," I said, although it was actually
anything but. "You heard what she said. We'll still
be friends. I'll still come here and you can come to
mine."

"It's bloody St. Anne's!" said Georgie, emotion
thickening her voice. "I don't want to go there. It'll
be like bloody Hawfield without boarding. 'Young
ladies don't do this, young ladies don't do that.' I
don't want to be a bloody young lady in a stupid
hat. What would you feel like, if it was you?"

I had no idea what I'd feel like. There was no

more chance of that happening than flying to the moon. I'd never given it a moment's thought. However, I could see why she was upset. St. Anne's Independent School for Girls was on the same street as our school and we all hated it. We referred to it as St. Trinians and mocked its pupils in their pretentious hats and gold-edged blazers whenever we passed them on the bus. Now Georgie would be on the receiving end of all this.

"I don't know. Not good, I suppose. Why is she doing this?"

"It's bloody Uncle Edward, isn't it? He says I need to be taken in hand. He looked at some of my books and said my work's rubbish compared to what Camilla does. He's a bloody interfering ..."

Georgie's words ended with a sob. She gave the fence post one last despairing kick and slumped to the ground where she sat with her face buried in her arms. I put a tentative hand on her shoulder.

"Don't worry, we'll still be friends. We'll still have all this," I said, gesturing at the space around us. However, I suppose this remark addressed my own potential loss more than Georgie's and she said nothing in reply.

I was going to sit down beside her, but then I felt the first, fat splashes of rain on my bare arms. The sky was now very dark and a brisk wind whipped through the apple trees, dislodging some of the immature fruit. Georgie showed no sign of moving, but I had no desire to get wet so I crawled into the den.

"Georgie, come in here! You'll get soaked."

Georgie looked up. It was raining quite hard by then, so it was hard to distinguish her tears. She shuffled across and I moved inside to make room. I didn't know what I would do if she started to cry again in such close proximity, but luckily she didn't.

"I've half a mind to run away," she said.

My heart leapt into my mouth. Was there no end to it? Was I doomed to deal with one crisis after another?

"No! Where would you go?" I asked. I was already quite clear that I would have to betray Georgie if she ran away. Something might happen to her, and I would never see her again.

"Oh, I don't know. I probably won't. But that's how it makes me feel. It's my life, but they think they have the right to control it."

I talked again about how we could make the best of this situation. I promised I would still come up to see her. I promised she could still come to mine and I would always invite her to everything.

I didn't lie and I didn't exaggerate. This was exactly what I believed at the time. We could make this work. It didn't have to be the end of everything – it simply couldn't.

We had to vacate the den eventually. We'd been running out of materials by the time we built it and this showed. It started leaking at the front first, but then we felt drips on our heads and shoulders at the back too.

"We'll have to sort this out next week," I said to Georgie as we hurried back to the house.

Georgie's mother was in the kitchen as we burst in, dripping puddles onto the floor.

"What on earth …?" she started to say, but Georgie gave her a look so fearsome that she closed her mouth again. Georgie grabbed me by the arm and dragged me out to the hall.

"Come on, Alice, we're going upstairs," she said. "And you needn't bother cooking for us, we're not hungry!" she shouted at the kitchen door.

Actually, I was hungry. Georgie's mother's cooking was not consistent, but she did have some good days and the smell that filled the kitchen that day boded well. There was no indication of burning and she appeared to be tending whatever it was that bubbled on the stove. However, Georgie was adamant. She was not going to sit with 'that woman' as she put it. She loaded up the record player and turned the volume to maximum, but I doubt Georgie's mother heard it from such a distance in that solid old house. It was an uncomfortable time in which we spoke little, and I was glad when it was over.

Term ended and I wasted no time in demonstrating to Georgie that nothing needed to change. As soon as my mother would allow it, I cycled up to Templars Way and dumped my bike in its usual place. However, as I walked up the drive I saw a familiar car parked outside the house. It was her uncle's. A huge wave of disappointment swept over me. What were they doing here again? I knew I could join them if I wanted to, but that was not what I'd imagined as I cycled up here. I had plans to repair the last den before it rained again. We probably needed to check the others too. Now none of that would be possible.

I turned on my heel and retrieved my bike. I would come again tomorrow, or very soon. All was not lost. It was still the first week of the holiday and there was plenty of time. It was hard to conceal my disappointment from my mum when I reappeared so quickly, but she didn't press me for information.

"Never mind, you can help me make these

cakes instead," she said. "Don't worry, there'll be plenty more nice days."

DECEMBER 2016

Alice doesn't know if it's the after effect of the photo, or the fact that they've finished the first bottle of prosecco and started on another. It's not as cold as the first, but that doesn't seem to matter. Whatever the reason, she feels unexpectedly calm. She might even say happy. All the tension has passed, like a storm in the mountains. One minute it's all threatening black clouds and the next the sun emerges to ask what all the fuss was about. They've been chatting in an amiable way for over an hour and, although the past has crept into the conversation, all is well. She has told Georgie about her mum, how she's moved to Yorkshire to be near to Angie and is still independent. She hasn't said how she feels about that. Then, Georgie spoils it all.

"So, are you separated then, or …?" The question hangs in the air, waiting to be answered.

"No, I'm a widow too," says Alice at last. She watches Georgie's face and sees the flash of recognition, the sadness.

"Oh, I'm sorry! I shouldn't have … was it quite recent? No, stop. I'm being insensitive."

Alice reassures Georgie that she doesn't need to consider her feelings. It's not like her and Matt. She knows she drank the last glass of wine too quickly, she knows it is loosening her tongue. But that's the trouble with alcohol. There can be a gap between recognising what is happening and doing anything about it. She knows she should stop at this point but her foot doesn't seem to be able to find the brake.

"We were about to split up when he died. The brakes failed on one of his precious cars. Yes, funny isn't it?" she says, although the expression on Georgie's face doesn't imply amusement. "He was about to go and shack up with his fancy piece when death intervened."

Georgie sits quietly, her hands in her lap. She has barely touched her glass of wine. Alice swigs down the last of hers and shudders. Where did all that come from? She has never used hackneyed phrases like 'shack up' and 'fancy piece' in her whole life. Is she in a play? If so, the script writer needs to be shot.

"Yes, it was the old story, I'm afraid. He was about to leave me for a younger model. It was all such a cliché! At least she wasn't his secretary - she was a rep - but honestly. I thought there was more to him than that. He was quite the opposite with cars - it was the older the better with them. I had to sell three so-called classic cars when he died and a garage full of spares. But I suppose he couldn't re-furbish me, could he? If I could've had a re-spray, maybe things would've been different."

"I'm so sorry to hear that," says Georgie. "Men can be such bastards, can't they?"

"Yes, but you'd never have known it with John. Never. Everyone thought he was the bee's knees. Including me. D'you know what? I haven't told anyone else, not even the kids. I couldn't do it. Their whole lives have been built on what they thought was happy family life. I couldn't take that away from them. And I didn't want all our friends to know he'd stopped loving me, stopped finding me attractive. Who wants to admit to that?"

"But that's an awful thing to keep to yourself," says Georgie. "You must've been so angry, and yet you had to behave as if everything had been fine between you. Even though he was dead. You need to talk about these things, or they …"

"Fester?" says Alice. "Yes, I know all about that. I had to sit through the funeral service, crying dutifully into my tissue, knowing that he'd been about to abandon me. And with that … that bitch sitting at the back. People kept asking me who she was. It wasn't normal for a work colleague to be sobbing like that. I had to make up a story about her losing her own husband recently to put them off the scent. It was like a set piece from Eastenders. Seriously, sometimes ... "

Alice stands abruptly, sways a little, then heads off to the kitchen with her empty glass. She's a little surprised at herself. The bitterness is still alive and well, and living not far from her conscious mind. That much is clear. But there's no harm done, she thinks. Georgie doesn't know any of her friends or family. She's not going to tell anyone, and it's been cathartic. It's true, it has been hard keeping all this to herself. But now she needs to be careful, she doesn't want to go too far. Maybe she should stop now, make some coffee. But she opens the fridge door instead.

When she returns, she stops in the doorway. Georgie is hunched over, her head in her hands. Alice may not be seeing too clearly, but she thinks Georgie's shoulders are shaking. What is going on now? She sits down as quietly as she can and sips her drink. It is only a moment before Georgie raises her head. She looks sad, but there are no tears.

"Oh, Alice," she says. "I'm sorry. I shouldn't have got you started on this. It's obviously still raw. And there was me, thinking you had a charmed life! You know, I was cross with you this afternoon, when you said you'd envied me as a child. I thought, 'how ridiculous!' To me, your life was everything I yearned for. Safe, orderly, loving. I thought that could only translate into some version of happy ever after, but there you go. Seems we both have our problems. Shall we talk about something else? Finish a lovely day on a positive note?"

So they do. They return to the photos and Alice tells Georgie she would like to print off the portrait of her and the study of light in the woods. Georgie looks pleased and proud and Alice feels her happy mood returning. She wonders if there is one more glass left in the bottle.

AUGUST 1964

I don't know whether my mum knew something
I didn't, or whether she was more intuitive than I
gave her credit for. Maybe it was neither of those
things. But the fact was, my attempts to return to
Georgie's house were frustrated for more than
another week. First it was the weekend and I was
dragged off to Maidstone to buy clothes. Then,
when the next week was beautifully warm and
sunny, ideal for playing in Georgie's garden, my
dad decided to take some leave and we made a
number of day trips.

Normally I would have enjoyed visiting my
cousins in Hastings. A trip to Dymchurch, with its

miniature railway and fantastic beach would have been even more exciting. But my parents steadfastly refused to allow me to invite Georgie or to remain with her while they went on their excursions without me. I moaned and I sulked, but all to no avail. By the time my dad returned to work it was Friday. I was punished for my bad behaviour by being confined to the house all day, helping my mum.

I probably could have ventured up to Georgie's the next day, but I didn't. The weather was dull and drizzly and something told me the snooty cousins and their disagreeable parents were even more likely to appear at the weekend. I bided my time. I would go on Monday. Georgie would be delighted to see me after such a gap and all would be well.

The first thing I noticed as I walked up the drive was a vehicle, but it was not the shiny, posh car I had dreaded seeing as the house came into view. No, this was a small truck with ladders sticking out of the back. A man in paint-spattered overalls was unloading something.

As I drew closer, I could see tins of paint on the gravel beside the house. Another man – a youth really, with hair down to his shoulders – was sanding the front door with vigorous, circular movements. It was hot again now, and his face was scarlet. Eventually he noticed me and stepped to one side.

"Hello, darlin'," he grinned. "Shall I do it for you?" He was indicating the door knocker, but I ignored him and reached across to raise it myself. For some reason I couldn't fathom, my face was burning too and I saw Georgie's quizzical expression as she opened the door.

However, all was fine from that point. Georgie seemed pleased to see me and accepted the explanation of my absence so far without question. Of course I expected to go straight out into the garden, but Georgie didn't seem too keen.

"It's really hot," she said. "Let's go up and play some music first."

So we did. I was astonished to see she had several new singles. 'A Hard Day's Night' was amongst them, and we played that over and over, triggering memories of the film and the fantastic time we'd had on my birthday. She also had 'The House of the Rising Sun' by The Animals, which I loved, and something by Dusty Springfield which I didn't.

"I know," she said, watching me turn it over then return it to the pile. "It's Camilla's. They all are, actually, but she said I could borrow them, so I did."

I felt a stab of jealousy then. A picture of Camilla sitting up here with Georgie, playing records and chatting just as we were, popped into my mind and refused to disappear. However hard I tried to displace it with other, less troubling thoughts, it teased and taunted me. At last, I could ignore it no longer.

"Do you like her?" I asked.

Georgie appeared to be thinking. "I don't know. She's alright, I suppose. I've known her all my life. I guess you get used to people. She's not bad once you get to know her."

This was not what I had wanted to hear, but it was my own fault. I should have kept well away from this subject. But now the little wound had been opened I seemed unable to stop picking at it.

"But do you like her … is it the same as … Do you like her as much as me?"

There, I had said it. Georgie looked surprised – no, more than that. She looked completely bemused; nonplussed.

"Blimey, Alice!" she said at last. "That's an odd question. She's my cousin and you're my friend. It's not the same. What's that all about?"

I was hugely embarrassed then and angry at myself. Now I appeared needy and clingy, just when the relationship had become more balanced.

"Sorry," I said, blushing again. I seemed to spend half my life willing away great surges of burning heat across my face. "I'm in a funny mood. Ignore me."

"Probably hormones," said Georgie, but this was a subject even more likely to provoke embarrassment. Although I had at last developed a couple of tender, tiny breasts and a few stray hairs under my arms, there was no sign of my periods starting and I felt this deeply. I could not be admitted into the sisterhood of grown-up girls until I had reached this milestone. I was excluded from hushed conversations in the form room and significant trips to the toilets, where strange rituals were performed in the end cubicle, the only one with a bin.

"Shall we go into the garden now?" I said.

Georgie agreed, although I was disappointed at her lack of enthusiasm. She was equally indifferent outside, seemingly content to watch while I carried out the much-needed inspection of the dens. She was devoid of ideas for materials to patch up the many holes that had appeared and returned to sit in one of the new deckchairs on the paving.

"It's too hot," she complained, but I knew this

wasn't the reason. There had been hot days before when we had worked like Trojans, hauling great sheets of corrugated iron around and stacking bricks. I didn't understand what had changed, but I couldn't ask. I had already shown myself to be a silly, immature and jealous person so I had to keep quiet and hope this was a temporary situation.

Eventually, I abandoned the idea of restoring the dens to their former glory today. I joined Georgie on the terrace. I wasn't very keen on sitting still, but it was quite pleasant to watch the birds as they visited the new bird table on the lawn. After a while, Georgie's mother appeared with some drinks for us. She placed them on a little table then returned with a bottle of white wine and a glass.

"Ah," she said, taking the third of the four deckchairs. "This is the life, isn't it? It's almost like being on holiday."

I smiled, but it wasn't like any holiday I'd ever had. In my family you did things on holiday. If the adults sat around at all, it would only be for brief periods and only one at a time. Somebody had to be available to play with my sisters. How could you go for long walks along the cliffs with the dog, explore the caves, or visit the next cove along if your parents were sitting in deck chairs?

However, I said nothing. I watched out of the corner of my eye as she filled her glass and drank more than half of it almost immediately. I hoped there would be no repetition of New Year's Eve. It seemed to be very early to start drinking. I looked across at Georgie but she appeared unconcerned. Her head was thrown back and her eyes were closed. It was then that I noticed she was wearing eye shadow.

I left well before tea time, inventing an excuse that I have since forgotten. There was only so much sitting around I could do, and I didn't want to watch Georgie's mother drink the whole bottle of wine, which appeared to be a likely outcome. Georgie seemed to understand. We decided I would return in a few days if it cooled down. At least, that is what I suggested and she agreed.

"Yes, that would be best," she said. "Too hot for working today."

I walked down the drive fighting back my dismay. Stop being so silly, I told myself. It's nothing to worry about. Georgie's just not in the mood for mending the dens today. It's hot. It's nothing to do with what I said. I must have made a sad little picture as I wandered off to retrieve my bike. My shoulders slumped and my eyes were fixed on the ground, watching my feet kick up angry little clouds of dust as they scuffed the sun-baked gravel.

"Oh-ho! What've we got here then?"

I jumped visibly as I rounded the corner and bumped into Hilary. I had no idea he was expected. I tried not to ask Georgie too often and she rarely volunteered any information about him.

"Well, well! It's George's little friend from the village. Off home so soon?" he continued, completely barring my way with his height and his presence.

This was terrible. I was utterly unprepared. All the witty reposts I had rehearsed in such detail deserted me in my hour of need.

"Yes, it's too hot," I managed at last.

Hilary shaded his eyes and looked at me. He was wearing a leather cowboy hat and he looked … I could think of no suitable adjective other than 'sexy' when I thought about it later as I wrote my diary. This made my stomach feel strange and I scribbled out the word so hard that the page ripped.

"Well, it certainly is that," he said. He stepped back and surveyed me from under his fringe. "Did anyone ever tell you, you look like a little fawn?"

"No, I don't think so. Sorry, I've got to get back," I stammered and dodged around him. I grabbed my bike and scooted it out into the road.

"Farewell, little fawn," he called.

It was one thing sanitising my diary but quite another controlling my thoughts. My stomach was dancing around like a mad thing. It was fine to be in love with George Harrison, an icon I was never likely to see, let alone meet. It was much more alarming to have these feelings for a real live person, a person I might encounter and speak to.

And then there was his behaviour towards me. I knew teasing when I saw it, but what kind of teasing was this? Was it the nice kind of teasing employed by my dad, or my Uncle Jack? When we'd last been to Hastings, he'd pretended not to recognise me. He'd asked my parents to introduce me to the young lady they'd brought with them. This had made me laugh and blush, but I knew it was kindly meant. It didn't seem like that, but nor did it seem like the unkind teasing dispensed by my classmate Dawn Burton during the first few days of the academic year. She'd offered to take me down to the office so someone could take me back to primary school where I obviously belonged.

However much I deliberated, I could come to no conclusion. Maybe this behaviour was something peculiar to big brothers. Maybe they had their own brand of teasing and this was an indication that Hilary saw me as something akin to a little sister. But if that were the case, why did I feel so strange when he talked to me? I slept very badly that night, my dreams full of unexpected meetings with tall figures in cowboy hats, sometimes recognisable and sometimes not. Over and over again I found myself struggling to understand what they were talking about. Sometimes they gave me tasks I was unable to perform, sometimes they simply stood in the corner of gloomy, panelled rooms, looking dark and enigmatic.

Although the weather cooled significantly during the next few days, I didn't return to Georgie's house. I made excuses to my mum and to myself, but I knew it was the thought of meeting Hilary again that kept me away. I returned to walking around the fields with the dog for hours at a time, pondering all the complicated issues that beset my life. I took my new transistor radio – probably my best birthday present ever – and tried to let the music transport me somewhere else. The Beatles were still riding high, but I also liked Gerry and the Pacemakers and The Four Seasons. Sometimes, I lay in the long, scented grass with my eyes closed. The music soothed my ears and the warm weight of the dog pressed against my side. Then, for a short time, I could be my old, uncomplicated self again.

However, after nearly two weeks, as my stomach returned more or less to normal, I became increasingly bored. I decided it was time to take the plunge. After all, Georgie would wonder where I was. She might be worrying that she'd upset me. Certainly she'd be bored herself, with no-one to spend time with, rattling around that great big house all on her own. It was a cloudy day, dry and much cooler than the last time I'd visited. It was perfect for working on the dens but I warned myself not to expect too much. If Georgie wanted to spend time in her room, then that's what we would do. That would have the added advantage of ensuring there were no unexpected meetings with Hilary. I still experienced an odd little tingle in my stomach when I thought of him, and this made me uneasy.

My heart sank when I saw the familiar, shiny car in the drive. I would have turned round and left, but Georgie's mother was outside with Georgie's uncle and I paused a moment too long. They were looking up at the front of the house. It had been transformed. Gone were all the flaky paintwork and crumbling brickwork around the windows. It was all bright and new, with white paint everywhere apart from the door. This was a deep, glossy blue. Obviously it looked a lot better, but I felt a tug of regret for the house I'd come to love. It had been scruffy but I was comfortable there. It had felt like home.

Georgie's mother turned round before I had a chance to creep away.

"Alice!" she said, as if it were a total surprise to see me. "Georgie will be pleased. I think she's up in her room."

For a minute, I thought it might all be alright. Maybe the obnoxious uncle had come on his own. I hurried up to Georgie's room and opened the door with a flourish. Georgie was there, but so was Camilla. They were both wearing smart clothes and they sat on the bed together. The bright pages of a magazine were spread out between them like a feast. Georgie's face gave her away as she looked up and saw me. Surprise was closely followed by embarrassment and something else that may have been guilt. Certainly it was not the broad grin I was used to. I froze in the doorway, my hand welded to the handle.

This didn't stop my eyes darting around the room. There was something new. Some sort of bed had appeared by the window, next to the window seat. There was an expensive-looking suitcase on the floor beside it, and two pairs of shoes were neatly lined up, their shiny toes just protruding.

Suddenly, I felt like a stranger, an intruder, but I couldn't simply turn round and leave.

"Alice!" said Georgie at last. She sounded exactly like her mother. "You remember Camilla?"

Of course I remembered Camilla, although I wished I didn't. I muttered something affirmative but it remained impossible to cross the threshold.

"We were just … we're … would you like to join us?"

At last, the door handle released me. I entered the room, but there was nowhere to sit - apart from the new bed. Nobody suggested that, so I sat on the floor. Normally this would not have been a problem, indeed either one of us would often do this, to allow the other to stretch out on Georgie's narrow bed. But now I felt doubly excluded and the atmosphere was tense.

"So, what've you been up to?" asked Georgie eventually, closing the magazine. Her voice was bright but it wasn't the way she would normally speak to me. She sounded like somebody else.

"Um, nothing much. Family stuff," I added as an after-thought. "What about you? Have you been in the garden much?"

A cloud passed across Georgie's face. There

was that strange, embarrassed expression again. What was going on?

"Er, no, not really," she said. Her face was actually colouring now. This was very unusual for Georgie. "The thing is … there's been … we've had some men in and ..."

"Oh, yes, I saw them the other day," I interrupted, relieved. "Are they doing the back too? I suppose you have to be careful, with the paint and ..." I stopped. Georgie's pained expression had not lifted. In fact she looked positively distressed. "What's the matter?" I said.

"It's the garden. Look, it wasn't my choice. We've had some gardeners in and ..."

Suddenly, I knew what she was trying to tell me. It was as clear as if she'd written it on a poster and pinned it to the wall. I jumped up and ran downstairs. I heard voices from the lounge but the kitchen was empty so I carried on, out through the back door. The grass near the house had been mown again and the new deckchairs were arranged with military precision. The paving stones were clean and weed-free, but I cared nothing for any of this. I ran up the path, past the willow tree, and came upon a scene of devastation. The whole area had been cleared. The bramble bushes were flattened, the shrubs were tamed and all our dens were gone. They had metamorphosed into heaps of scrap, lined up and awaiting removal. I could barely catch my breath.

I walked slowly up to the top of the garden. I clasped my arms tightly around my middle to contain the pain that threatened to break out, to engulf everything. The pain that might express itself in something others could hear. There was a real risk that I might emit some kind of terrible howl, like a dog sitting beside its dead master. The apple trees were still there, but where our final den had been there was a wooden platform and on that was a little wooden house. It had a pointed roof like something you would see in Switzerland, and a sort of balcony with steps leading up to it. I hated it and loved it at once.

I stood there, trying to take everything in. Clearly someone had spent a lot of money on wrecking my life and it looked as if they hadn't finished yet. It must be that horrible uncle. I searched for a better adjective, but nothing bad enough came to mind. I was about to leave, to sneak down to the side gate and disappear without saying goodbye, when I heard something. The snap of a twig or the rustle of grass, I don't remember. I turned round quickly, expecting to see Georgie and Camilla, but it wasn't them.

"Hello, little fawn."

I have no idea what came over me then. I don't suppose the decision to clear the garden had been anything to do with Hilary, but he was standing there and the horrible uncle wasn't.

"For God's sake! I'm not a fawn! A fawn is either a baby deer, or, if you choose to spell it differently, a mythological creature with the legs of a goat. I'm not ..."

Unfortunately, I was unable to continue my speech. I had practised it in my head at home, trying to sound witty and grown-up, but it had come out all desperate and wrong. Now tears constricted my throat and strangled my words. I tried to escape, but Hilary blocked my way, his hands held up as if to protect himself from the force of my tearful indignation.

"Whoa! Whoa! I'm sorry! Didn't mean to upset you, little ... Georgie's friend. Look, I've forgotten your name – useless with names – and I only meant ... It's your eyes, you see. You have big, brown eyes like Bambi. That's all I meant. Am I forgiven? Please ...?

With that, he dropped to one knee on the grass and held his hands together as if praying.

"Ok," I mumbled. I tried to leave again. He was being stupid now. All I wanted was to get away so it wouldn't matter if the dam broke and the great rush of emotion I was holding back came spilling out.

"What is it then?" he asked, and then, when I failed to reply, "Your name. What is it? I promise not to forget, and I won't need to call you Georgie's friend or … or anything else. Ok?"

"It's Alice."

"Ah, Alice. Of course. I remember now. And I promise not to say anything about mad hatters or white rabbits. I'm sure you've had enough of that."

This provoked a watery smile, but altered nothing. I needed to leave. Nothing but the solace of my own room, or maybe a circle of flattened grass in the middle of the field, could satisfy me now.

"That's better. I don't need to ask what you think of the improvements. And what about this?" he asked, gesturing at the little house.

"I preferred it all the way it was," I said. "But anyway, I have to go now. My mum ..."

"They call it a summer house, you know," said Hilary thoughtfully. "And it's summer. Come on, let's just go and take a look inside. Let's see if it's worthy of its moniker."

Somehow, I found myself climbing the four or five steps up to the platform, with Hilary close behind me. It seemed rude to refuse, especially as he'd been so sorry for upsetting me. He walked over to the door and rattled it, but it was locked.

"Damn and blast!" he said, an angry expression flashing across his face, but I was actually quite relieved. It would have been interesting to see inside on another occasion, but now I could leave without being impolite.

"Well, thanks for trying, anyway," I said. I hurried down the steps, leaving him standing there. He didn't even call goodbye as I left, but that was the least of my worries. This was further evidence that adults were strange beings and he was certainly one of the strangest I'd met.

DECEMBER 2016

When Alice awakes the next morning she thinks she may have got off lightly. She actually feels ok. Then she sits up and swings her legs round and realises her body was tricking her. A great wave of nausea sweeps over her and she only just makes it to the en-suite. When the vomiting seems to have exhausted itself, and her, she crawls over to the wash-basin. Yes, she crawls. The last time this was necessary she was either young enough for it to be acceptable, or pregnant. Clearly, neither of those excuses can be employed today.

She pulls herself up and splashes water on her face. She cups a little in her hand and washes out her mouth. Then she tries to brush her teeth, but somebody appears to have swapped her electric toothbrush for a miniature road drill. The noise echoes around her head and makes it pound, so she has to switch it off and use it manually.

Normally, her morning routine would take about twenty minutes. She has never especially enjoyed standing in the shower for hours. Today it takes nearly double that time. Every movement needs to be planned and executed with the utmost care and at half the normal speed. She views everything from within a bubble of pain and sickness. It distorts her vision and accentuates every sound. She wishes she were dead.

When she eventually makes it downstairs, Georgie is up and about. She looks fine. How could that be? Alice shuffles over to the kitchen table and sits down carefully. She waits until the fabric of the kitchen has settled back into its usual formation then she groans.

"I think I overdid the prosecco last night," she says. "I feel like death."

Georgie agrees that Alice is not looking her best. She offers to make her breakfast, but the thought of food nearly sends Alice scuttling off to the downstairs toilet. Not that scuttling would have been easy. Eventually, her stomach settles again and she accepts both water and coffee. Georgie appears to have more recent experience of dealing with monumental hangovers so Alice lets her take charge.

It is well into the afternoon before Alice feels remotely human. Pain-killers, lots of fluids and a short sleep have helped with the pain and sickness, although she still feels as if any kind of sudden movement could cause her skull to shatter. She lies on the sofa with a mug of herbal tea Georgie has conjured up from somewhere. It certainly wasn't in any of Alice's cupboards. It tastes disgusting, but Georgie has been so helpful she feels obliged to drink it.

"I'll cook tonight," says Georgie. "Don't worry, I won't do anything rich."

Alice tries to protest, but there is no point. It is quite clear that she is in no condition to boil an egg, let alone cook a meal for the two of them. She doesn't even know what it would be. She'd intended to drive to the supermarket but that will be closed by now. Georgie doesn't seem to think this will be an insurmountable problem, though.

"I'll have a root around in your cupboards. I'll find something. You concentrate on getting better. Leave it all to me."

Alice moans that she feels like a terrible fraud.

This is all self-inflicted after all, but Georgie will hear none of it. She goes out to the kitchen and, before long, sleep has wrapped Alice up in its comforting arms once more.

When she awakes, it is to the smell of something cooking. To Alice's relief, the nausea seems to have disappeared completely and she actually feels hungry. She wonders what Georgie has found to cook, and she doesn't have long to wait before she finds out, as Georgie appears with a tray.

"Ah, the patient looks a bit better," she says, putting the tray on the coffee table. "It's just a hearty soup, I'm afraid."

Half an hour later, Alice feels almost normal. Georgie's soup was perfect. It was simple but delicious, packed with vegetables and pulses. There was a rustic herb scone to compliment it and provide the carbs her body needed. Alice can't imagine how she managed to prepare all that in such a short time and with such limited ingredients. She is grateful, but simultaneously discontented. Why can't she throw things into a pan and produce something like that?

Georgie takes their bowls and says she'll clear up later. She won't allow Alice to go near the kitchen.

"Now," she says. "There's something else I need to tell you."

Alice sits up a little too sharply and receives a sharp stab in her right eye to remind her that her body is still bearing a grudge. She winces. What is Georgie about to say? She's not in any condition to hear bad news.

"I just thought I should set the record straight," says Georgie. "You know we were talking about our childhoods? Well, it wasn't just that my parents split up although I know that's what I told you. It was much worse than that. Things were terrible before we moved. I'm afraid my father was an appalling man. There's no other way to put it. He was evil. He was self-centred, jealous and violent. He used to hit my mother – not through drink or anything like that – it was his temper. He had to have his own way."

Alice doesn't say anything. Georgie seems fired up and needs no encouragement.

"The thing was, my mother had money. Her own family were very well-to-do and the house was hers too. I found out later that he lost loads of it. He gambled on the stock exchange and he wasn't very good at it. Then he started tricking clients out of their money – he was a solicitor – and he was fired and eventually charged. He only got six months, but that was long enough. My mother sold the house, used most of it to pay off creditors, and we moved to Templars Way. We were only renting it at first. You know the rest."

"Did he ever hit you?" asks Alice. She is trying to fit this information into her memories of Georgie as a child. Did she seem damaged?

"No, he didn't, although it was terrifying when it happened. I used to hide in my room."

"That's awful! Your poor mother! She didn't deserve that," says Alice.

"No-one deserves that, Alice," says Georgie, and her expression provokes a prickling sensation all over Alice's scalp.

AUGUST 1967

It seems remarkable, given the intensity of our relationship, that I saw Georgie only a few more times that summer and then not at all. Not for almost three years. I tried to keep it going at first, but it became a long, protracted goodbye that hurt more each time I saw her. The house and garden were being ripped apart and put together again with such speed and disregard for all the memories they contained, that it seemed our friendship was left behind in the debris. We were stranded on a little island that was sinking fast, becoming overwhelmed by a rising tide beyond our control. Neither of us seemed to be the same person we had been just a few short weeks before. We had to separate or drown. That's how it seemed to me.

So I went back to school and Georgie didn't. She went off to St. Anne's with its ludicrous uniform and parents who cluttered up the road with their fancy cars. I never saw her, although I looked every day for ages, yearning for and dreading the possibility in equal measure.

I had a tough time those first few weeks of term. After all, it wasn't Georgie who had to fend off all the questions. 'Where's your friend then, Alice?' was only the start of it. Once it came out that she had moved to St. Anne's, it seemed that some of the snobbery that implied had attached itself to me. It was well known that we saw each other out of school, so I was guilty by association. I found myself alone both in school and out, barely able to live with the great aching void in my life. I was angry and bereft; full of regret. I found it hard to look forward when everything I cared for seemed to have been snatched away so easily.

But, in time, my classmates forgot. I forged new friendships. It had to be done. There was a girl called Jean who nobody liked to sit beside as her uniform was shabby. She was glad of my company for a while, and I discovered that she didn't smell at all. Then, as the memories of Georgie faded into the dull, yellowing paintwork, I teamed up with Elizabeth and her crowd and that arrangement worked well for the next year or more.

Before I knew it, I had celebrated my fifteenth birthday and the long summer holiday stretched ahead of me once again. It was the Summer of Love. The sexual revolution had started, people were experimenting with drugs and all the social norms were being challenged. At least, that's what the papers said, often in hysterical tones. Doubtless it was true of some places, for some people. It certainly wasn't the case for me, neither was there very much evidence of it in my small town. My life was governed by the same rules that had been in place for my parents. Girls who had sex before marriage were at best reckless, and at worst lacking in morals or self-respect. Drugs were to be avoided at all cost and addiction was the likely outcome of even a single foray into this world. I accepted these beliefs as truths and vowed never to risk my future or my reputation.

But I was not immune to the cultural revolution that was part and parcel of that era. How could I be, when I was overwhelmed by a flood of new music unlike anything I had ever heard before? I spent hours in my special place in the field behind my garden, my radio pressed against my ear. I longed for Jimi Hendrix and Pink Floyd to be played. I loved The Turtles and the other West

Coast bands. I imagined myself in San Francisco, floating around an un-named park with flowers in my hair. But The Beatles were still my first love. 'All You Need is Love' was amazing but, even better, my sisters had saved some of their pocket money and contributed towards a copy of Sgt. Pepper for my birthday. It was my first LP and I played it whenever I could gain access to my parents' new stereo system. My inner life seemed to be complete.

It was around this time that I started to hang around with a girl called Maggie. My old friend Elizabeth had become mad about horses and tried to include me in her weekly visits to a local stables, but it wasn't for me. I found the size and strength of the horses alarming. I gained little pleasure from spending hours raking dung-impregnated straw from stalls in return for five or ten minutes leading a snorting beast around in a circle. Elizabeth assured me that I would progress to riding before long, but the prospect of sitting astride something so tall and muscular led me to a decision quite the opposite of that she had anticipated. I stopped attending and we drifted apart.

Maggie was very different to other friends I had made. She was a town girl. She lived in a cramped little terraced house with her widowed father, an assortment of older brothers and sisters and an irascible old grandmother who sat in a corner of the tiny front room and chain-smoked. I have no idea how they all slept there. The house was chaotic, not particularly clean and smelled of cooking and cigarette smoke. I was not especially comfortable being there, but Maggie was fun. Maggie knew about things that were a mystery to me. Maggie swore without even noticing she was doing it and she knew boys. Being with Maggie was exciting and just the right side of risky, so I put up with her less than desirable home. If I went there after school, I sprayed perfume on my clothes afterwards so my parents wouldn't notice the lingering smell of tobacco.

Now that I was fifteen, I was allowed to take a Saturday job. I worked in Woolworth's. Most weeks I was assigned the stockings and tights counter, where everything was priced at an amount ending in eleven old pence. The till was capable only of receiving the total, which had to be worked out on a little pad held on my belt by a piece of string. It took me some weeks to work out that three pairs of stockings at 2/11 (two shillings and eleven pence) was an easy calculation if you simply rounded up and subtracted the three pence at the end. After that, I became quite efficient. The work was exhausting as the shop was busy throughout the day and our breaks were very short.

We were not permitted to relax in the absence of customers, but were expected to tidy and replace our stock even if that was unnecessary at the time. Despite all this, I was glad of that job. Suddenly, I had money of my own.

So all my Saturdays were taken. There was no question of being allowed out in the evening and everything was closed on Sundays, but now the holidays had arrived and, with them, opportunities. I had money in my purse and a friend who lived in town.

"Who is this girl?" asked my mum when I announced I was going to meet Maggie. "Do we know her?"

I told her Maggie had been in my class since day one. I told her she was a nice girl and we simply hadn't been friends for very long.

"Hmm," said my mum, but she could think of no reason to object. "Don't be back late then."

My stomach churned with pleasurable anticipation as I sat upstairs on the bus in a fug of cigarette smoke. It would not have been cool to sit downstairs with all the old ladies and mothers with small children. I was going to town on my own. I was going to meet a friend. This was the sort of thing I had heard other girls talk about. It was the sort of thing I never did, together with having boyfriends and going to youth clubs. I was heartily sick of being the girl who never did anything and now it was all going to change. I was going to make it change.

Maggie met me off the bus. She was wearing a very short mini dress and lots of make-up. I was wearing a lime green skirt I had made on my mum's sewing machine and a white skinny top. I hadn't dared apply any make-up as that would have been noticed immediately. Maggie looked me up and down.

"Come on," she said.

She dragged me off to the bus station toilets where she produced her own make up and applied it liberally to my eyes. I looked like a small nocturnal animal, but I was delighted with the result.

"You'll do," she said. "Come on, let's go to The Cab."

My heart leapt into my mouth at this. The Cab was a coffee bar – La Cabana – in the High Street. It was where all the hip people went – people older than Maggie and me – and it had never occurred to me that we would end up there. I had envisaged wandering around the shops, perhaps having a look in the single clothes shop to sell anything fashionable. Maybe we would sit on one of the benches by the clock tower where other kids sometimes loitered. Maybe some boys would talk to us. This was in a different league, but how could I refuse?

As we approached The Cab, Maggie must have sensed something. Maybe she was expert in reading body language. Maybe it was the fact that I had suddenly become very quiet.

"Look, don't worry, I'll order," she said. "It won't be that crowded on a Monday. It's crazy on Saturdays – you can wait forever to get a seat. D'you want coffee?"

With only the slightest hesitation, I agreed. I had tried coffee a couple of times and didn't really like it, but this was a coffee bar. What else would it sell? It would be embarrassing to ask for something inappropriate and show myself up still further.

"Well, I'll need some money then," said Maggie.

We found a table quite near to the door. Although Maggie was right and the place was not full, I could see there was a second room at the back. A blue curtain of smoke hung around the arched entrance to this space. Although it was darker than where we were sitting, it looked a lot more crowded. Occasionally, bursts of laughter drifted out with the smoke, as if the room had reached its capacity for amusing conversation.

Maggie took my purse and left me alone. I had nothing with which to occupy myself and I sat bolt upright, like a person with severe toothache waiting for the dentist to call their name. After what seemed to be an age, Maggie returned with two steaming cups of coffee.

"What a bummer!" she said. "Bleedin' machine started playing up, just when I was getting served. Anyway, here we are. Cheers!"

She lifted her cup in mock salute and took a sip.

"Fuckin' hell! That's ridiculous," she gasped, putting the cup down again and fanning her tongue. "This place is going to the dogs, but there's nowhere else to go. What d'you think of it, anyway?"

I said I thought it was very nice, then quickly amended that to 'cool.' Such words didn't fall naturally off my tongue, but I had been trying to learn them. If I was going to join the world to which Maggie appeared to have a passport, I would have to use the right language.

I relaxed a little as our coffee cooled and we chatted about things we had done and boys we had met. It was a very one-sided conversation. There was a boy called Dan who regularly sought out

Maggie on the way home from school. Now he had started to bump into her at other times. She professed not to like him and mocked the fact that he rode a bike, but she seemed to talk about him an awful lot.

"I was sure he was going to ask me out," she said. "I could tell he wanted to, but he chickened out. Just as bloody well! As if!"

"Would you say 'no' then?" I asked.

"Of course I fuckin' would! Where's a boy like that gonna take me? He wouldn't get served anywhere with all that bum-fluff on his chin!"

I had never seen Maggie's admirer, but I wished he would come and follow me on his bike. He sounded ok to me. I wouldn't have minded if we went to the cinema or even to the park. I wouldn't have minded if he had just walked along beside me, pushing his bike and chatting as he did with Maggie. Apart from my cousins, I had not spoken to a single boy for at least two years and they were beginning to seem like a different species.

We lingered over our coffees. Maggie told me not to finish the last half inch or so.

"They'll come and take your cup, then you either have to buy another one or give up the table," she said, impressing me with her understanding of social rules. All the same, there was a limit to how long anyone could sit with one cup of coffee and we seemed to have reached that when Maggie's reserve of anecdotes dried up.

"I'm going to the bog," she announced and strode off towards the room at the back. She was a large girl, tall and well-built. She looked much older than me and she walked with an air of confidence I knew I would have to emulate if I needed to go to the toilet. I watched her go, then turned to the large window at the front. It was bright and sunny outside and I looked forward to breathing something other than smoke. I decided I could manage without visiting the toilet. Walking through that murky back room, with its crowds of older kids who laughed such a lot, might be a step too far.

I paid no attention to the group of four or five who left the back room and passed by my table on their way to the door. I had stopped looking through the window, but I was studying my fingernails, trying to appear as if I didn't feel uncomfortable sitting there alone.

"Oh, my God! It's Alice, isn't it?"

For a split second, I assumed there must be another Alice in the room. Nobody in here could possibly know me, but then I recognised the voice. I looked up.

"You go on, I'll catch you up," said Georgie to the people she was with. She stood back and surveyed me. "It's so cool to see you! Amazing! How are you? You look fab!"

Luckily, my body no longer dispatched all its spare blood to my face at critical moments. That had stopped a while ago. However, I seemed to have made little progress in other respects.

"I … I'm fine, thanks. And you? Your mum …?

Oh, God. I'd asked after her mother. I must have seemed about fifty rather than fifteen. But if Georgie had drawn any conclusions from my very un-cool response, she was much too well-bred to show it.

"She's well, thanks. Still painting. Still mad. She'll be delighted when I tell her I've seen you. She was always saying what a lovely girl you were."

I didn't know what to say. Memories I thought I had tucked away somewhere safe and unobtrusive jumped out suddenly and clamoured for attention. They were much closer to the surface than I'd thought. It really was Georgie. She was a lot taller and exceptionally attractive, but still the same in essence. Her hair was now wavy and almost waist-length and a patterned scarf encircled her forehead to hang in chiffon waves on one side. She was wearing a full-length gypsy skirt, nothing like anything I would have worn. But her eyes were the same and her smile was the same. All I could do was smile in return.

Georgie's eyes flicked to the door. "Look," she said, "I'd better go. But it would be so cool to catch up some time. Do you come here often?"

I was about to say that yes, I did pop in from time to time, when I noticed that Maggie had reappeared. She was looking at Georgie with an expression that could only be regarded as hostile.

"Um, no, not really, but I could ..."

"Not to worry. I'll call you. Are you in the book?"

I told her we were and she hurried off, swinging her tapestry bag over her shoulder with a flourish.

"Who the fuck was that?" asked Maggie, glowering after Georgie as the door swung shut behind her.

"Oh, just a girl I knew at school."

"Fuckin' snobs, that lot. Think they own the place, just 'cos they can afford to buy drinks all day."

I didn't feel inclined to defend Georgie at that point. After all, she wasn't really going to call me, was she? In all likelihood it would be another three years before we were in the same room again, if at all. Or, and this would be worse, I would see her and we would have to pretend not to notice each other. We had nothing in common apart from that one, magical year. I was never sure whether she felt quite the same about that as I did anyway.

"Yeah," I said. "Bloody snobs. I hate them. Who do they think they are?"

DECEMBER 2016

The following morning, Alice's body appears to have forgiven her. She has promised it there will be no repetition of the abuse and that's a promise she's certain she will never break. It appears to be yet another of the indignities of approaching old age, that you can't drink a little too much without suffering in a wholly disproportionate manner. She showers and dresses before going downstairs, expecting any minute to feel fragile again, but she seems to be fine.

That is, until she enters the kitchen. She'd retired early the night before, but assumed Georgie would keep her promise about clearing up later. She'd shown no signs of going to bed when Alice threw in the towel. Her heart sinks at the state of it. Georgie may be good at producing tasty meals out of nothing, but she is not a tidy cook. There are pans heaped up in the sink, the tops are covered with chopping boards and vegetable peelings and there is a semi-circle of flour on the floor with a trail of footsteps emanating from it.

Alice sighs and opens up the dishwasher. It is full, but nobody has switched it on and it is very poorly stacked. She has to take almost everything out and re-pack it before she can think of running it. Then she turns her attention to the rest of the chaos. There can be no coffee, no breakfast until it is done, until order is restored.

It takes over half an hour, but at last Alice has her kitchen back. The tops are gleaming and the dribbles of soup have been removed from the front of the cooker. The peelings are in their recycling box and the pans are washed, dried and sitting in a neat stack in their rightful place. She puts coffee on and is about to think about breakfast when Georgie appears. She is swathed in her terrible old dressing gown and looks as if she hasn't been awake for long.

"Oh, Alice! I'm so sorry!" she cries. "I fell asleep in front of the telly last night and it was three o'clock when I woke up. I thought I might disturb you if I did it then, but I didn't mean for you to do it. I'm such a messy cook!"

Alice tells her not to worry. It's the least she could do, given how brilliant Georgie was yesterday. She hopes it sounds sincere, as she knows it's exactly what she should be feeling. As long as Georgie can't see what she really thinks there will be no harm done. They have breakfast together, but there is a strange feeling in the air. Georgie goes to the sink, washes up her plate and mug then turns and leans against it, arms folded.

"Well, it's Monday," she says, brightly. "Time for me to get my life in order. I'm going to get ready then I'll pop out for a local paper. I need to get myself somewhere to stay."

Alice opens her mouth to protest, to say there really is no hurry, but she pauses a little too long and Georgie sees it.

"It's ok, Alice, you don't need to say anything. You've been brilliant! I can't tell you how much better I feel for being here. But I can't impose on you much longer, plus, I need to do it for myself. I need to start making plans and it's quite nice being back in familiar territory. Time to put down some new roots."

Alice thinks she can see a few tears in Georgie's eyes as she leaves the room. She feels quite sorry for her. But what she feels most is relief. Now she can look forward to her life returning to normal and she can start thinking about her own future. She supposes she should be grateful to Georgie for provoking that, but it's true that it's time for her to move on.

She occupies herself with more domestic chores while Georgie is out. She doesn't exactly eradicate signs of Georgie's presence – that would be rude – but she collects a few of her things together in one place in the hope that Georgie will notice them and take them upstairs. Then Georgie returns and sits at the kitchen table with a mug of tea, the local paper and Alice's pen from the telephone table. Alice leaves her to it and goes to clean her en-suite.

When she returns to the kitchen, Georgie has folded the paper. She hasn't returned the pen but Alice leaves it where it is. That can wait.

"Any luck?"

"Yes, I've got a couple to see this afternoon."

"Oh, that's … that's quick. Would you like me to take you?"

Georgie says no, she'll be fine, but Alice is feeling magnanimous now the end is in sight. She insists. She says it will be so much easier with the satnav to help, and anyway it will give her something to do this afternoon.

So it is settled, and Alice begins to enjoy her role. She sees herself in an advisory capacity, offering support and guidance. She may even extend that, once Georgie has found her own place. She has a vision of a neat little bedsit or flat, with a small but functional kitchen area and stripped pine floors. She will help Georgie move in and possibly persuade her to dispose of some of the contents of her car. Maybe she will take her out and treat her to some nice rugs and cushions to brighten it up. They will meet in town for coffee and Alice will invite her round for meals from time to time. It will be perfect.

AUGUST 1967

It was the Thursday after my trip to town. I had resisted the combined efforts of my mum, my sisters and even the dog to get me out of bed and it was past nine-thirty. Didn't they know this was what teenagers were supposed to do? The more they peeped round my bedroom door with spurious reasons to talk to me, the more I determined to stay where I was. So when Angie called me from outside my room just as I had fallen back to sleep, I was irritated, to put it mildly.

"Angie, I've told you a hundred times. Leave me alone!" I shouted.

"Fine, don't come to the phone then." I barely heard what she said, but it must have filtered through the layers of sleep that weighed me down in the mornings at that time.

I ran downstairs and reached the phone just as my mum was telling whoever it was that I was indisposed at present. She wouldn't have wanted to admit to having a daughter who stayed in bed half the morning.

"Who is it?" I mouthed.

"Oh! Pardon me. Here she is after all. She must be feeling better," said my mum to the phone through gritted teeth. Her eyes flashed in silent reproval. Apparently it was my fault that she felt the need to lie to people just to maintain appearances. I took the receiver, assuming it would be Maggie. She had promised to call sometime this week and wouldn't give a damn if I was still asleep mid afternoon.

"Hello, sorry about that. I was in bed."

"Oh, no! Listen, I'll call back. I'm really sorry ..."

I told Georgie it was fine. I was about to get up anyway. I told her all sorts of lies about how I hadn't been asleep and was simply hiding in my room because of my annoying family. I don't know how convincing I sounded.

"I still can't believe I've seen you. It's been such a long time," she said. She sounded genuinely pleased to be talking to me. "Shall we meet up? Now I know you go to The Cab I'll look out for you, but shall we say an actual time? How about tomorrow?"

So we agreed to meet in The Cab the following afternoon. It all happened so quickly, with such casual ease. It was only after I put the phone down that my body caught up with my brain and sent a flood of adrenalin into my bloodstream. Unsurprisingly, my mum was delighted. She'd stopped suggesting I try to make contact with Georgie years ago, but I knew she'd been very disappointed when it all fizzled out. Despite the obvious issues in Georgie's family, they had class. That was something money couldn't buy and it always impressed my mum, however much she would have denied it.

However, my pleasure was soon tempered by a range of problems. For a start, I had no idea what to wear. Although I was charmed by the notion of flower power, I had not attempted to embrace its look. My role models were Twiggy and other skinny, leggy models. They wore mini dresses in bright colours or with vivid geometrical patterns. Their hair was cropped pixie-style or hung in angular straight lines. My only concession to hippy fashion was a string of orange beads my dad had bought from a stall in Carnaby Street. I was a mod and there was no denying it, but Georgie was not. Would she look down on me? Would I seem like a shallow follower of fashion?

But that was only the half of it. What about Maggie? I had been actively cultivating my friendship with her for more than half a term, but I had no illusions about it. Maggie had lots of friends. She was that kind of person. It was obvious that she frequented The Cab on a regular basis and it followed that she could be there tomorrow afternoon. Then she would see me with the girl she had derided as being a snob. At the very least I would appear two-faced. She might even end our fledgling friendship and then I would have to find someone else. It would be nice to see Georgie, but it wouldn't lead to anything. We lived in different worlds. Was it worth the risk?

In the end, I couldn't resist Georgie and all she stood for. I never could. There was something about her life that pulled me in and kept me wanting more. It was like the drugs that I vowed never to try. I chose my single pair of jeans, the spoils of a hard-fought battle with my parents, and a plain T-shirt. I counted out what remained of my money and headed off to town in a mood that could only be described as fatalistic.

In the event, there was no sign of Maggie. To begin with, my head swivelled round in panic each time the door opened, but it was never her. Then, after I'd been with Georgie for fifteen or twenty minutes, I wouldn't have cared anyway. It was unbelievable how the intervening years disappeared. It was like the sun shining and burning off an early morning mist. One minute I was taut and anxious, worried about saying the wrong thing or giving the wrong impression, and the next I was relaxed and laughing. None of the many things that separated us mattered. We were still Alice and Georgie. Was it possible that we could revive our friendship?

That's what I was thinking as Georgie went to buy more drinks. Apparently it was perfectly fine to not to drink coffee in a coffee bar. I had asked for a Pepsi and she'd smiled as she rose to go to the counter.

"Still a fan of the fizzy drinks then?"

I laughed, and a contented feeling enveloped me. It was like getting out of the bath when I was small and being wrapped in a towel that had been warming on the tank. I wasn't the only one who remembered in such detail the precious days we'd shared. I sat back in my chair and half closed my eyes. I wasn't tired, not remotely. I simply wanted to savour the moment. It was then that I heard someone talking behind me. He was speaking quietly, but I could hear every word.

"So if you want some, he's getting it on ..."

"Not now," hissed Georgie. "I'm with someone. She's ... Look, I'll be half an hour. I'll come and find you."

Panic surged in my stomach. What were they talking about? It sounded like something secret. Could it be drugs? Could Georgie really be involved in anything like that? I told myself there must be another explanation. She looked completely normal. There were no pin-prick pupils or shaking hands and she appeared to be glowing with health. Drug addicts didn't look like Georgie looked.

Georgie put the drinks on the table and sat down.

"Look, you absolutely have to come up to the house. Mother is adamant. She always liked you best of all my friends, you know."

What could I say? Georgie hadn't had any other friends that I knew of, but that didn't seem an appropriate response. I said something about liking her mother too. I assumed the whole exchange was driven by politeness and Georgie would change the subject without making any firm arrangements. The snippet of conversation I'd heard still troubled me and I wasn't really paying full attention.

"So, what do you think? I promise my mother won't cook!"

Somehow, I managed to work out that this was a real invitation after all. I think Georgie must have seen I was struggling, as she helpfully repeated the details. Could I come on Sunday afternoon? Of course I agreed without hesitation. This was an unexpected bonus. I had resigned myself to never seeing Georgie's house and garden again. I had stashed them away for posterity and they remained, unchanged, in a corner of my mind. Now, it appeared, I was to be granted a second chance.

It was almost like history repeating itself. Here I was, nearly four years older than when I'd received the first invitation, and yet nothing seemed to have changed. I looked forward to Sunday with a different mix of emotions, but they were just as ridiculously intense. I remembered my feelings back then, when I was young and impressionable. I'd believed every exciting, scary detail Georgie had told me about her father and the Russians. Now all my later suspicions were confirmed: she'd made that up. She told me about her parents' messy divorce as we sat in The Cab and how embarrassed she'd been. Embarrassed enough to make up a fantastic story. It was much less usual for parents to separate in those days.

There was no reasonable explanation for the way my stomach behaved throughout the two days I had to wait. Georgie was only a girl, I told myself. The house was only a house – and it wouldn't be the same house now, anyway. Georgie's family may not have been ordinary, but they were not embroiled in the shadowy world of spies. Their secrets were much more mundane. And Hilary. What of him? Well, he wouldn't be there, would he? He must have left university by now and presumably he would have left home too. I had long since consigned him to the category of childish crushes, along with Mr Peterson, our young Science teacher, and the lead singer of The Small Faces. All these things were true but my body refused stubbornly to pay them any attention.

At last, Sunday came and I played the part of a girl popping out to spend an hour or so with an old friend.

"It's no big deal," I told my mum, when she gave my casual appearance a look that required no further interpretation. "I'm only going to say hello. I doubt I'll be there long."

I have no idea whether I fooled her. I didn't fool myself. My choice of outfit was the result of hours of deliberation. In the end, I decided that it was important not to appear too keen. Despite my initial rush of enthusiasm at the re-kindling of our relationship, I couldn't escape the fact that the odds were against its continuation. I convinced myself that Georgie had invited me on her mother's behalf and that this would be my last visit to that house. If I looked as if I'd spent hours getting ready I would be at a disadvantage from the moment I stepped through the door.

Georgie's house was more or less hidden from view until you took the first curve in the drive. There were trees along its boundary with the road and, even from the top deck of the bus, only the roof was visible, with its elaborate chimneys and the weather vane that pointed always to the north. That didn't stop me from craning my neck to catch a glimpse of it for months after she left my school, but to no avail. There was nothing to give me the slightest clue about what was going on inside. As I left my bike in its usual place and walked in what I hoped was a casual manner down the drive, it was very nearly three years since I'd last seen it.

At first, I was struck by how much more ordinary everything seemed. I had hardly left childhood behind and it was a shock to find that my idealised version of the past was different to reality. True, it was a lovely old house and way beyond anything my family could afford, but my memory had turned it into something more than that.

I had raised the knocker and let it fall before I noticed that there was now an electric bell. Luckily, I had only just begun to worry about whether to press that too when the door opened. There stood Georgie. She was wearing a loose, brightly-coloured top over flared jeans and her feet were bare. She was beautiful; there was no other word for it. Suddenly, my decision to affect a casual look seemed like a huge mistake, but Georgie was grinning.

"Hello! Come in, please," she said, stepping aside to let me in. I followed her into the hall and found that it, too, had shrunk. Nothing was actually different, apart from a telephone table that hadn't been there before and the smooth, regular motion of the pendulum in the grandfather clock. That now showed a more or less accurate time but I doubt it was this that made me feel as if I were looking at everything through a different lens.

"Come on, let's go and find my mother," said Georgie. For a minute, I thought she would take me by the arm as she always had when we were young and she was impatient, but she didn't. "I think she's painting, just for a change!"

We went into the kitchen and I saw that the old, wooden back door had been replaced by a French window. There were new cupboards along one wall. The long, oak table remained in its place, but now it was largely clear and I could see the warm depth of its grain.

"She's probably in here," said Georgie. She opened the French window and I followed her into an enormous glass structure that took up at least a third of the terrace. A sofa that I remembered from the lounge was against one wall with a small tabby cat curled in one corner. Most of the space was filled by a cluttered trestle table and a number of easels. Canvasses were stacked against another wall and the clay bin was in one corner.

"Alice! Darling!"

Georgie's mother advanced, arms outstretched and gave me a lingering hug. She looked younger than I remembered, with no hint of the dark circles that used to make her seem permanently tired. She smelled of a combination of linseed oil and another spicier scent, but not tobacco smoke. That was different too. She released her grip then stood back to examine me.

"My goodness, how you've grown up. And look at your hair! Quite the little fashion model aren't you?"

I didn't know how to reply to this. My new, short haircut was the subject of considerable controversy in my house. Seeing how beautiful Georgie looked with her long, wavy hair falling from a central parting had made me start to regret it. My hand drifted up to my neck, which still felt cold sometimes even though it was summer.

"Mother, you're being embarrassing," said Georgie. She turned to me. "Come on, let's go up to my room."

I stayed a couple of hours - much longer than I expected. Slowly, my memories of Georgie's house came to some kind of compromise with the images on my retina and a truce was called. It was different but familiar at the same time. In particular, Georgie's room, although boasting new furniture, had retained all its charm. I began to feel at home once more.

I sat on the bed as I used to, while Georgie played some of her new records and we chatted. She told me about St Anne's and the trouble she'd had settling in at first. She told me about making new friends and that it wasn't true that all the pupils were stuck-up. I found that I could hear this without experiencing the great surges of jealousy that had afflicted me when we were younger. I even asked about Camilla and was pleased when Georgie declared her to be 'a bit straight these days.' However, there was one subject that neither of us raised. I waited for Georgie to mention Hilary and then, when she still hadn't by the time I rose to leave, it was too late.

"I'll just pop and say goodbye to your mum," I said to Georgie as we reached the bottom of the stairs. By this time, I felt as if I could do this without being taken, but Georgie followed me. As soon as we entered the kitchen I could hear voices. One was clearly Georgie's mother. It was slightly raised and a fraction higher than normal. The other was indistinct, but male.

"Look, you don't ..." began Georgie, but I had already reached the open French door and I could see the second participant in the conversation. It was Hilary. He looked slightly thinner than I remembered but otherwise unchanged. Georgie's mother seemed tense and uncomfortable when she noticed me standing there, but she dredged up a smile. Hilary continued to glare at Georgie's mother and didn't even glance in my direction.

"I'm off now," I said. I had to say something, having stumbled into what was obviously a difficult situation. "It was lovely to see you again."

"Well, it was lovely to see you too. I do hope you won't be a stranger," she replied. "George, will you see Alice out?"

I lifted my hand in a half-hearted wave and followed Georgie back through the kitchen and into the hall. She opened the front door.

"Look, I'm sorry about my brother. That was very rude of him. I hope you won't think ..."

I stopped her. I assured her it didn't matter at all that Hilary had ignored me.

"It was you I came to see – you and your mum," I said, and I meant it. The unexpected encounter with Hilary had left me completely calm and unmoved. This was proof that I had matured, that I had left all my childish fantasies behind me. Georgie gave me a brief hug as we said our goodbyes and I walked home feeling more positive than I had for months.

AUGUST 1967

The first room is not in the best part of town. Alice notes the bins sprawling on the pavement and the untidy, weed-infested front gardens of many of the properties. However, she forces herself to smile and remain positive as the satnav informs them they have reached their destination. A young man with a shiny suit and a clipboard is waiting for them.

Alice tries, she really does, but it is impossible to be anything but depressed at the thought of living in this house. What was formerly a family home has been sub-divided into a series of rooms with shared facilities. Although Georgie would have a wash-basin and a microwave, she would have to share a bathroom and a run-down kitchen that looks like something from Alice's student days. A young man with unrealistically defined biceps pushes past them, muttering something about milk.

"Georgie, you're not living here!" she whispers as the agent begins to talk about terms. She takes her by the arm in a strange reversal of what used to happen when they were children, and practically drags her back to the car.

The next property looks more promising. It is in a much nicer street, with trees at intervals and traffic-calming measures in place. The houses are a series of sturdy Victorian semis and small terraces, mostly well-maintained. The room is in a property about half way down and Alice is pleased to see the neat hedge and litter-free front garden.

"This looks more like it," she says. Georgie is quiet. Maybe the thought of living in the appalling room they've just viewed has left her speechless.

There is no agent this time. The owner of the house lives here and rents out the attic conversion only. He explains this as he puffs his way up the two flights of stairs. The acrid smell of cigarette smoke lingers in his wake. The second staircase is a particular challenge as he is clearly unfit and it is both narrow and steep, but eventually they make it.

"Here we are then, me ducks," wheezes the potential landlord. He looks as if he needs to sit down. His face has become a very alarming colour.

The attic space has been sympathetically converted, if the newspaper advert is to be believed. In practice, this means that some of the rough roof beams have been left exposed and there is mock oak laminate flooring throughout. There is a tiny area that could be used for minimal food preparation and a small but functional en-suite. There is a double bed and the landlord explains that the sofa also converts. He is still breathing heavily and looks as if a lie-down on either of these alternatives would be very welcome. Everything looks new, but cheap. Although there is nothing wrong with it, it is far from the mental picture of a snug little nest Alice has created for Georgie.

"It seems fine," says Georgie.

"Well, I'm glad you like it, deary," says the landlord. "It'll be so nice to have a bit of company. I've been on my lonesome since my better half passed over. It's no fun spending every evening by yourself, is it?"

"Er, no," says Georgie. Alice can read her mind

as if her thoughts were being typed up like the news headlines on the tv, scrolling across the foot of the screen. 'Help, I don't want to spend my evenings with this man,' she's thinking.

"Well, we have a couple more to see," says Alice. "Thanks so much for showing us round. We'll be in touch." She says this with such decisiveness that all three of them are back by the front door within a minute and they are in the car in another.

"Oh, my God," says Georgie. "Thanks, Alice. It wasn't a bad space, but can you imagine it?"

"I expect he was harmless," says Alice.

"Yes," says Georgie. "But I'm not convinced I would've been for long, especially if he kept calling me 'deary'."

That evening, although they are no further forward with Georgie's accommodation, there is a changed atmosphere. It is as if Georgie has already gone, is already living somewhere else. She is a visitor rather than a guest. Alice has never thought about the difference before, but there is one. Georgie must feel it too, or she's aware of her impending departure and wants to tie up loose ends, to ensure Alice has the full story. She talks about her mother and how she struggled in the year following their move to Templars Way. She describes the bouts of drinking and how she nearly fell apart completely at one point.

"You didn't see the half of it," she tells Alice. "If you thought it was all to do with her artistic temperament, you couldn't have been more wrong. She was so angry. When it was just the two of us, guess who was on the receiving end?"

Alice takes a moment to reorganise her memories. She sees how easy it is to fit everything you see into your chosen ideal, especially as a child. She had embraced the woman who drifted around the house in eclectic clothes, a paintbrush in one hand and a cigarette in the other. She was exciting, she was glamorous. She sees that she chose to ignore the absence of food, the absence of love and care Georgie received. She had dismissed her own mum and dad as boring when they were actually doing a much better job of being parents. Then she remembers something.

"She did use her art to help her, though," she says. "I saw a picture once. It was of a man in a pool of blood, surrounded by knives. I was so shocked. I was convinced the Russians had killed your father and that was her way of expressing it. I tried to find out more, but of course I never did."

Georgie laughs uproariously and Alice can't help but join in. How silly she'd been as a child, how gullible.

"Yes, I remember that one," says Georgie. "We had a ceremonial bonfire in the garden before we left Templars Way and I believe it went on first. It was bloody awful!"

They are quiet for a while, both lost in their own memories. Alice is relaxed and beginning to think about bed. She may even read for a while, now that the thought of someone else being in the house is almost comforting.

"Alice?"

Mmm?" says Alice. She begins to rise. She foresees a short conversation about tomorrow. That is almost comforting too, but any comfort is dispelled as she sees the anxiety on Georgie's face.

"There's something I must ask you. I wasn't going to, but it's been eating me up, not knowing. About six months before we moved to Kent, Hilary tried to kiss one of my friends. She told me, but she obviously didn't tell anyone else. She never came to my house after that. I didn't know what to think then. I didn't know what it meant. She was quite mature, but obviously it was … Anyway. Was he ever … did he ever try to ...? Alice, did he ever assault you?"

Alice feels herself plummet backwards into the softness of her chair.

"No," she says. "No, never. There was nothing like that at all!"

AUGUST 1967

I began to lead a double life. It was stressful but exciting, trying to see both Maggie and Georgie without either of them knowing about the other. I'm sure Georgie wouldn't have minded me having other friends. She was never possessive about our relationship or any other as far as I knew. But that wasn't the problem. I didn't want Georgie to see me out with Maggie because of who Maggie was. In much the same way, I didn't I want Maggie to see me out with Georgie, because of who Georgie was.

Maggie was a girl of sharp edges. She met the world head-on and there was never any doubt about what she thought of it. Her skirts were very short, her heels were very high and her tight, low-cut tops advertised the allure of her large breasts without a hint of modesty. She was not the kind of girl my parents would approve of and she was the polar opposite of Georgie. I knew all this, but I was reluctant to let her go. My contact with Georgie was very intermittent and, although I loved being with her, our relationship lacked the one thing that I craved above all else. To be specific, it lacked any opportunity to meet boys. Georgie showed no sign of inviting me to hang out with her friends. Thus, if I was ever going to catch up with the majority of my classmates and have a boyfriend, I needed Maggie.

Maggie's potential as a means to this end was illustrated just days after my visit to Georgie's house. We were in town, but neither of us had any money for The Cab, so I wasn't unduly bothered about bumping into Georgie. We were wandering around, taking a long time looking in shop windows and fast running out of things to do. I think Maggie had only agreed to meet me as she thought I might have some money, but I was keeping her occupied by asking about her new boyfriend.

We had just crossed the road to continue down the other side when we were approached by two boys who blocked our way. I didn't recognise them.

"Hello, Maggie," said one.

"Fuck off, Vincent," said Maggie. "If I wanted to talk to you I'd come and find you in infant school."

Vincent smirked and his friend laughed, a short yelp of a laugh, like a dog that had been kicked.

"They still not dropped then, Brian?" said Maggie. "Never mind, give 'em another few years."

She shouldered her way between them, but I took the easy way and darted into the road to pass by. My heart was beating fast and I was hoping they would follow. Maybe one of them would talk to me.

"Pair of twats," said Maggie. She looked over her shoulder. "Got rid of them, anyway."

I sighed inwardly, but this interaction, although abortive, was a good sign. Maggie might attract more interest as we progressed. I decided to revisit the subject of the boyfriend. She'd only met him at the weekend, so I had plenty more questions in my repertoire.

"How old is this Kevin then?" I asked, expecting her to answer that he was or seventeen or eighteen.

"Dunno for sure. I'd guess he's around twenty-one. He's been working a few years."

I was shocked. This was a man, not a boy.

"And he's got a car," she continued. "Tell you what, I ain't going with no spotty schoolboys again. Not after that!" She gave me a look that I was obviously supposed to interpret for myself. I took a guess.

"Is he a good kisser?"

Maggie snorted. "A good kisser?" she said. She seemed about to say something else, but obviously thought better of it. "Anyway, gotta go now. Things to do, people to see. Bysie-bye!"

She left, tripping off down the High Street with a purposeful air. Her shiny white handbag bounced against her hip. I watched her until she disappeared then looked at my watch. It was nearly an hour until my next bus, but there was nothing I could do about that. I continued to wander up and down on my own. At one point I thought I saw Vincent and Brian up by the clock tower and increased my pace, but they were nowhere to be seen by the time I got there. Eventually, I gave up and returned to the bus station where I sat on a bench until my bus came. My feet hurt and I hadn't achieved much, but it had been a start. Maggie was the key to my new improved social life, of that I was sure.

Eventually, I had to force myself to make the first move with Georgie. There had been no invitation to her house for a while and I feared the relationship would fizzle out altogether, just as it had done all those years ago. Of course it would be easier to phone and arrange something but, for some reason, I couldn't. Maybe it was fear of rejection. Every time I picked up the receiver my mouth dried up and I found myself slamming it down before I'd even finished dialling. I decided to drop in casually. It would be a nuisance if she were out, but I would live with that.

It was Friday, just after lunch. I told my mum I was bored and going out for a bike ride. She looked a little surprised as I would normally walk the dog in these circumstances, but she kept her thoughts to herself. Doubtless my parents put my reluctance to tell them anything down to normal teenage behaviour. The fact was that my life was so complicated at that time, that I found it too risky to discuss anything with anyone. My social life, such as it was, seemed like an edifice of deception and lies of omission. One ill-advised word and it was liable to crumble.

When I got to Georgie's house, I dumped my bike at the entrance as always. It was a perfectly nice bike, new and shiny, but this seemed like a habit I couldn't break. I walked slowly down the drive, rehearsing what I would say when the door opened. It would be ridiculous to pretend I was just passing, as there were only a few more houses after Georgie's, then a mile or two of tree-lined road before the outskirts of the next village. No, I would tell the truth – or at least a version of it. I would say I was bored, went out for a bike ride and suddenly had the bright idea of paying Georgie a visit. That would have to do.

There was no car in the drive but that wasn't an issue in itself. Even I was allowed to stay at home without my parents now. There was still a good chance that Georgie would be home. I rang the bell, running through my words once more to ensure they sounded plausible. I opened my mouth as the door began to open, but closed it again when I saw that it wasn't Georgie standing there. Neither was it her mother.

Hilary looked as if he had just fallen out of bed. He was wearing jeans and an unbuttoned shirt. I couldn't help noticing the way the dark hairs on his chest resolved themselves into a fine line that led down to his belly button and beyond. His hair was untamed and looked a lot like Georgie's had before she grew it very long. Little corkscrew curls fell onto his shoulders. There was dark stubble on his cheeks and chin.

I watched as recognition dawned. He rubbed his eyes.

"Wait, don't tell me," he said. He ran the fingers of one hand through his hair, causing it to stand up even more wildly. "It's Alice. Tell me I'm right, won't you?"

I confirmed he was right and asked for Georgie.

"Ah, well. You see, that's where there's a problem. But it's only a little one," he said, demonstrating the size of said problem with his index finger and thumb. "George has gone out with Ma to get ... well, the truth is, I don't know what they went to get, but that doesn't matter, does it? The thing is, they won't be long. Could be a matter of minutes. Why don't you come in and wait?"

I began to say that I wouldn't stay, that I was only here on the off-chance, but Hilary stopped me.

"This is because of the other day, isn't it?" he said.

I didn't reply. I had a fair idea what he was talking about, but no desire to discuss it.

"You know, when you were here and I was ... when Ma and I were ... Truth is, I was being a bit of a boor. Didn't even recognise you. I had a real hard time from George afterwards, I can tell you. Come on, let me make you something … cup of coffee? Please?"

So I agreed to go in and wait. I slipped my shoes off in the hall and sat on the new sofa in the now rather smart lounge. Hilary disappeared, to return a few minutes later properly dressed and with his hair slightly less wild.

"What can I get you then?"

"Actually, I'm not really thirsty," I said. "I'll just wait a couple of minutes and then I'll go if they're not back."

Hilary sat down beside me.

"Well then, if you won't allow me to provide you with refreshments, you'll have to talk to me instead. It's more than my life's worth not to look after you. You can't imagine what it's like, living with those two. They do nothing but boss me around. I swear, my life isn't my own."

I couldn't help smiling. Of course he was exaggerating, but I could imagine that the combined personalities of Georgie and her mother could be hard to resist.

"That's better," said Hilary. He looked at me intently. "I remember that smile. I remember those eyes, too. I seem to remember I upset you the last time I remarked on them. D'you remember? I called you Bambi."

"It wasn't 'Bambi', it was 'little fawn'," I said.

"You're absolutely right. So it was," said Hilary. He was still looking at me and smiling. It made me uncomfortable to be under such scrutiny and I tried to avoid catching his eye. "Unforgivable," he continued. "The problem is with you young ladies, you're not aware of what you're doing to us poor unfortunate chaps. You look at us with those big eyes and we lose our senses. Come up with all sorts of nonsense. It's not our fault, don't you see?"

Somehow, Hilary was nearer to me than he had been when he first sat down. His body was close enough for me to feel his warmth. I crossed my legs and leaned away from him, but then, when I shifted further along the sofa, he followed me. He draped his arm along the cushions behind me. I felt the pressure of it. I felt very hot.

Suddenly, Hilary stood up and went to stand by the fireplace. He leaned on the mantelpiece and looked down at me.

"So. How's school then?"

Strangely, the whole tone of the conversation changed. It was as if somebody had flicked a switch to reveal an entirely new Hilary. He asked me about my GCE subjects and which I preferred. When I said English was my favourite he looked pleased and quizzed me on my set books. I relaxed and even began to enjoy myself. Hilary was clever and amusing and he was interested in what I had to say. He had been teasing me before and it was nothing to worry about.

After I'd been there nearly half an hour, I decided not to wait any longer. Hilary was apologetic. He said he'd appeared to have kept me there on false pretences. I smiled.

"It's fine. I wasn't doing anything else," I said. "I'll come and see Georgie another time."

"I do hope you will," said Hilary and I could tell he meant it.

I went into the hall and bent to retrieve my sneakers. I'd left the laces tied, so it took a while to untie them. As I stood, I realised that Hilary had come up behind me. He had one hand resting on the wall above my head.

"So, am I forgiven then?" he said. There was something about his voice. Something soft and a bit husky. My heart began to batter its way out of my chest.

"I ..."

"It's alright, you don't need to say anything,"

said Hilary. His other hand appeared from nowhere and his fingers brushed my jawbone, titling my head up.

In one movement, I ducked under his arm and grabbed the door handle.

"Sorry, I've just remembered something, somewhere ..." I stammered. I yanked open the door and half ran, half walked down the drive. I dragged my bike out of its bush and pedalled home as fast as I could. I ignored my mum's query and ran upstairs where I threw myself on my bed.

I knew it wouldn't be long before I heard the hesitant little tap on the door.

"Are you alright, love?"

"Yes, I'm fine. Stomach ache. You couldn't do me a hot water bottle could you?"

My mum bustled off to make herself useful. She liked that. My period wasn't due for a few more days, so I would have to hope I didn't get any significant pain when it arrived for real. Another deception. Another lie. But what could I do? I couldn't tell her that Hilary had very nearly kissed me. For he had. There was no question about it. I had never been kissed, but there could be no other explanation for his behaviour, for that strange look on his face. My mind was in utter turmoil.

For the whole of that weekend, I mourned the loss of Georgie. I couldn't return to her house after what had happened, could I? I couldn't tell her about Hilary and it would be intolerably embarrassing to see him again. He must have been having a mad moment to want to kiss me. No, it was impossible to see any of them ever again and that was heart-breaking. Luckily, Hilary must have kept quiet about my visit and Georgie was probably busy with her friends so I had no invitation to refuse. I spent hours in my room, lying on my bed and re-living those moments with Hilary, over and over again.

By the time Monday came, I was beginning to change my mind. I began to think I'd been stupid. I'd panicked and run away, but why? Maggie's boyfriend was in his twenties. Other girls in my class had talked of older boys. The more I thought about it, the more I wished I'd behaved differently. I started to imagine an alternative end to the events in the hall. In this new version, I let Hilary's hand linger on my face. I let him pull me towards him. I let him drop his lips onto mine. It was all a little vague after that, as I wasn't sure what proper kissing involved. I had heard talk of tongues being involved, but that sounded disgusting. There would be nothing disgusting about my first kiss. More importantly, now I knew who it would be with.

I spent the whole day in a dream. It's lucky that people's thoughts are not visible, that they're not played out just above their heads like a little film for all to see. My mum would have been shocked to see multiple re-plays of a passionate embrace between Hilary and me. She couldn't have known what I was now beginning to believe, that Hilary had fallen in love with me. It didn't seem possible, but what other explanation could there be for his behaviour? I replayed the events of that memorable day last week. He'd clearly been dying to kiss me on the sofa, but he must have told himself I was too young. That's why he stood up so abruptly and started talking about exams. But then our conversation had led him to believe that I was much more mature than he thought. Either that, or his feelings were so strong that he couldn't resist.

This made everything different. If love was involved I had nothing to fear. This wasn't like whatever Maggie was doing with Kevin in his car. I had more than a suspicion that Maggie had actually had sex, although she hadn't said as much. No, this would be a real relationship. It would be like something from a film, or Pride and Prejudice. There would be some kissing, but no question of anything more than that. If Hilary's feelings were as I thought, it followed that he would respect me.

I was hugely relieved and excited. This amounted to a revelation. I only wished I'd experienced it earlier, as my idiotic and infantile escape from Georgie's house presented me with a significant problem to overcome. Now I had to manufacture another opportunity for Hilary to kiss me. I also had to find a way to let him know that I understood how he felt, and that I felt the same. Otherwise he would give me a wide berth the next time I appeared. I could hardly blame him for that.

When I wandered downstairs to eat, three pairs of eyes widened. Love appeared to have rendered me pale and ill-looking.

"Oh, you poor old sausage. Is it a bad one?" asked my mum.

"A bad what?" asked Janey.

"Never you mind!" snapped my mum. "You'll find out soon enough. Alice, do you want me to put something on a tray? Then you can go and lie down again."

I nodded. I did feel rather strange. My stomach was churning so much that I'd hardly been able to eat for days. My mum told me to go back to bed. She followed with the tray a few minutes later.

"If this doesn't settle down soon I think we may have to get you a doctor's appointment. You look like death warmed up."

I agreed, but as soon as she left I forced myself to eat everything on the tray. After all, I couldn't have Hilary seeing me like this, could I?

DECEMBER 2016

Somehow, they seem to have fallen into a routine. It's comfortable and actually quite enjoyable. For the past few days they have visited rental agencies and viewed a series of wholly unsuitable rooms. These visits have been punctuated by periods in coffee shops, pubs and small restaurants. Georgie has almost stopped protesting about Alice paying for everything now, beaten down by Alice's determination to make the process as pain-free as possible.

For all that, they are no further forward. Although Georgie expressed a mild interest in a couple of the rooms, Alice put her foot down.

None of the possibilities, even those that Georgie favoured, have met her standards. She dismisses Georgie's insistence that her budget is unlikely to fund anything more up-market than what they've already seen.

"It's out there somewhere," she repeats whenever Georgie seems inclined to accept something inferior. "We just have to be patient and look harder."

They are back in Alice's favourite coffee shop, the one where they first met up, over a week ago now. Alice notes with pleasure that Georgie looks a lot better than she did then. She has touched up her roots and her skin looks much more healthy. There were some reasonable clothes amongst the endless bags of laundry and Alice has bought her a new coat. Georgie was aghast when Alice brought it home but was finally persuaded to accept it when Alice lied that it had been substantially reduced and was too good a bargain to miss.

So now they can sit together in places like this without Alice worrying about other people's opinions. Clearly they are not equal in a financial sense, but nobody will be aware of this. Apart from Georgie, of course, but Alice has found an incontrovertible argument for her.

"You'd do the same if it was the other way

round, wouldn't you?" she says, and Georgie has to agree.

They have just about finished their drinks. Alice has also eaten her lemon muffin, but Georgie has only made a small inroad into her shortbread. She didn't ask for it, but Alice has taken to ignoring her when she appears to be abstemious for no good reason. She would look better with a little more weight on her. Alice leans back in her chair. The cafe is almost empty and the staff won't hurry them if they take their time.

"D'you remember the dens?" she asks.

"Oh, yes! How could I forget? They were a work of art. You can't believe how much I complained when they demolished them. I was terrified of telling you."

Alice is shocked. "Surely not!" she says. "You were always the boss in that relationship. I'd never met anyone so confident."

"Or a good actress," says Georgie. "Most of it was an act, especially when we first moved. My world had crashed around me but I couldn't let anyone know that, could I? So I decided to reinvent myself. I thought, 'nobody knows me, so I can be anyone I choose.' I stood in front of the mirror for hours, practising what I thought a confident expression looked like."

"Well, you did a bloody good job," says Alice. She still finds it hard to believe.

"I know. The funny thing was, after a while I didn't have to try. The new Georgie became me, most of the time, anyway. But that didn't stop me being scared of telling you what my bloody uncle had done with the garden. It was mostly your project, after all."

Alice considers this. Was she really the leader in their enterprise? At the time it had seemed like an entirely co-operative endeavour. She can't remember having to persuade Georgie to play outside. It was understood: that was what they did whenever it was dry and not intolerably cold. But then what did Georgie do with Camilla when she came? They dressed up and read magazines in Georgie's room. Is it possible that Georgie was humouring Alice all that time?

"Are you going to eat that?" she asks, looking at Georgie's shortbread. Georgie's expression is pained. She shakes her head imperceptibly.

"No point in wasting it then," says Alice as she picks it up.

They are quiet as they drive home. Alice is wrestling with the idea that Georgie's persona was something she adopted, worked on over time. This has caused yet another crack to appear in what had seemed the solid edifice of the past. If both Georgie and her mother were not what they seemed, what else might she have wrongly interpreted? This is a worrying thought, but she can't explore it with Georgie. That would risk resurrecting the one subject she is determined to avoid.

Georgie seems content to sit quietly and watch the countryside roll past as they approach Alice's village. There is nothing she hasn't seen many times before, given the number of trips they have made in search of a room, but that doesn't seem to matter. Alice forces herself to think of something else. Is there enough food in the house? Who will make dinner tonight? This, too, is becoming something of a routine.

As soon as they enter the house, Alice can tell something is wrong. She always leaves the heating on when they go out, but there is no warm air to greet them. It is a cold, dull day and the temperature inside is not much warmer than it is outside. She puts her hand on the hall radiator. It is stone cold.

"The heating's off," she says, slipping her coat back on. "I'll just go and check."

The boiler is in the kitchen. A red light on the front is flashing. Does it normally do that? Alice doesn't think so, but she is not sure. She knows how to set the timer and override the settings, but otherwise this anonymous metal cuboid is a mystery. Thus far it has carried on doing its job without any intervention from her.

"Shall I have a look?" says Georgie.

"Um, I don't know. Perhaps I should call someone," says Alice. After all, this is a gas boiler. Georgie could blow them both to pieces. Suddenly, Georgie takes her arm.

"Look," she says, and points to the ceiling. There is an alarming bulge above the boiler, with a dark, circular stain at its centre. It looks like an angry, monochrome boil.

"Quick, get me a screwdriver and pass me the washing up bowl," says Georgie. Alice hasn't a clue where to find a screwdriver and Georgie seems to sense this. "Scissors then, or a knife. Anything sharp."

She drags a chair across and reaches up, directing Alice to hold the washing up bowl as high as she can. She works the point of the scissors into the wet plasterboard and soon there is a steady flow of water splashing into the bowl. When it has reduced to a regular drip, she climbs off the chair.

"Right, that'll stop the ceiling coming down,"

she says. "Keep an eye on it while I go and see what's causing it."

Alice is transfixed. This is another version of Georgie. Georgie who is practical, who knows what to do in a crisis. There was a time she could have seen herself like this. She'd always been interested in how things work, always liked to solve problems. But that's the trouble with living with a man like John. He was so good at everything. There was no room for her to learn by trial and error and she bowed to his expertise. She watches the drips falling into the bowl as instructed until Georgie re-appears.

"I think I've stopped it for the moment, but you'll need a plumber to sort it long term. It's the joint to the radiator in my room – the guest room. I've tightened it up, and if you give me a carrier bag and some tape I'll do a bodge job on it for tonight – it'll save paying emergency rates."

Alice doesn't know what to say.

AUGUST 1967

Normally, when presented with a problem, I would make a plan. This had always worked in the past, even if the outcome wasn't always what I expected. At least I felt as if I had some control. Not this time though. Although I spent hours in my room, or wandering around the fields with the dog, I could see no solution. There were too many unknowns. How could I manufacture a situation in which Hilary and I would be undisturbed in Georgie's house? I would need detailed information about all their plans for days in advance. This was clearly out of the question. No, I would have to rely on luck and that didn't suit me at all.

The simple laws of probability told me that, in order to maximise my chances of being alone with Hilary, I had to spent more time at Georgie's house. That meant I had to overcome my reluctance to call her and invite myself up there. I made a chart showing the remaining days of August – there were only ten of them – and marked each day according to the strategy I would employ. A star indicated a good day for an apparently unplanned visit. A 'T' indicated I would phone and try to invite myself to the house. I drew a line through the only Saturday to fall in that period, as I would be working.

There were a maximum of six possible interactions on my chart. I decided it would look strange if I made contact every day so I had to leave some days fallow. Before long it would be September and everything would change. Georgie would go back to her school, I would go back to mine and the opportunities to see each other would dwindle. I had to make the most of my chances or lose Hilary. He was only human after all. I hadn't managed to work out whether he was still at university or about to start work, but he would meet other girls sooner or later. Would his love for me be strong enough to prevent him becoming attracted to one of them?

I was plagued by jealousy of these hypothetical girls. They would be older than me, more experienced. They would be practised at kissing, flirting and all the other feminine arts I had yet to learn. Although I read my weekly copy of Jackie magazine from cover to cover, absorbing all its wholesome tips on getting a boyfriend, I knew that there was no substitute for the real thing.

But, it seemed, I had a plan after all. It wasn't much of a plan – it was little more than a timetable – but it was better than nothing. I forced myself to call Georgie on the days marked with a 'T'. I cycled up to her house on the starred days but all to no avail. Georgie was very busy at the moment. Of the two occasions I called, I only spoke to her once and she was on her way out.

"Oh, you've just caught me," she said. "We're going to Streatham. Ice-skating. I wish you'd called yesterday, you could've come. Anyway, sorry, must dash, they're waiting for me. Call me. We'll arrange something. Bye!"

I pushed aside a picture of a jolly trip to the ice rink. I couldn't allow myself to become distracted. Oh, if only I'd allocated a star to this day instead of a 'T'! Then I might have arrived at Georgie's house after she left, her mother might have been out and Hilary might have opened the door. I might have watched as conflicting emotions battled for supremacy on his face. His love for me would be overwhelming, but I had rejected him. Could he bear to be rejected again?

But then he would look into my eyes and he would dare to hope. There would be a connection. We wouldn't need to speak. It would be like Mr Darcy and Elizabeth Bennett, when at last their destiny as lovers was fulfilled. He would stumble down the couple of steps to the drive and hold me. His hair would fall forward and frame his face and his eyes would glisten with love. Then we would kiss, and it would be the most wonderful moment of my entire life.

I gave myself a mental shake. Enough of this dreaming. It wasn't too late, was it? I could still pop up to the house. At least I knew that Georgie would be out. Almost certainly, Hilary wouldn't know that I'd already called, but it wouldn't matter if he did. Once we were together, we'd have no secrets and that would be such a relief. I'd tell him everything. He'd laugh and call me silly and cute, but he'd be secretly pleased at the lengths I'd gone to.

Fifteen minutes later, I stood at Georgie's front door. The editors of Jackie would not have been impressed, as I'd followed none of their advice on making myself more attractive to boys. I figured that time was of the essence and that Hilary

wouldn't care that I wore no make-up or perfume.
I wasn't even wearing my ring with the two inter-
twined hearts, despite the fact that it was pretty
well guaranteed to help me find love. If he loved
me, those things wouldn't matter. I rang the bell. I
waited. I rang the bell again, and let the knocker
fall heavily. No-one was in.

Then it was Saturday. The days were fast
running out and, to make matters worse, Georgie
and a couple of her very well-groomed friends
came into Woolworths and bought tights from me.
I knew I'd told her about my Saturday job, but she
pretended to be surprised to see me. I would have
quite happily opened a packet of stockings and
used them to throttle her friends. They could have
had one each. That would stop them smirking and
whispering to each other behind their hands.
Having ruled out the possibility of cold-blooded
murder in such a public place, I considered asking
them if their posh school taught them any
manners, but I didn't. I served Georgie with a
smile and thanked the god of retail outlets who
kindly sent me a rush of customers who couldn't
be ignored.

At the start of the day I had entertained the idea
of going to The Cab after work. I might see
Georgie and this might lead to an invitation. I
might even enjoy myself. The Cab remained open

during at least part of the evening and there was live music from time to time. But now this was out of the question. If Georgie was there, she would be with her obnoxious friends. I caught the bus home and spent the evening watching tv with half an eye. The rest of the world was out there having fun. I imagined Hilary sitting at home in similar solitude and yearned for the time when we could keep each other company.

In the end, I abandoned my timetable. There was insufficient time for fallow days. I bombarded Georgie with calls until she agreed I could come to the house on Monday, which was a bank holiday. I had the distinct impression that she wasn't keen, but I was immune to such considerations by then. I squeezed my copy of Sgt. Pepper into my rucksack, gave myself a short lecture and cycled up to the house. My stomach was up to its usual tricks at the thought of seeing Hilary. How would he react? Would he snub me?

Georgie opened the door, but only partially. She stood in the gap and she wasn't smiling. This was nothing like the old days, but I found this didn't matter. These weren't the old days. This was about the start of something new, something much more important.

"Look," she said. "I know we said today, but actually I'm in the middle of something. Totally forgot this Latin assignment. Has to be in first day of term. Would you mind awfully …?"

My disappointment was such that there was a real risk that I would cry. My nerve-endings were so super-charged, so close to the surface, there was no telling what my body would do. My mother considered my wild mood swings to be the result of problems with hormones and it suited me to go along with this at home. But that would cut no ice here and now. The effort it took to keep my tears at bay rendered me speechless.

Suddenly, I heard Hilary's voice calling Georgie. I'd always thought that Victorian novelists were guilty of ludicrous exaggeration when their heroines swooned at times of high emotion, but now I knew what they meant. I felt the blood drain from my head and it was only with enormous will-power that I forced myself to remain upright.

"George, are you playing or not? It's your turn."

Georgie looked as if she'd like very much to be somewhere else. She winced, but had no time to say anything before the door opened wider and there stood Hilary.

"Aha!" he said. "That's excellent timing. Now we can play pairs."

Before I knew it, I had been bustled through the

kitchen and conservatory and into the garden. The lawn was smooth and flat these days, and I saw a number of small metal arches, placed in a pattern. Georgie's mother sat at the table, where there were glasses and a large cut glass jug of something mixed with ice.

"Have you played before?" asked Hilary, handing me a long-handled mallet.

I had to admit that I had never played croquet. I didn't know anyone else who had either. My only knowledge of the game was the version played with flamingoes and hedgehogs, and I was hardly likely to mention that. As it turned out though, I wasn't the only croquet virgin to be playing that afternoon.

"We found it when the gardeners cleared out the last shed," Georgie's mother told me. "We're not very sure of the rules, but we'll muddle through."

So we played. Hilary insisted on being my partner and, although I felt awkward at first, it was enormous fun. Even Georgie relaxed after a while, and I forgave her for lying to me. It didn't matter now. All that mattered was that I was with Hilary. He clearly bore no grudge as far as I was concerned. On the contrary, he made sure I had a glass of delicious home-made lemonade and showed me how to hold the mallet correctly. He stood behind me and leaned forward to position my hands. I could feel his hot breath on my neck.

It took ages for both Hilary and me to hit our ball through all the hoops, but, at last, we were declared the winners. Hilary shook my hand with mock solemnity and said I was the star player. I caught a glimpse of Georgie from the corner of my eye and was surprised at her expression. Surely she couldn't be jealous? Clearly I needed to carry out some repair work on this relationship, or I would lose my link to Hilary.

I retrieved my rucksack from the conservatory and pulled out Sgt. Pepper.

"Look," I said, approaching Georgie. "I got this for my birthday. Would you like to hear it?"

Georgie agreed, although not with the enthusiasm she would once have shown. We went up to her room and she put it on her record player.

"Look, I'm sorry ..."

"It's fine. Don't worry," I said, raising my hand to ward off any more apologies. "I know I've been a bit of a pest. It's just that I love coming here so much ..."

Georgie looked stricken.

"I know, and I love to see you. It's not that. It's

difficult."

I leant across and placed the needle on the record. Paul's voice joined the jangly guitars, to be followed shortly by the brass, then John's nasal tones and the cheers of the crowd behind them. It didn't matter how often I played it, it sounded new every time.

"Let's just listen," I said.

By the time we'd played the whole album, our relationship was restored. Georgie hadn't heard some of the tracks and she was visibly impressed. I had a sudden idea.

"Would you like to borrow it for a few days?"

"Oh, yes! If you're really sure, that would be great! But won't you miss it terribly?"

I would, but it would be worth it. Now I would have an excuse to come back another time. I assured Georgie I'd played it so many times that I could probably listen to it in my head with no need for the original. She laughed.

"I'll probably be the same. It's the most amazing thing I've ever heard!" she said, putting it on again from the start.

I told Georgie there was no need for her to let me out. I left her sitting on the floor with her legs crossed and eyes closed, nodding gently. I went downstairs to say goodbye to her mother, who was watching something on the tv about Brian Epstein, the Beatles' manager, who had been found dead the day before.

"Sad, isn't it?" she said, when she looked up and saw me standing there. I agreed, and watched the end of the piece with her.

"Probably drugs," she said, as I stood up to go. My stomach contracted as I remembered the conversation I'd heard in The Cab. Should I say something to her? But no, this would not be the right time. She might be grateful to me, but Georgie wouldn't. In any case, there were probably other explanations. It could wait. Maybe, once Hilary and I were together, he would know what to do.

I had intended to go back into the garden to catch one more glance of Hilary and to say goodbye, but it wasn't possible. Georgie's mother decided to see me out, so I had no choice but to leave then. I wandered off down the drive but I was not too disappointed. My copy of Sgt. Pepper was being played this very moment and it ensured at least one more visit. Added to that, Hilary had been more than friendly and I had patched things up with Georgie. This had been a good afternoon's work.

As I rounded the corner and walked towards the gate, I was shocked to see that my bike was not in its usual place. Could it have been stolen? It seemed inconceivable. Someone would have to be passing on foot to see it, and even then they would need to have entered the drive. I began to panic. It was the first decent bike I'd owned and my parents would be angry and upset if I'd lost it.

"Whoo-hoo!" called Hilary. He freewheeled through the gate. My bike was much too small for him, and his knees were sticking up in a comical fashion. I laughed, mostly with relief. He skidded to a halt in front of me but didn't dismount.

"Hope you didn't mind," he said. "Haven't been on a bike for years."

I found this hard to believe. I'd carried out a little research on Cambridge University and discovered that everyone travelled by bike. However, I said nothing.

"Did you have fun today?" he asked.

"Yes, it was great, thanks."

"We made a good team, didn't we? You and me against the world, eh?"

I smiled. This was clearly an exaggeration, but I liked it when Hilary joked. He was funny.

"You're doing it again," said Hilary. His voice

had gone husky again, just as it had before. My heart seemed to have realised what that meant even before I did.

"What?" The word came out as a whisper. Hilary let my bike fall to the grass at the edge of the drive and took me by the arms. I saw him glance towards the house and then he shuffled me over to a place nearer the gate and behind a bush. I knew what was going to happen and I was so excited yet so scared.

"You're a naughty girl. I've told you before about smiling like that," he said. "Now I'm going to have to kiss you. It's entirely your own fault."

Suddenly, his arms encircled me and pulled me to him. He was practically crushing me, but I didn't protest. Then his face was close, very close, and his mouth was on mine. At first, I was overcome with joy, but only for a moment. This wasn't the gentle kiss I had dreamed of. Hilary's tongue forced its way between my teeth and I thought I would gag. His hands were low, clasped around my buttocks and pulling me in towards him. I could feel him moving against me and I knew this was getting way out of hand.

I squirmed, tried to detach my mouth from his, but this seemed to make things worse. One of his hands crept round to the front and he pushed his fingers hard between my legs. It hurt. Panic made me strong. I wrenched my head away and pushed against his chest.

"Stop it!" I shouted. My voice was high and loud, almost like a scream. If we'd been any nearer the house somebody would have heard me, but we weren't and nobody did.

"You fucking little prick-teaser," said Hilary. His face was all red. "You can't lead a chap on then change your mind. Come here, you know you want to."

I didn't want to, but I was shaking so much I couldn't speak. I backed away, but there was a bush behind me and he grabbed me again and tried to kiss me. I twisted my face away and that must have made him angry, as he pushed me to the ground.

That was when I realised what was going to happen. Until then, I had been functioning at some sort of primitive level, like a rabbit being chased by a fox. It was all adrenelin and heartbeat. Now my brain caught up. Hilary dropped to his knees beside me and held me down with one hand while stroking my hair with the other.

"Don't cry, little fawn," he said tenderly. I hadn't even realised I was.

Before I had the chance to say anything - to

plead with him, to explain that I didn't want to do this, that it was all a mistake - he had undone my jeans and forced his hand into my pants. I could feel his fingers working their way down. Now it really hurt and I heard my own voice crying as if it were someone else, a long way away.

I didn't hear the car at first. I was locked away in my capsule of fear and pain, but Hilary did. He stopped. Withdrew his hand.

"Fucking hell!" he said, rising to his feet. Then I heard the sound of car doors slamming and I knew I'd been saved. I scrambled to my feet and fastened my jeans, although my hands were shaking so much I could hardly manage it.

I stood there, still frozen, watching Hilary like a mouse watches a cat. I thought he would do something, say something about what had just happened, but he didn't. He brushed some dried grass off his jeans and walked back to the drive. I heard his footsteps receding and I heard him swear and kick my bike as he passed it.

DECEMBER 2016

Half an hour later, the panic is over and Georgie has taken the Volvo to pick up a takeaway. Alice paid for it on her card, but welcomed Georgie's offer to collect it so she could return the floor to its normal pristine condition. Georgie has done something to the pressure in the boiler so they have heating again, too. She has explained it all in some detail, but Alice has no intention of trying to remember what she said. No, she has a much better idea. It is an idea that has been incubating for a day or two, but now its little beak has tapped its way through the shell and it is standing there, waiting for its feathers to dry. All she has to do is work out how to express it.

But not now. Not tonight. There is no rush. She sits down and tries to think of something else, then sees her laptop and pulls it towards her. She has taken to leaving it on the kitchen table so Georgie can use it. She flips up the lid and, as the screen flashes on, she sees it has failed to close down after the last session. This keeps happening and she thinks she must remember to ask Georgie to look at it.

The screen is showing her emails. She scans them, then realises it is not her account at all, but Georgie's. She is about to log out when something catches her eye. It is a message from someone called Veronica and the subject is 'visit'.

She knows she shouldn't. She knows this is not remotely appropriate, but she can't help herself. She clicks on the message and reads the conversation between Georgie and this person. It appears that Alice is not alone in having accommodated Georgie. She stayed several days in Bournemouth prior to turning up here and, by all accounts, had a lovely time.

Angrily, Alice pushes away her stupid jealous feelings. What is wrong with her? She's not a child. Does she want to drive Georgie away? Of course she will have other friends, and she didn't choose to look for a room in Bournemouth, did she? No, everything is fine. She logs out and shuts down just as she hears Georgie turn her key in the front door.

Alice has difficulty containing her excitement as they eat their takeaway meal. She knows she must be sensible, she knows she must choose her time carefully, but it is not easy. It all seems so obvious now. However, Georgie seems to have relapsed into her previous mood. She has been like this for a couple of days, now Alice thinks about it. She has been quieter than usual, even more reserved.

"Penny for them?" she says. She hates how easily these platitudes seem to be queuing up to be spoken these days, but she seems to have lost her way with words recently. All those years of writing things for other people. All those persuasive techniques. All those novels she never wrote. Now there seems to be nothing left for herself.

"Oh, sorry," says Georgie. She has hardly touched her meal. "You must think I'm very rude. It's just … you know I asked you about Hilary the other day? I was so relieved when you said nothing happened, but I thought … you must've wondered …?"

Alice freezes. All the old emotions come flooding back. They've lost their power to shock now, all these years later, but they have never disappeared. She has to say something in response, but she has never spoken of this. Not once. Not with any of the girls she got to know at uni, not with any of her boyfriends, not even with John. Saying nothing has kept it all contained and it's much too late to let it out now.

"I did wonder," she says at last, "but I didn't want to probe. You looked so … I don't know. It was obviously very difficult for you. But if you want to talk about it, of course ..."

"I think it's best, don't you? To get things out in the open? He's been lurking in the background, hasn't he? The bastard. He still manages to spoil things, somehow."

Georgie swallows. She blinks back tears. She goes on to tell Alice about Hilary being 'sent down' from Cambridge as she puts it. Apart from doing little academic work, he pursued a teenage waitress in the town for weeks, despite the fact that she had rejected him.

"Eventually, he waited outside the cafe back door and grabbed her when she went to the bins. He was so arrogant, he thought she couldn't really mean it when she said she wasn't interested. She reported it and there were enough witnesses who'd seen him hanging around day after day. It was all hushed up of course, but he couldn't stay, so we had to put up with him. It was like having a monster in the house."

Alice wants to ask Georgie if he did the same to her, but she can't. She knows her voice will betray her. She knows she won't be able to stay calm if the answer is as she fears.

"Oh. Was it him? When you were talking about your dad hitting your mum the other night … I got the impression it had happened to you too. I guessed it was Gordon. Was it Hilary?"

Georgie nods. A tear escapes and trickles down her cheek.

"Yeah, towards the end. After Cambridge chucked him out it got worse. He'd always been rough with me, but he was vicious after that. He started on my mum too. Like father, like son I suppose. He'd grown up seeing my father yelling at my mother and grabbing her by the arm, hauling her around. It's hardly surprising."

Alice doesn't know what to think about that. Is Georgie excusing Hilary's behaviour as a product of his upbringing? She knows there is a link between the two, but does that absolve him? Surely he had the choice to reject his father's legacy rather than continue it?

Georgie is very quiet now. She looks as if it wouldn't take much to reduce her to tears again, but Alice can't risk any further revelations tonight. If Georgie wants to tell her something else, something Alice has wondered about for many a long year, it will have to wait. She needs to shore up her defences again. She needs to be in control. She collects up the debris of their unfinished meal and consigns it all to the bin. She thinks about opening a bottle of wine, but quickly dismisses that idea.

"Come on," she says to Georgie. "Let's go and sit in the lounge. I'll do the rest of this later. I bought something in town the other day, and I think you'll like it."

It is nearly an hour now, since Alice led Georgie into the lounge and sat her down. It is fifty minutes since she put the cd into the stereo and pressed play. It is five minutes since the last strains of 'Day in the Life' morphed into the weirdness of the final ninety seconds of the wonder that is Sgt. Pepper's Lonely Hearts Club Band. Now they are silent. It is nearly fifty years since the first time they listened to this music together, and it might as well have been yesterday.

SEPTEMBER 1967

I wish I could record that my resilience and maturity carried me through. I wish I could say that I soon realised what I would have known if I had been less innocent: that Hilary had an unhealthy interest in young girls. I wish I could remark on how sensible I was, in taking no responsibility for what had happened. But, unfortunately, that was not the case. After the shock began to wear off, I was tormented by Hilary's words. 'It's entirely your own fault,' he'd said, and I couldn't argue with that. I had walked into the situation with open eyes. More than that, I'd plotted and planned to make it happen.

I had wanted him to kiss me. I had wanted it really badly. I must have been giving off signals to that effect, without even trying. No wonder Georgie had looked so cross. I was probably flirting like mad, fluttering my eye-lashes and biting my bottom lip without realising I was doing it. Obviously all my Jackie tutorials had worked after all. I'd wanted a boyfriend, and then when I'd got one, it had all gone wrong. I must have given the impression that I was happy to allow more than a gentle kiss, or Hilary wouldn't have behaved like that. I hadn't heard the expression 'prick-teaser' before, but it didn't take much working out.

As if all this wasn't bad enough, I was afflicted by terrible dreams. They were a grim combination of romance and menace. I kept awaking with a start, covered with sweat and breathing fast. It was no comfort that the precise content of these dreams often escaped me. I knew what they were about well enough.

It has to be said that my ability to deceive stood me in good stead in the immediate aftermath. I was so worried about my parents finding out what I'd done that I managed to act my way through the best part of the following week. How could I possibly live with them knowing what sort of daughter they had? I'd given Hilary the green light to do the kind of things people like Maggie and Kevin did. I obviously had no self-respect after all. I might pretend to be one kind of girl, but there was another, dirty girl hiding inside me, not far from the surface.

By Thursday, I was coming to terms with the fact that I was probably never going to be happy again. My friendship with Georgie was doomed and I would have to steer well clear of boys, at least for the foreseeable future. There was no telling what messages I might give out unwittingly. I couldn't bear the thought of another episode like the one with Hilary. Apart from the fact that it had been terrifying, it wouldn't be long before I gained a reputation. Alice, the girl who led boys on then backed off. Alice the prick-teaser.

As usual, I sought solace in lonely walks and music. But there was one thing missing: my Sgt. Pepper LP. Although I could have lived with never seeing Georgie or any of her family again, I couldn't live without my favourite music of all time. It played in my head whenever there was a little space for it, but I wanted the real thing. I wanted a soundtrack for my misery. I knew I could save up for another copy, but I had made the mistake of telling my mum where it was. She would be sure to become suspicious if I didn't retrieve it and my sisters would be hurt.

At first, I had the idea of asking my dad to pick it up on his way home from work, but he wasn't keen. He hadn't met Georgie's mother since the disaster of New Year's Eve all those years ago and he probably thought it would be embarrassing. There was no alternative. I would have to go up there, but I couldn't leave this to chance. I wouldn't set foot on Georgie's drive unless I knew she would be home and I wouldn't set foot in the house at all. I would get my record, say goodbye and then I would leave. Georgie might wonder what had caused me to become so frosty, but I couldn't help that.

So I phoned her. She was really friendly. She couldn't stop thanking me for lending her the record. She was going to buy her own copy, she loved it so much. Yes, of course, she completely understood that I wanted it back. We agreed that I would come to the house at about midday the next day. She said I could stay for some lunch but I had no intention of doing any such thing. I had twenty-four hours to come up with a reasonable excuse not to, but I said nothing to hint at that.

"Are you sure you'll be there?" I asked.

"Yes, of course. I'm positive," she said. Did I catch a note of surprise in her voice? I may have imagined it. I was past caring anyway.

The next day, I cycled up to Georgie's house. As I turned left into Templars Way I started to shake and breathe so quickly that I had to pull up. Hot and cold flushes swept over me. I heard a rumble of thunder in the distance and acknowledged it as a fitting backdrop to my mood. I tried to breathe more evenly. Eventually I was able to continue, although the shaking didn't stop completely and I was constantly aware of the rapid beating of my heart.

I took my bike right up to the front door and leaned it against the wall. I might need to make a quick escape and I was leaving nothing to chance. I took a couple of deep breaths and pressed the door bell. There was no answer. I tried to look through the patterned glass but it was impossible to see much. I rang the bell twice more, for longer each time. I could hear the bell ringing in the hall but there were no answering footsteps. I could feel my breath becoming shallow again.

I looked at my bike standing there. It seemed to be urging me to jump on and ride away, and that was a tempting proposition. But, if I did, I would have to go through all this again another time. Georgie's mother's car was in the drive and she never went anywhere without it. They must be in the garden. It would be safe.

I wheeled my bike round to the side entrance and propped it up there. Then I opened the gate and walked down the narrow path between the house and the fence. Normally I would have run, calling out a cheery greeting as I did, but I crept down that path like a thief.

I was two thirds of the way down when I heard voices. I couldn't see anyone, so they must have been obscured by the conservatory that stretched to the end of the house on this side. One of them was Georgie and she didn't sound happy.

"I've told you, I can't. Alice is coming any minute. Will you leave me alone!"

I could hear Hilary's voice, but I couldn't hear what he said. Not to begin with, anyway. But then he must have moved closer for I heard exactly what he said next.

"I don't know why you keep inviting her. She's a boring little leech. No, not a leech - she's not interesting enough to be anything that sucks blood. She's a limpet. She attaches herself to you and sits there, doing nothing."

Tears rushed to my eyes and stung as if they were acid. I found it hard to catch my breath. Could that really be Hilary speaking? Hilary who had paid me so many compliments, listened so intently when we talked? Despite what had happened, I still believed he liked me. Maybe too much, and maybe in a way I wasn't ready for, but this was a complete shock. At that moment, it seemed as if the whole world was one great big deception. Nothing was what it seemed. I ran back to my bike, careless of whether anyone heard me, and cycled home in a daze. I have no idea how I managed to arrive safely. I'm sure I was quite unaware of anything but my own misery, but the stars must have been in my favour that day. Certainly nothing else was.

"They weren't in," I told my mum. Lying was second nature to me now. Sometimes I found it easier than telling the truth. At least I could manage the things I made up. I had lost control of the rest of my life and the chances of getting it back receded further by the minute.

"That's terrible," she said. "Fancy inviting you then not being there."

It was habit that led me to leap to Georgie's defence, rather than the fact that she was entirely innocent. That she had actually been there, waiting for me to arrive.

"Something must've happened," I said. "They must've been delayed or something. I'll call later."

I think the veneer might have been wearing a little thin that day. It was hardly surprising, given what I'd just heard. In any case, something caused my mum to keep a close watch on me. I knew she was monitoring what I ate for lunch, so I forced it down, despite the fact that everything had the taste and texture of cardboard. I helped with the washing up and was about to go up to my room for a nice little cry when she stopped me.

"I thought you were going to call Georgie."

"I will!" I snapped. "Stop bloody well going on about it! It's only a bloody record!"

There was a fearful silence. If there had been any tumbleweed to hand, it would have rolled across the kitchen floor and down the hall, blown by a gust of shock and disbelief. My sisters were aghast. My mum appeared to have turned to stone, a tea towel in one hand and a colander in the other. She was a statue in honour of domestic efficiency. I had sworn at her. I ran upstairs and slammed my bedroom door. There was my bed waiting for me, the pillow quite probably still damp from yesterday's tears. I lay down and waited, but even my ability to cry had deserted me now.

Nobody disturbed me for hours. I would have preferred my mum to come up and berate me. I deserved it, after all, just as I deserved everything else that had happened to me. What an idiot I'd been! Hilary had been playing with me like a cat with an injured mouse. He must have been having such fun watching his sister's little friend make eyes at him. I imagined him sharing the joke with his friends, whoever they were. I was pathetic. There was no other word for it. Well, there probably was, but I couldn't be bothered to look it up.

I must have slept some of the time. I was dozing when my dad came into the room and turned on the light. I had pulled the curtains, not wanting to invite any part of the cruel outside world into my miserable cave. I sat up and blinked as he perched on the edge of the bed.

"You know you've really upset your mum, don't you?"

I nodded.

"She doesn't deserve it, Alice. Whatever's going on between you and Georgie, it's not her fault. Do you want to tell me about it?"

I shook my head, but I'd misjudged my ability to cry. It had only been on hold after all. I threw myself on my dad's chest and sobbed until I was exhausted. Then, through my tears, I told him a completely fabricated story about Camilla being mean to me and Georgie failing to stand up to her. I surprised myself. Obviously I borrowed aspects of what I'd heard in the garden, but a lot of it came entirely from my imagination. I was quite impressed.

My dad went back downstairs to be replaced by my mum shortly afterwards. I apologised and she accepted it. I had a little cry in her arms so she wouldn't feel left out, but actually I felt a lot better by then. In a way, Hilary's vile remarks had helped. Now I could forget about the lot of them, for once and for all. I just needed Sgt. Pepper back.

The next day, I ate a hearty breakfast then I called Georgie. I apologised for not turning up the day before and blamed stomach ache. I was confident that she and my mother were unlikely to compare notes on my period problems and it was a very handy excuse. She told me they would all be out until about three, but if I came after that she'd be there.

It usually took about ten minutes to cycle to Georgie's house, so I waited until three and set off. I rode slowly, rehearsing what I would say to Georgie. I wanted the very last words I ever said to her to be special. I didn't want to say something mundane like 'see ya' or 'bye'. I wanted her to ponder on the meaning of what I'd said, maybe even to learn something. These were lofty thoughts, but, unfortunately, they were not matched by any good phrases. I pulled into the drive and forgot all about memorable valedictions as I rounded the corner. The drive was empty.

I looked at my watch. It was only quarter past. It was annoying to wait, but I could imagine my mum's response if I arrived home empty-handed again. I didn't want a repeat of yesterday. I propped up my bike by the front door and sat on the step. I had only been there a few minutes when I heard the crunch of wheels on the gravel. At last! A few more minutes and it would all be over. I jumped up, but it was not Georgie's mother's car that roared into sight and skidded to a halt, kicking up gravel and dust. It was a battered, souped-up Mini, painted in bright colours. Seconds later, a scooter followed.

"Hello, sweetheart," said the driver of the scooter. "Nobody in?"

I told him that the family were expected back any minute. I was half inclined to leave, as both the scooter driver and the occupants of the mini were young men about the same age as Hilary. My head knew they were unlikely to attack me, but my body was sending out frantic warnings of danger. As it happened, they took little notice of me. The scooter driver chatted to the occupants of the mini through the open window and they all smoked cigarettes. There was quite a lot of looking at watches.

When the final butt had been flicked onto the gravel, the scooter driver looked at his watch once more then returned to his machine. He flicked up the stand, wheeled the scooter past the mini and parked it at the far end of the drive. He turned to me.

"Listen, love. That scooter is for the guy who lives here. You know him? Posh bloke."

I nodded. I would have supplied the name for him, but my brain had banned my mouth from saying it.

"He's bought it, but we can't wait any longer. Are you gonna see him?"

I swallowed. I said I might. I said I would see someone in the family, anyway. My voice was small and high, like a little child's.

"Tell him he can pay me the rest tomorrow. I'll come round. Oh, and tell him not to take it out yet. The brakes are a bit soft. Tell him I'll look at them when I come round. It won't be anything much. You got that?"

I nodded again.

"You sure?" He must have thought I was mentally deficient. Certainly I was behaving as if I might be.

"What are you going to tell him?"

"You'll come round for the money tomorrow and don't drive it because the brakes are soft. And you'll fix the brakes when you come."

"Ten out of ten!" said the young man. He actually seemed quite nice, but I had to be careful not to smile or make eye contact in case I gave him any unintended encouragement and he got the wrong idea.

While he was talking, the passenger in the mini had clambered into the back. The scooter driver took the passenger seat and wound down the window.

"You will tell him?"

I nodded. It was the best I could do. I just wanted them to go. I wondered if I should become a nun, then I wouldn't have to engage in social interaction with any males. If this was going to happen every time I met a boy, my life would be a misery. But then, the fact that I was a confirmed atheist would not be in my favour. I sat back on the step and put my head on my arms.

There can't have been more than a couple of minutes between the mini pulling out and Georgie's mother driving in. They may have even passed each other on the road for all I knew. Georgie leapt out of the car, full of apologies as I rose to meet her.

"Don't worry," I said. "But look, I'm sorry. I have to be somewhere. Could you just …?"

I don't know whether it was my expression, my tone of voice or something else, less discernible. Georgie obviously picked up some signal, though. She hurried past me and let herself into the house without another word. Her mother and Hilary remained in the car. I didn't need to be an expert in body language to tell they were arguing, even though I couldn't hear anything. I hoped they would both stay there, but Georgie's mother got out.

"Well, at least you can bring in the shopping!" she said to Hilary, before slamming the door.

"Are you coming in, sweetie?" she said as she passed me. She looked tense.

"No, I'm … I've got to get back," I said. I had half an eye on the car. Hilary was still sitting in the passenger seat. I couldn't bear the thought of him being anywhere near me, but I didn't want to go into the house. I had divorced it and everything associated with it. It would feel like a betrayal. My eyes veered wildly between the front door and the car and my heart was going crazy. For God's sake! How long could it take to find an LP?

At last, Georgie appeared. She handed Sgt. Pepper to me.

"Sorry, couldn't find the sleeve," she said. "It's been on the record player since you left!"

I don't know what I said then. It wasn't anything significant or memorable, that's certain. I put the record in my rucksack and went to get my bike. Georgie watched me.

"Are you alright?" she asked.

"Yeah, I'm ok. It's just the usual," I said, laying a hand on my abdomen.

"Nightmare," said Georgie with a sympathetic grimace. "Call me when you're better?"

I nodded, she smiled and it was over. She went inside and pulled the door to, although I don't think she closed it completely. I was just about numb, but I still had to get my bike past Georgie's mother's car. She had parked it very badly, and there was only room to pass on the passenger side. I took a deep breath and hurried past, but the car door opened. That's when I remembered what I had to tell Hilary. I had missed my chance to tell Georgie or her mother. Now I would have to speak to him again.

DECEMBER 2016

Alice awakes early. She is suffused with echoes of last night's rosy glow, together with a warm tingle of anticipation. It is like the opposite of a hangover. She showers and dresses as quietly as possible. She wants to have the kitchen to herself for a while. She wants to sit alone, drink coffee and think about what she will say; how she will say it. She has thought of little else since she awoke and she is aware that even some of her dreams have been rehearsing this morning's scenario. But none of that matters. She may only get one shot at this. She pictures Georgie's expression when she asks her. The surprise, the relief, the gratitude.

Downstairs, she is pleased to find the kitchen empty. She makes coffee and drinks it, being careful not to scrape her chair on the ceramic tiled floor. She is on her second mug when it comes to her: there are two things she has to say to Georgie, not one. She should have been braver yesterday, when it was obvious Georgie wanted to continue talking. She remembers Georgie's face when she talked about Hilary, when she called him a bastard. How it scrunched up with anger. As a child, Alice had never been sure whether Georgie was exaggerating when she spoke of Hilary. Now she knows. There was no exaggeration. He was a sexual predator, a paedophile. He was violent and controlling. He was a vile and hateful person.

Alice pictures him now, approaching her with the smile that can still turn her stomach. 'You're a naughty girl,' he'd said. 'Now I'm going to have to kiss you.' These words have stayed with her, and for years she believed them to be true. It was all her own fault. How many potential relationships had he ruined? It was only when she attended a feminist discussion group at university that she realised the truth of what had happened to her and was able to start the long climb out of the hole Hilary had dug for her. The trouble is, she's still climbing. Yes, she's angry, and so is Georgie.

That's why she has to know. Then they will be sisters again.

She can't eat, but she waits patiently. Now she has decided to say it, the precise words don't matter. They will find themselves when the time comes. They are all in there, waiting to be spoken and she knows she can trust them.

At last she hears the shower running in the room above and prepares herself. She puts on the kettle for Georgie's tea and gets out the mug she seems to like. The door opens.

"Morning," says Georgie. "Sorry I'm up late. I had a lovely sleep."

Alice had intended to make Georgie's tea and possibly even her toast before saying anything, but she seems to have no control. The words are there and they won't wait for anything, least of all breakfast.

"Georgie, I need to talk to you. Come and sit with me, please."

Georgie does as Alice asks. She looks a little alarmed so Alice tells her not to worry.

"It's just that I've been thinking a lot recently, especially after what you told me about Hilary. I've got two things I need to say, and I'd be really grateful if you'd just listen. I'm sorry if that's controlling, but I need a run at this or I may never say it."

"Ok," says Georgie. She still seems anxious but Alice can't help that.

"I'll do the easy bit first," she says. "I'd like you to stay. I don't mean just for another week, or until after Christmas or New Year. I mean I'd like you to move in properly. The house is all paid for, courtesy of my cheating husband's very substantial assets, so I wouldn't charge you rent. You could contribute to the bills, food and stuff, when you were … What do you think?"

Georgie's expression has changed. She looks very uncomfortable now.

"Um, well. I don't know," she says. She is running her hands through her hair. "That's an amazing gesture, Alice. I don't know what to say. I hadn't even thought of it. Are you sure you've thought this through?"

Alice assures her she has given the matter many hours of thought and she is sure they could make it work. She pushes aside her disappointment at Georgie's failure to leap at the chance. She sees that she is shocked, and that she may feel pressured into making a decision too quickly.

"Listen," she says. "It's just an idea. Of course you need to think about it. Like I say, I've had a few days to mull it over. Take as long as you like."

Georgie thanks her again, but suddenly remembers something she urgently needs to do in town. It's something about pensions and tax she tells Alice, but she won't elaborate. No, she doesn't want to use the house phone or Alice's laptop. She prefers to talk to a real person. She hurries out of the kitchen, leaving Alice stranded almost in mid-sentence. Now the moment has passed. She wanted to say the two things together, so Georgie would feel, as she does, that they are linked. Alice feels a warm rush of indignation. This is very thoughtless of Georgie. What can be so important that she can't spend a few minutes talking? And how ungrateful! You don't make excuses to go out when someone has just offered you a home. She takes a deep breath and follows Georgie upstairs.

DECEMBER 2016

We didn't find out until Monday. Sundays were family days in our house and we rarely interacted with the outside world. On that particular Sunday, I slept in until after ten. Then, when I drifted downstairs, my family tip-toed around me as if I were a rather unstable hand-grenade, cunningly fashioned to resemble a teenage girl. Someone had clearly had a word with my sisters. They looked at me with wide eyes and kept out of my way.

After we'd eaten our normal roast dinner, my dad announced they were taking the dog out. They were going to the heath, a favourite family haunt, a few miles away. It was a wide stretch of common, dotted with gorse bushes and stunted trees. It was ideal for walking the dog and, as a child, I loved to go there. There was something about the air, the size of the sky. It made me want to run and shout. However, I hadn't been with them for ages and nobody expected me to come.

"Ok if I come too?" I said.

There may have been a slight pause before both my parents said how lovely that would be. I was particularly sensitive to any perceived slight at that time, but I chose to ignore it. I thought it would do me good to re-wind my life, to pretend everything was normal. To pretend, just for a while, that I was the Alice they all thought I was.

Somehow, the dog always knew when we were going to the heath. He bounced up and down and revolved in excited circles until we put him in the car, then he panted hot, disgusting breath over my shoulder the whole journey. I didn't complain. I was determined to be positive and, at least to some extent, I succeeded. I threw sticks until the poor creature could barely drag himself to get them. I had a somewhat stilted conversation with my mum about going back to school. I drew the line at playing with my sisters, but they didn't try very hard to persuade me and I didn't blame them for that.

By the time we left to go home I felt a lot better. It wasn't that the future seemed any more rosy, but I thought I could put it on hold for a while. Nobody knew what had happened. I could go back to school and carry on as before, although I wouldn't bother trying to keep up with Maggie. I would team up with Dorothy, or maybe Suzanne. They were both serious, rather studious girls. I had always considered them to be somewhat dull, but maybe there was more to them than I'd thought. I would have to concentrate on my studies now that there was nothing else to do, so at least my exam results might be improved.

We weren't due back at school until mid week. If it had been a school day I would have found out earlier. There might have been a police car in Georgie's drive. I would have seen the tree, probably fenced off. The first year girl who got on the bus at Georgie's old stop might have said something. She would have been breathless with excitement, keen to tell everyone about what had happened to the family up the road. But none of those things occurred, as I stayed at home all day and so did my mum and sisters. I spent the day in blissful ignorance.

It was my dad who came home with the news. He had to drive along Templars Way to get to the station, and he passed the spot. Obviously he didn't know who was involved at that point, but one of his fellow commuters told him. Apparently he thought of phoning from work but decided against it. It would be better to tell me himself.

So that's what he did. My sisters were put in front of the tv with strict instructions not to move and the three of us went into the lounge. We sat down. By time that I knew something terrible had happened and I assumed it must involve Georgie. If it had been someone in our immediate family – my remaining grandmother, or an aunt or uncle -

my mum would have been in a much worse state. She was quiet, and her expression was sad, but there were no tears. I shook so much that my teeth chattered. My stomach was in knots. So much for my resolution to divorce myself from Georgie. The thought of losing her now made me realise what a hopeless plan that had been.

"There's been an accident," said my dad.

"Georgie?" My voice was tiny.

"No, love. It wasn't Georgie. It was her brother. It was Hilary. He was on a scooter and he seems to have lost control. Went into a tree. I'm afraid he didn't make it."

Relief washed over me. If I hadn't already been sitting down, it might have knocked me over. I had to bury my face in my hands in case my expression was inappropriate. My mum got out of her chair and sat beside me on the sofa. She put her arm around me.

"There, there. Let it all out," she said. I felt obliged to make some crying noises, but actually I felt totally numb. I found this reaction rather strange. I said I'd prefer to be alone and went up to my room, where I sat, staring into the middle distance. Hilary was dead! He was dead and I had no idea what I felt. I had gone to sleep hating him the night before, but now I would never see him again. How could I carry on hating someone who was dead? Now I would never be able to tell him how he'd made me feel. All those words I'd chosen. I wasn't expecting to tell him any time soon, but I thought I might have the chance one day. What a waste of time.

After a while, my thoughts turned to Georgie and her mother. Georgie had always said she detested Hilary, but did she really? What would it be like to have your brother die? I tried to imagine the two of them supporting each other, but it didn't seem very likely. Georgie would hide herself away in her room and her mother would probably turn to drink. I was glad I'd managed to get Sgt. Pepper back before it happened. It would have been very difficult to ask for it now.

The next day I hardly ventured from my room. Nobody bothered me apart from my mum. She popped her head round the door at regular intervals, sometimes to tell me about food but sometimes for no apparent reason. I think she was worried about me and I tried to take that into account, but when the door opened for about the tenth time I snapped.

"For God's sake, Mum! I'm ok. I'm not hungry and I'm not thirsty. I don't want to walk the dog and I don't need anything from the shop. I just want to be left in peace!"

"Alice, there's a policeman here to see you."

All the blood in my head suddenly decided that life would be much more attractive in my feet. There was a strange roaring sound in my ears.

"He wants to ask you some questions. You're not in trouble, love. He said that. I said you weren't feeling up to it but he insisted. He says it's urgent."

Slowly, I rose to my feet. I may have wobbled a little, as my mum insisted on taking my arm. We went downstairs and into the lounge, where a policeman sat in my dad's chair. He had taken off his helmet, and his hair was flattened in a circle around his head but still curly on top. I tried not to look too often in case he thought I liked him. My mum sat on the sofa and I sat opposite him, in her chair.

"This is my daughter, Alice," she said. "Alice, this is Constable Garrett."

Constable Garrett cleared his throat. He probably wasn't a lot older than Hilary. He had placed a small notebook on the coffee table and now he took a pencil out of his top pocket. He looked at me and smiled sympathetically.

"I know this may not be easy for you, but I have to ask you to think about the afternoon of last Saturday. Did you visit the house of the May family, on Templars Way?"

"Yes," I said. This was hugely stressful, but a small part of me found it oddly exciting. It was like being in a detective drama on tv.

"Where you there when a scooter was delivered?"

"Yes."

"Can you tell me about that?"

I told the young policeman exactly what had happened. I explained all about arranging to collect my copy of Sgt. Pepper and how Georgie had been late. He wasn't a very fast writer and I think he may have missed some of that out. Then I told him about the young men arriving in the mini and on the scooter.

"They said they had to go. They couldn't wait any longer," I said.

"Did they say anything else?"

"Yes, the one on the scooter said to tell Hilary he would come back tomorrow for the money and to tell him not to ride it as the brakes were soft. He said he'd come and fix them."

I could tell by the policeman's expression that I'd confirmed what he'd already been told. He nodded slightly as he wrote it all down.

"And then what happened? Did you wait?"

"Yes, I wanted my record. But anyway, it was only a few minutes 'til they came. Georgie went to find it, the record, and her mother – Mrs May – and Hilary were in the car. They were … they were talking. Then Mrs May got out and told Hilary to bring in the shopping, but he didn't."

"What did he do?"

"Well, he just sat there. Then Georgie came and gave me my record, so I said goodbye to her. I pushed my bike past the car and then Hilary opened the car door at the same time. That's what reminded me of the message. So I told him."

"What did you tell him? Please try to remember what you said, if you can."

"I know exactly what I said. I know I got it right, 'cos the man on the scooter made me repeat it back to him and that made me a bit cross. I said, 'Some men delivered a scooter for you. One of them's coming back tomorrow for the money, but you mustn't ride it yet as the brakes are soft. He'll fix them when he comes."

"Now, this bit is really important," said Constable Garrett. "Are you absolutely sure that's what you said, and that Hilary heard you?"

"He must've heard me as he swore about it. I

think he was in a bad mood."

"What did he say?"

"He said … he said," I looked at my mum. "It's quite a bad swear word."

"That's ok, it's evidence," said my mum. She looked rather pleased with herself.

"He said, 'fucking hell'."

Constable Garrett appeared to be suppressing a smile. "Is that all he said?"

"Yes, that's all. Anyway, I went then. I'd already said goodbye to Georgie, and Hilary … well he wasn't very friendly."

"Thank you, Alice. That's very helpful and very clear," said Constable Garrett. He looked through his notes. "I don't think there's any more questions, but if anything else comes to mind, tell your mum and she can get in touch."

I went back upstairs, but I hovered outside my room until I heard him leave. My mum let him out of the front door, which was reserved for visitors of some importance.

"I don't think they'll call her," said Constable Garrett. "It tallies exactly with what we've been told. Looks like he took a risk and paid for it."

It was weeks before the funeral. Apparently

there had to be an inquest in a case such as this and Constable Garrett was right. I wasn't called to give evidence. The man who had sold the scooter would have been, no doubt, but the fact that I had corroborated his evidence meant he wouldn't be blamed. We saw it in the local paper afterwards. 'Death by misadventure,' it said. Although I was fairly sure I knew what that meant, I looked it up anyway and found there were two meanings. The legal meaning was 'Death caused by a person accidentally while performing a legal act without negligence or intent to harm.' That seemed reasonable, whilst the alternative definition was less so. 'An unfortunate incident; a mishap,' it said.

My parents insisted that we attend the funeral. It was my first, but the novelty value was outweighed by other feelings. What strange symmetry life offers us sometimes. How elegant, that my contact with Georgie should begin and end with the same ceremony. Of course it was quite a grand affair. I had no idea they had such High Church connections, but I daresay Georgie's uncle Edward played a part in that. The service was in the town's largest church, but even this was only just big enough to hold the congregation. It went on for what seemed like hours, with interminable prayers and eulogies about what a superb fellow Hilary had been.

We were almost at the back. I could barely see Georgie and her mother, but I caught glimpses of them occasionally, mostly during times of transition between sitting and standing. They were both dressed entirely in black as was the norm. Unconventionality didn't extend to funerals, it seemed. We were not intending to go to the graveside, nor to whatever social event had been arranged for afterwards. We were there to show respect, said my mother. That was all.

That's why I assumed there would be no opportunity to speak to Georgie and I had made no preparations for what I might say. I had sent her a card weeks ago, expressing my condolences and saying she could call me any time, but she hadn't. I assumed she found it too difficult, knowing that I had been involved in the sequence of events leading to her brother's death. Or maybe she had enough friends to support her without me. I was working hard on repairing the damage to my own life and may not have been much use to her anyway.

There was a final hymn, and then Georgie and her family processed down the central aisle. Our eyes met, and there was nothing but affection in her expression. Unless it was regret. We had to wait ages for everyone to walk past us, and we were heading away when I felt someone touch my arm. I turned.

"I'm so glad you came," she said. "I wanted to call you, but it's been … well, you can imagine. It's not just all this. We're moving. It's simply impossible for my mother now, being there, having to drive past the place it happened day after day. We're going to live with my uncle until the house is sold and then we'll get somewhere else. But I will call you then. I promise!"

She looked round, and it was clear that everyone was moving off for the burial.

"I'd better go." Then she pulled me to her for a brief but tight hug. Her eyes were shining as she let me go and stepped back. "Alice, don't carry the world on your shoulders," she said. And then she was gone.

I never saw her again. She never called, and I couldn't contact her even if I had thought it was a good idea. It probably wasn't. Everything that had tied us together was gone. Now the gulf between us could no longer be bridged by childhood, or history, or music. There was no Hilary, there was no house. My feelings for Georgie were entirely positive as I lay in bed that night, knowing that I had reached the final full stop in that story. If I had any regrets, it was only that she had stolen my thunder and come up with a memorable farewell.

But I guess I could forgive her for that.

DECEMBER 2016

Alice is about to tap on the guest room door but sees that it's not properly closed. She gives it a little push and peeps inside. Georgie looks up in surprise, that old guilty expression sweeping across her features. As well it might. Alice has never seen such a mess, such chaos. Georgie appears to have been sorting out her possessions, as there are piles of clothes on the bed and teetering towers of books, magazines and papers on every available surface. And boxes. So many boxes. Cardboard boxes, carry boxes, plastic crates. Some are empty but some are full and lined up against the one available wall. It is impossible to believe that all this once fitted into the back of a Volvo estate.

"I ..." says Georgie, but Alice enters the room and raises her hand.

"I'm sorry, Georgie, but I need to say this. I said there were two things. I know it might've been a surprise – my suggestion – but I really think it could work. This might help you to decide, so if we can just ..."

"Alice, I'm so grateful, you must understand that, but I don't think ..."

"Will you just listen?" shouts Alice. She surprises herself and she certainly surprises Georgie, who takes two or three steps back and sits on the bed, her face a picture of distress. "I'm sorry. I'm sorry I shouted, Georgie, but you keep interrupting me. It's ... I need to say this. Just listen. Please."

Georgie agrees. Alice would like to sit down, so the conversation can feel more normal, more friendly, but there is nowhere to sit.

"It's about Hilary. I lied to you before. There was something," she says. She has to clear her throat before continuing. "Do you remember that day we played croquet?"

Georgie's hands fly to her mouth. "Oh, no! I

saw how he was with you, but you came straight up to my room. How did it … how did he …?"

So now the floodgates are open. The words come tumbling out. Alice was right, they were there all the time, just waiting to be set free.

"He caught me at the end of the drive. I don't know how to say this bit. I was so stupid! I thought he loved me. He'd been so kind to me, so attentive. I thought he wanted to be my boyfriend. I can't believe I was so naïve, but when it was obvious he was going to kiss me, I let him. I wanted him to. Then it all got out of hand, very quickly."

"Oh, God! Did he … he didn't rape you, did he?"

"No, but only because you had some visitors arrive, just in time. He would have. He had me on the ground. It was disgusting. It put me off boys for ages. I felt so dirty. I thought it was all my fault. That's what he said. He said I was a prick-teaser and that lived with me for a long time. Even now, I sometimes wonder whether I helped to cause it."

"No!" Georgie cries. "He was an adult. You were still a child. I'm so sorry Alice. That's what I've been dreading, all these years. I feel so guilty."

"Why?" asks Alice. "It wasn't your fault. You've just said it. He was an adult."

"I know, but I invited you in the first place, didn't I? I liked you and I wanted to be friends with you. You were different to other girls. I knew what he was like, but I took a risk. I thought the fact that you looked so young would protect you. And then, when we met up again … well, I've no excuse. He'd hadn't stopped trying it on with me by then, but I thought … Well, that's the thing, isn't it? I didn't think. I didn't think you'd keep coming back, but I couldn't seem to stop you."

So now Alice knows she was right. Hilary did abuse Georgie too. She hurries to her side and pushes a heap of clothes onto the floor. She sits beside her and pulls her close. This is entirely new territory and it calls for something more than words – or at least something to supplement them.

"Don't blame yourself," she says. "He was a predator and we were his victims. Both of us, Georgie. You and me. I don't know what he did to you, or whether you even want to tell me, but it doesn't matter. We have that in common. Our lives have been changed by it, scarred by it, but we're both still here, aren't we? We can support each other now. We have an understanding that no-one else will ever share. Say you'll stay, please?"

Georgie stands. Alice feels her arm drop as it falls from Georgie's bony shoulders.

"I can't," Georgie says, turning to face her. "I'm sorry, but it doesn't change anything. I need to move on. I thought it would work, coming back, but it hasn't. I was going to tell you later, but I may as well say it now. I'm going to see a friend in Bristol. Well actually, it's not a friend, it's Camilla. My cousin – you remember her? They've got this huge old farmhouse about five miles ..."

"I don't need to know about her fucking house!" says Alice. She knows she is losing control, but there's no stopping this tide of anger. One small, detached part of her brain remarks on the way her vision has become distorted. People talk about a red mist, but it isn't a mist at all. It's like one of those mirrors in an old-fashioned fairground. Everything is pulled into a weird, mis-shapen circle, with Georgie at the centre, untouched.

"Oh," says Georgie. "Ok. I'm sorry. Look, I really do have to go into town and then, well, I think ..."

"So you're leaving then? Just like that? After all I've done for you? D'you know, I've never told a single soul what I just told you! Can you imagine what it cost me to say those words?"

Alice is aware that her voice has risen in both pitch and volume, but she can't help it. She doesn't even sound like herself. It's as if a different, shrill Alice has been locked up all those years and, now she's out, there's no telling what she will say or do.

"Alice, please. It was never going to be for long. You know I'm grateful ..."

"No you're not! Not really! You don't even know the half of it. I saved you, Georgie. You and God knows how many other girls. If it wasn't for me ..."

"What?" says Georgie. "What do you mean? What are you saying?"

"Exactly that," says the shrill Alice, the Alice who can't be stopped. "I didn't tell Hilary about the brakes on that scooter. Why would I? After what he'd done to me? I didn't know what would happen, but I didn't care and I still don't. I'm glad he died, Georgie, and I should think you would be too!"

There is a terrible silence. It is broken only by the thudding of Alice's pulse in her head, in her ears, in her chest. The moment seems to last forever, but then Georgie gives herself a little shake, as if she has been in some kind of trance.

"Oh, my God," she says. "You're serious, aren't you? You killed him. I can't listen to any more of this. There's something wrong with you, Alice. Something seriously wrong."

She hurries to the door with a backward glance that Alice finds hard to read. Is Georgie scared of her? She hears the pounding of Georgie's feet on the stairs. Seconds later, the front door slams and then the Volvo starts up with its customary rattle and cough. Wearily, Alice rises and walks to the window. She is just in time to see the Volvo hurtling out of the crescent.

So Alice is left alone. Suddenly, everything is clear. What an idiot she has made of herself. Again. She has bared her soul, told Georgie the secrets she has shared with no-one else - not even with John, although there were times when she felt she could trust him with her life. Now she is vulnerable and exposed. The person she was beginning to believe in has proved to be exactly the same as everybody else in her life. No-one is what they seem. Everyone leaves her.

Five minutes later, Alice gets into her car and drives off in the opposite direction to town. She doesn't want to see Georgie's car. She doesn't want to pass all the places they've been to together. She thinks about the note she left on the kitchen table. It was written in a hot flush and anger and betrayal but its words appear calm and civilised. At least she has that skill left. It merely tells Georgie it is best if she leaves today, as soon as possible. It asks her to leave the keys Alice has given her on the hall table. It expresses her hope that she has a good stay with Camilla. There is nothing else to say.

But then she wonders. Is she doing the right thing? Why is she making it so easy for Georgie to skulk away? She could have waited for her to return, screamed at her, told her a few home truths. How dare she use Alice like this? Either she has been saving money on accommodation all this time or she has made contact in order to lay her last few ghosts to rest. In any case, it has all been about Georgie. She cares nothing for Alice or her feelings, that is obvious.

Alice's hands grip the steering wheel so tightly her fingers begin to ache. Goodness knows how fast she has been going. She slows right down and tries to think. She could easily turn round and still be home before Georgie. There are ways to pay her back. She deserves it after all. If they'd never met, if Georgie had never picked Alice out as the girl least likely to be of interest to her perverted brother, everything would have been different. She wouldn't have had so many failed relationships. John would never have stood there with tears in his eyes, telling her she'd driven him away with her jealousy and need to control.

There is a lay-by ahead so Alice swerves into it and brakes hard. Only the advanced breaking system and top of the range tyres prevent her from skidding into the verge. She stops the engine and sits there, trying to control her breathing. She closes her eyes. She imagines apologising to Georgie on her return. Patching it up with fake expressions of remorse. She sees herself creeping out to her old car at night, when she is asleep. She sees herself siphoning out some of the brake fluid with the turkey baster and squirting it into the shrubs. She sees herself replacing the fluid with water. She knows it's not foolproof. She knows Georgie might feel the brakes becoming soft and pull up in plenty of time. But she might not. She's a fast and somewhat reckless driver. Who knows what might happen?

But actually, she is surprised to find she isn't angry enough to want to act this out for real. Maybe she's just too old and tired. Maybe we are allocated a finite supply of anger and resentment in our lives and hers is all used up. Maybe she simply can't be bothered. No, she will sit here for a while, then she will drive to the outlet centre and spend some money on clothes she doesn't need and a meal she won't enjoy, before going home to her empty house. Tomorrow, she will blitz the place from top to bottom and try not to think about the fact that Georgie is free to go and enjoy the company of somebody else. After all, it's a risky business tampering with people's cars. Somebody might get suspicious. She might not be so lucky a second time.

The End

A NOTE FROM THE AUTHOR

Thank you so much for reading this novel. I really hope you enjoyed it. Presumably, if you are reading this, you got to the end, so that's a good sign. There are many advantages to being an independent author – no-one to tell you what genre to write in, no deadlines to keep – but it can be a lonely business. Unless someone leaves a review, I have no idea whether they loved my novel or hated it and gave up after the first chapter. So, if you enjoyed An Unfortunate Incident, I would be very grateful if you could leave a quick review and tell your friends. Independent authors like me have no publicity machine but rely almost entirely on word of mouth.

Also, you might enjoy some of the other novels I have written. All are available from Amazon and you can read more about them on my website: julie.mclaren.com or my Facebook author page.

As you will see, I don't stick strictly to one genre, but most are psychological thriller/suspense novels and I hope you will give at least one of them a try.

Thanks for your support, it is very much appreciated.

Julie McLaren

Made in the USA
Columbia, SC
28 July 2017